"You broke his heart."

"I know," Ronni whispered.

"Did you know his last word was your name?" Hayden was relentless—he couldn't let this go.

Her head shake was barely perceptible.

"Well, it was. 'Take care of Nick and Ronni,' he said. And I swore I would, even while I was cursing you left, right and sidewise under my breath…. Look at me!"

Ronni lifted her face. A haze glimmered in her eyes. Hayden's chest tightened but he continued, "I hate you for that. What you did to my brother was inexcusable. He was scared, too. He needed you. And you weren't there for him."

She nodded. And part of him wished to hell she'd argue with him. Rant about how she'd been justified. Make lame-ass excuses. Because her quiet but obviously deeply felt pain was getting under his skin.

Like a splinter, he needed to cut it out. Before he got infected—caring again about the woman who'd taught him that it was better to beat a hasty exit before your heart got involved.

To think he'd once been jealous of what Ian and Ronni had shared…

Dear Reader,

Life is messy. People aren't perfect. Sometimes we believe we know what we'd do if we found ourselves in a certain situation, and then life puts us there...and we don't do what we thought we would.

Ronni Mangano is in a tough situation. She wanted to divorce her cheating husband, but then he was injured. She's spent the past few years caring for the man who made her feel like "less." Her teenage son deals with the stress by acting out.

Enter Hayden Hawkins, with whom she hasn't spoken since the death of Hayden's brother, Ian—her son's father—thirteen years earlier. Hayden's a charmer, a woman magnet who adores the female species. But his relationships come with a thirty-day out clause. After watching his brother deal with a broken heart before his death, Hayden decided love wasn't worth the pain. Better to love 'em and leave 'em wanting more than getting hurt.

The last thing Ronni and Hayden expect is to fall for each other. Because she's the kind of woman he doesn't go near: a married woman. A woman tied by obligation, guilt and, yes, even a little bit of love, to a man in a permanent vegetative state.

When you've been numb for so long, even pain is a welcome sensation. Joy and pleasure are things you only read about. Loving Hayden promises all those things and more. But they can't give in to temptation.... Or can they? Hayden's a thirty-day guy. Ronni wants a *semper fi* guy.

But sometimes we have to wade through bad stuff to get to the good.

I'd love to hear from you! Please visit my website, www.susangable.com, email me at Susan@susangable.com or send me a letter at P.O. Box 9313, Erie, PA 16505.
Friend me on Facebook, too.

Susan Gable

As Good as His Word
Susan Gable

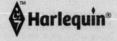

TORONTO NEW YORK LONDON
AMSTERDAM PARIS SYDNEY HAMBURG
STOCKHOLM ATHENS TOKYO MILAN MADRID
PRAGUE WARSAW BUDAPEST AUCKLAND

Recycling programs for this product may not exist in your area.

ISBN-13: 978-0-373-71708-8

AS GOOD AS HIS WORD

ABOUT THE AUTHOR

Susan Gable is a bibliophile. Or perhaps book-a-holic is more accurate. The sagging, groaning bookshelves in her office attest to her compulsion. Her own books—the ones she's written—have been nominated for and won numerous awards, including the National Readers' Choice Award. She lives in Erie, Pennsylvania, where she enjoys the summers and tolerates the winters because they provide an excellent excuse to stay inside and read or write.

Books by Susan Gable

HARLEQUIN SUPERROMANCE

Don't miss any of our special offers. Write to us at the following address for information on our newest releases.

Harlequin Reader Service
U.S.: 3010 Walden Ave., P.O. Box 1325, Buffalo, NY 14269
Canadian: P.O. Box 609, Fort Erie, Ont. L2A 5X3

To my son.
Who knows exactly why this particular book
is dedicated to him.
Love you always, bud.

Special thanks to:

The DoubtDemon Slayers, Jen and Di.

CHAPTER ONE

MEETING WITH A PROBATION officer required a certain look. A jacket and tie.

A body-hugging yellow spandex superhero costume beneath his street clothes hadn't been part of his plan.

But a spur-of-the-moment trip as Captain Chemo to the hospital bedside of a sick kid, combined with a stuck zipper on the costume, hadn't left him with any other option. He'd been forced to pull a Clark Kent.

Hayden Hawkins glanced at the clock in the dash and muttered a few choice curses.

He was going to be late. He whipped his new Camaro into a parking space opposite the Erie County Courthouse.

Climbing out, he grabbed his sports jacket from the backseat, then shrugged into it.

Despite the mid-May weather's perfect seventy-two degrees, a bead of sweat trickled down the middle of his back as he fed quarters into the parking meter.

He jerked upright with a disgusted sigh. He'd spent time in Panama in a Marine uniform, a fully loaded pack on his back, and it hadn't seemed this hot.

Either he was getting old and soft or spandex was the devil's fabric.

Determined to prove both points wrong and make up lost time, he sprinted across Sixth Street and up the stone steps in front of the courthouse.

At the security checkpoint, Jeannie, a shapely brunette sheriff's deputy, smiled as he placed his cell phone and change into a tray to pass through the X-ray machine. "Hayden Hawkins. Here to see your brother Alan?" The handcuffs dangling from her belt swayed, emphasizing her hips as she stepped from behind the counter.

They'd been playing this game for almost a year now, ever since she'd started at this post. His oldest brother, Alan, worked in the district attorney's office, and when Hayden had time off from his position as a high school gym and health teacher, he sometimes met him for lunch. Today was a school day—only eighteen school days left in the year—but he'd taken a personal day, getting a sub to cover his classes.

Hayden grinned at the woman. "Maybe I'm here just to see you."

She fluttered her hand over her chest. "Oh, be still my heart. Hayden Hawkins, making a special visit just to see me?" She leaned closer. "You looked flushed. You feeling all right?"

"Being around a beautiful woman does that to me."

She snorted. "Nice try, Romeo, but your reputation precedes you. Move along."

"You can't believe everything you hear through the gossip grapevine. Unless it's good. Then you can believe it."

"I believe you've got a short attention span, and I'm looking for something more than thirty days, sport."

He winked. "Be the best thirty days of your life."

She laughed. "I hear that's a distinct possibility, but I'll still pass."

"I'll ask again next time."

"You know what the definition of insanity is, right? Get through the metal detector, you're holding up the works."

He glanced at the empty lobby behind him, then pointed at the handheld scanner lying on top of the security machine. "Sure you don't want to hand search me?"

"Go!"

"Admit it. You'll be heartbroken the day I come through here and don't hit on you." He sauntered through the metal detector with nary a blip—for which he counted his blessings. The last thing he needed at the moment was a hand search, pretty deputy or not.

He blew Jeannie a kiss as he headed down the hallway. She shook her head and laughed again.

He waved over his shoulder as he turned the corner to the elevators. One was for police and prisoners only. He hesitated, finger over the public elevator button.

Upstairs, his brother Ian's son was in trouble. The son Hayden had promised to keep an eye on.

Apparently he'd done a lousy job of it.

Nor had he recovered from the shock of hearing the kid's mother's voice on the phone. Ronni Davidowski Mangano. The love of his brother's too-short life.

The woman who'd broken Ian's heart while he was fighting for his life.

A voice Hayden hadn't heard in thirteen years, despite his ongoing relationship with her son, Nick.

Time for a forced thaw in their long-standing cold war. Nick needed him.

Needed *them*.

Hayden jabbed the button.

IT COULD BE WORSE.

Ronni Mangano wanted to snatch back the errant thought the moment it formed. Life over the past few years had an uncanny way of proving it could, indeed, be worse.

Tempting fate didn't seem like a wise move at the moment.

She was exhausted already, so one more thing could be the proverbial straw....

She glanced sideways at her fourteen-year-old son, Nick, slumped in the seat next to her.

Or rather, one over from her. He'd intentionally left the plastic-coated, wire-mesh seat on the bench between them empty.

She reached across the space to poke him in the leg. The khaki pants she'd ironed only an hour ago already looked rumpled. Not the image they were going for today. "Sit up," she murmured. "And fix your tie."

With a dark glare that swept first her, then the stark waiting room, Nick pushed himself upward. He yanked on the blue tie she'd retrieved from a box of his stepfather

Scott's things in the basement storage room after they'd discovered that the tie Nick had worn to a family wedding only last summer was too short.

"Whatever, Mom."

Ronni clamped her molars together and went back to studying the gray-tiled floor. The bench opposite them, like the one they occupied, was bolted to the floor.

All in all, not such a welcoming place.

But then, she imagined the Juvenile Probation Office in the Erie County Courthouse wasn't meant to be welcoming. And bolting the furniture to the floor made sense when dealing with teenagers, who at even the best of times could have hair triggers.

And being in the probation office on a gloriously sunny May day didn't exactly constitute the best of times.

The door to the hallway opened, and a uniformed officer escorted in a boy who couldn't have been more than twelve.

In handcuffs.

Making Ronni wonder what such a baby-faced kid could have done to warrant cuffs. And if his mother felt half as despondent as she did. As much of a failure…

See, it could *be worse.* Nick in handcuffs was something she never wanted to see. Though since he'd been arrested—he'd been caught with a backpack full of spray paint, along with some pot he still insisted belonged to a friend—at some point he must have been cuffed. Hopefully, he'd learn something from this and get off the path he was currently on.

The officer guided the kid to a seat, looming over him.

Ronni jiggled her leg, checking her watch. Hayden had said he'd come.

Had given his word.

What if he didn't?

She'd swallowed her pride and thirteen years of silence to contact him when, at Nick's intake meeting, there'd been mention that the judge might consider appointing Nick a Big Brother.

A volunteer to provide the boy with a proper, stable, male role model.

And she'd blurted out Hayden's name. The "rules" since Ian Hawkins—Nick's father—had died had been that she ignored the Hawkinses, and they ignored her. Not that she hadn't deserved their contempt. She had. *Did.* Their scorn and anger was justified.

Exceptions to the "pretend you don't exist" rule had been made for phone contact with Lydia Hawkins, the family matriarch, when making plans for Nick's bimonthly and holiday visits with them when he'd been younger. Those phone calls had been polite but to the point. Now they all texted or called Nick directly on his cell. The most she ever saw of them was through the living room window when one of them dropped Nick back at home.

But Hayden had always been Nick's favorite uncle. After *dada, unk* had been Nick's second word. Hayden had spent tons of time with them, both before and after Ian's diagnosis with leukemia.

Until Ian's death had changed everything.

Once Hayden had finished his stint in the Marines—he'd enlisted immediately after Ian's death, putting his college education on hold—he and Nick had maintained a decent enough relationship. By then Nick had been almost six—old enough to take to a ballgame and other outings. Hayden also saw him at the Hawkins family gatherings she'd always made sure Nick attended. The older Nick got, the more he mentioned Hayden with the sort of awe and enthusiasm that made Hayden her first thought, as opposed to saddling him with yet another man who might be in and out of his life. Why draft a stranger when Nick had so many uncles?

Besides, Hayden taught at Millcreek High School. Not the same school Nick attended, but still…he had plenty of experience in relating to teenagers.

Her son needed someone to talk to. Because God knew he wouldn't talk to her.

The hallway door opened again.

Recognition took only a millisecond. The angular jawline, the vibrant blue eyes, the short-cropped, quasi-military-cut-but-spiked-in-the-front chestnut hair…

Hayden Hawkins, Ian's ten-months-older Irish twin, his wild-child partner-in-crime, walked in.

Trouble had never looked so damn good, except when it had been the two brothers together. Hayden Hawkins personified the boy—now the man—your mother had warned you about.

Ronni had somehow forgotten that whole bad-boy

thing when he'd come to mind. Damn. Maybe she should have gone with one of Ian's other brothers?

Alongside the row of chairs, he leaned against the wall, crossing his arms over his yellow-and-blue paisley tie. His biceps stretched the lightweight fabric of his beige sports coat.

The oft-admired summer-day blue of his eyes turned icy, spewing venom in her direction.

Not surprising that thirteen years later, he still carried a grudge.

For a moment, her chest constricted, making it hard to breathe.

He jerked his chin down. "Sorry I'm late. Ran into some…traffic."

Nick jumped out of his seat. "Unk. What are you doing here?" He cast a wary glance from his uncle to his mother.

Hayden's gaze softened, but his tone was firm. "Nicholas. Perhaps a better question would be what are *you* doing here?"

Her son studied the shiny toes of the new black dress shoes they'd purchased only yesterday. The old ones had been another casualty of his recent growth spurt. "Uh…"

The door to the inner offices opened. A woman with a folder in her hand called out, "Nicholas Hawkins?"

Ronni shot to her feet. "Yes, ma'am."

After introductions and handshakes, Mandy Curtis, Nick's probation officer—*there* was a phrase a mother never wanted to hear—escorted them down a hallway and into a cramped office. She directed them to a round table in the corner. Ronni took the chair on one side of Nick, Hayden sat on the other.

"Okay," Mandy announced, "we're going to cover all the terms of your probation." She pulled papers from the file she'd carried, and started going over them.

Because Nick had agreed to plead guilty, and because it was his first—and please, God, hopefully last—brush with the law, he'd been placed on "informal adjustment," which meant he didn't have to actually appear before a judge in court. Judge Madison, however, was aware of his case and had established the parameters for his probation. If Nick failed to comply with all the terms, or failed two of his drug screenings, he'd be brought before the judge.

Which Mandy implied would be a seriously bad thing.

The paperwork also indicated that if Nick didn't toe the line, he could be removed from home and placed in juvenile detention.

Ronni's stomach rolled at the thought.

Nick was basically the only family she had left, and she wasn't about to lose him—not to drugs, and not to the court system. This *had* to work.

Mandy read aloud from the document. "You live with your mother, and obey all her rules and regulations. You will let her know who you are with, where you are going and how you can be reached."

Ronni leaned forward and tapped the copy she and

Nick were reading. "Huh. Look at this. I think I like this setup."

Her son scowled at her.

They covered further ground, including the amount of time Hayden agreed to spend with Nick. He could spend more time, but the judge had asked he commit to a given amount.

"Why?" Nick asked. "I get all the other stupid rules. The drug tests, the curfew, the community service, all that crap. But why is Unk part of my probation?"

Mandy leaned closer. "Because the judge thinks, given your stepfather's…" She glanced at Ronni. Ronni could tell she was carefully weighing her words. People tended to tiptoe around what had happened to Scott. "… situation, that you need a man in your life. Someone you could spend time with. Talk to."

"I don't want Unk to hang with me just because some judge told him to."

That had been one of Ronni's other fears about a Big Brother volunteer. That Nick would resent someone who viewed him as a volunteer opportunity. Or an obligation.

"Hey." Hayden bumped his fist into Nick's tightly clenched hand on the table. "We already spend time together. This just means we'll get to do more stuff this summer. That's a good thing. I can think of much worse punishments, can't you?"

Nick lifted his shoulders.

"Informal adjustments, which you agreed to, give Judge Madison a lot of leeway in what he orders. You can still change your mind and appear before him in court if you'd rather."

"No!" Ronni and Hayden said at the same time.

"All right. I'm going to take Nick down the hall. He's going to get his picture taken, and then he's going to have his first drug test."

"Frikkin' joy," the boy muttered under his breath.

"I'd like the two of you to read over the paperwork again while we're gone. Make sure you understand everything."

When the door closed behind them, the silence was deafening. With each passing moment, the air in the room grew thicker. Tension tightened Ronni's shoulders as Hayden stared at her.

She looked like hell. Seeing her for the first time, up close and personal like this…she wasn't the Ronni Hayden remembered.

This was a shadow of that woman. A ghost.

Dark smudges she'd tried, unsuccessfully, to hide, accentuated the lack of spark in her eyes. She'd lost weight—not in a you-look-great way. More like someone who'd been sick. Or who just didn't care enough anymore to eat properly.

The hard mileage life had dealt her showed.

Karma was one hell of a bitch. Served her right.

And yet, for the briefest moment, he wrestled with the urge to lift her from the chair onto his lap and wrap his arms around her.

For a while she'd been his second-best friend on the planet.

But that had been before she'd broken his brother's heart while he'd been dying.

Clearing her throat, she asked, "Are you sure you want to do this? We could ask Finn or Greg. Or one of the others."

"Hell, no." The stupid urge vanished, replaced once again with the bottled-up anger that had simmered for years. "*I* made a promise to Ian on his deathbed, remember? Oh, wait a minute. That's right. You weren't there, were you?"

A flicker of outrage animated her eyes for a split second. Then it went out, and she looked away from him, shoulders slumping, gathering the oversize purse on her lap into an odd embrace. "No," she said softly. "And believe me, that's something I'll regret to *my* dying day."

All the times he'd confronted her in his imagination, this wasn't the response he'd pictured. "Why?" he demanded. "If we're going to work together to help Nick, then I need to know why."

She shrugged. "I was young. Barely eighteen. The man I loved, the wild, rowdy, bigger-than-life man who'd stolen my heart, was fading, inch by inch, in front of my eyes. I was scared. The idea of watching him die…" She raised her shoulders again, shaking her head so hard her chin-length, chocolate-brown hair flapped. "I ran. Not my finest moment."

"No, it wasn't. He loved you and Nick. More than anything."

"I know."

"You broke his heart."

This time she whispered. "I know."

"Did you *know* his last word was your name?"

Her repeat head shake was barely perceptible.

"Well, it was. 'Take care of Nick and Ronni,' he said. And I swore to him I would, even while I was cursing you left, right and sidewise under my breath. Look at me," he ordered.

Ronni lifted her face and her eyes glimmered. His chest tightened but he continued, "I hate you for that. What you did to him was inexcusable. He was scared, too."

She nodded.

"He needed you. And you weren't there for him."

She nodded again. And part of him wished to hell she'd argue with him. Rant about how she'd been justified. Make lame-ass excuses, not like the things she'd said so far.

Because her quiet but obviously deep-felt pain was getting under his skin like a splinter.

And he couldn't afford that.

Like a splinter, he needed to cut it out. Before it got infected.

Before *he* got infected—caring again about the woman who'd taught him that it was better to beat a hasty exit before your heart got involved.

Got shattered.

Once, he'd been jealous of what Ian and Ronni had shared. But in the end...

If that was what love got you, he wanted no part of

it. *Love 'em and leave 'em wanting more* had worked just fine for him. He offered women thirty days of fun, romance and pleasure. Nothing more. They knew going in that it would end and when.

He cleared his throat. "We don't have to be best pals this time around. Hell, we don't even have to like each other."

A jolt of shock registered in her face, and she leaned back a fraction of an inch, recoiling from his words.

"But we do have to work together. For Ian. For *Nick*." He stuck out his hand. "Deal?"

She slowly extended her own, and he took it, stunned by the tremors in it.

"Deal," she said. "For Ian. But mostly…for Nick. I'd walk through fire for that boy. Hell, I'd dance with the devil himself."

Hayden forced a roguish grin. "You don't have to dance with the devil, darlin'. Just with me."

CHAPTER TWO

LEAVING HIS MOTHER ALONE with Unk...probably not a good idea. Nick had seen the fire Unk had shot at his mother when he'd entered the probation office.

"We should get back," Nick told Mandy. She'd escorted him to have his picture taken, and then turned him over to a male PO—probation officer—for his pee-in-a-cup, drug-test adventure.

Now she leaned against the wall, arms folded across her chest. "What's the rush?"

Nick lifted one shoulder.

"What's the story with those two, anyway?"

He didn't answer.

"Talking's not that hard, Nick. Pretty sure you've been doing it for years. Open your mouth, words come out. I get the impression those two are not the best of friends, despite your mother suggesting him as your buddy rather than a Big Brother."

Nick found that hard to believe. That Mom had suggested Unk, had suggested any of his father's family... He was glad she had, but also shocked. "They haven't spoken since my father died."

"How come?"

"My mom broke up with my dad a few weeks before

he died. The rest of the family, especially Uncle Hayden, kind of blames her…like my dad didn't want to keep fighting the cancer without her." It had left him in the middle. Like a kid whose parents had divorced and hated each other's guts. Though neither side ever made an unkind comment about the other in front of him, still… he'd felt robbed growing up. Felt even more robbed recently as he'd watched his uncles bring new women, like Aunt Shannon and Aunt Amelia, into the Hawkins family. New women who were welcomed with open arms.

"They told you that?"

He shook his head. "She did. Not exactly like that."

"That's gotta be a lot of guilt for her to carry."

This time he raised both shoulders.

"What about your stepfather? Tell me about him."

Nick clenched his teeth. "I don't have a stepfather anymore."

"And how do you feel about that?"

"Thought you were a probation officer, not a damn shrink." He managed three steps down the hallway in the direction of Mandy's office before he was jerked to a halt, her hand wrapped around his forearm as she spun him to face her.

"Good juvenile PO's are part teacher, part cop, part shrink and part ass-kicker. I'm here to help you, but don't push me." She leaned closer, her clipped words carrying a hint of mint that didn't match the scowl creating wrinkles between her eyebrows. "What I'm *not* is your mother. Don't run from me again. I can be your new best friend, helping you get your life back on track, or I can be your worst nightmare. Your choice. Got it?"

He nodded.

"Good." She released him.

He rubbed his arm where she'd gripped it, following her back to her office. She barreled right in, but he paused in the doorway. No longer sitting where he'd left her, his mom stood in the tiny space between her chair and the table, facing the wall, one hand to her ear. The other hand gestured in the air. "No. I don't care what Vera says. Do *not* allow them in there. Look, I'll be there as soon as I can."

Nick sidled into the room, jerking his head in his mother's direction while staring at his uncle. Unk shrugged.

Nick looked closer at him. Sweat beaded across his forehead, and a pale red tint coated his face. Maybe Nick should have been more concerned about Unk than his mom. Maybe Mom had given him holy hell instead.

"You all right?" Nick asked quietly. "You're dripping sweat like you've just run Presque Isle."

"Couldn't be better. This moment is a dream come true." Uncle Hayden frowned at him, hooking a finger inside his collar. "It's just hot in here."

Mom snapped her cell shut and crammed it back into her purse, gingerly sitting on the edge of the chair as if she wanted to pop out of her skin, never mind the seat. "I'm sorry," she said to Mandy, moving the paperwork in front of her. "Can we cover the rest of this as quickly as possible? I need to go."

"Problem?" Mandy asked.

Mom sighed. "Just another fire to put out at the nursing home."

Nick's gut tightened. The nursing home, combined with his mother's expression, equaled bad. "What's wrong?"

Mom glanced over her shoulder at him. "Grandma Vera's causing havoc again. She's got a news crew there, wanting to do a Memorial Day story about Scott. Vera just doesn't get it. He wouldn't want that."

"No kidding." The last thing his stepfather would want was his story plastered across the news.

And the last thing his mother needed was a nosy reporter asking too many questions about the man who'd helped raise Nick. His stepfather's secrets were best kept that way. Mom had enough problems. She didn't need gory details that would hurt her.

The sick feeling in his stomach got worse. Nick crammed his hands into his pockets.

"No problem." Mandy lifted her set of papers—papers that might as well be handcuffs as far as his upcoming summer vacation went. "We're almost done, anyway."

Ten minutes later, the three of them, him, Mom and Unk, waited for the elevator together—*together*. Something he'd never thought he'd live to see. Maybe getting snagged by the cops that night wouldn't turn out to be the worst thing ever. Unk shifted on the balls of his feet, while Mom studied the floor indicator numbers. They sneaked sideways looks at each other.

When the elevator stopped, the adults stepped forward—then both stepped backward, muttering apologies. Nick pushed past them, stepping into the far corner. Unk stuck his palm across the sensor, holding the doors while his mother boarded. His mom stood all the way to the right, in front of the buttons. Unk stayed on the left side.

Wow, this was almost as much fun as the drug test.

For years, Nick had hoped that one day his father's family would make peace with his mom. She'd always told him not to hold his breath. Apparently she'd been right.

Unk dragged the sleeve of his sports jacket across his forehead.

The elevator motor whirred as they descended to the ground floor. Nick tapped his foot.

The air grew heavier with every moment. When the doors opened, Nick bolted between the adults, heading for the exit. He barreled past the security checkpoint and out the main exits. Across the street, the metallic specks in Unk's new Camaro glinted in the sunshine. That was as good a place as any to wait for his mother. Better the college side of the street than the courthouse.

"Nicholas!" His mother's raised voice caught up with him when he hit the middle of Sixth.

He crammed his hands into his pockets and kept going.

From the top of the courthouse steps, Ronni watched

her son trudge the rest of the way across the street. "I swear, there are moments when I understand why some animals eat their young."

At her side, Hayden snorted. "Try educating a hundred of them on a daily basis."

"No, thanks. You chose that career path, not me." Finding out through the grapevine—the one that ran right through the chair at her beauty salon, Do-Ron-Ron—that Hayden had become a high school phys ed and health teacher after the Marines and college had been quite a shock. "Not what I expected you to pick, that's for sure."

"Really?" He balanced one hip on the metal handrail beside the staircase, sliding down it before gracefully regaining his feet.

She shook her head as she caught up with him at the bottom. This was the role model she'd chosen for her son? "Really. I figured you'd either stay career military, or do something...I don't know. More exciting."

"Trust me, a hundred teenagers a day is plenty exciting. It's like working in the middle of a minefield. Or driving down a highway potentially laced with IEDs. You never know if one of them is going to go off."

Ronni's life had been loaded with IEDs. Nick's legal issues were only the latest. If Scott's injuries had been caused by an actual IED, she'd probably have just a little less guilt over the whole thing.

But only a little. She did guilt well.

She caught up to her son, who had stopped to admire

a blue sports car. "All right, Nick, let's go. I need to get to the nursing home ten minutes ago."

"Drop me off at the house first. You know I hate going there."

"The house? I'm dropping you off at *school* first."

"Aw, Mom. Let me take the rest of the day off."

Ronni counted to three silently before responding. "You think you deserve a reward for going to court? Wrong."

He kicked the pole of the parking meter. "Why do you always have to be such a bitch?"

"Excuse me?" Hayden's polite words belied the growl under them. He stepped around Ronni, straightening up so fast she feared the seams on his jacket would split. "I don't think I heard you. Did you just call your mother a bitch?"

Nick lifted one shoulder.

"Drop and give me twenty."

The only thing that dropped was Nick's mouth. Ronni checked to make sure hers was closed. She'd been about to chastise her son when Hayden had barreled in.

Nick laughed. "You're kidding, right?"

Hayden stepped even closer, so that he had to be toe-to-toe with the boy. Hard to tell from her vantage point behind Hayden. He leaned down, spoke softly. "Do I look like I'm kidding?"

"Y-you're not my father."

Ronni jockeyed for a better position, trying to see her son's face.

"Lucky for you. I'm pretty sure if your father heard

you speak to your mom that way, he would have separated your head from your shoulders. Push-ups would be
the least of your worries. Where do you get off, talking
to any woman like that, let alone your mother?"

The teen shrugged again, then took one step to the
side, turning beseeching eyes to his mother.

Hayden twisted his head, pinning her with a chal-
lenging stare. One eyebrow rose in question.

She felt two inches tall. Totally inadequate. A feeling
she ought to be accustomed to, especially where Ian's
family was concerned. Hayden had overstepped. But
she damn well couldn't afford to show Nick any chink
in their ink-barely-dried partnership. If he thought he
could divide and conquer them, they'd be toast. He'd
done it a million times with her and Scott.

She cleared her throat. "You heard your uncle. Drop
and give him twenty."

Hayden's head jerked a fraction of an inch in acknowledgment. Battle lines were being drawn, and she'd
chosen to stand with him.

Unfortunately, that still didn't make them allies.
Somebody she could count on to have her back.

Nick's eyes widened. "No way. Here? On the
sidewalk?"

"On the grass if you prefer," Hayden told him.

"This is stupid." But Nick grudgingly lowered himself to the ground.

"Be glad the college finished classes last week and
there aren't a bunch of cute coeds hanging around to
watch you. Count 'em off. And next time I hear you

speak to your mother that way, it'll be fifty." Hayden moved closer to the car, gesturing for her to follow.

"You had me worried there for a second," he said softly. "Thought you were going to let him off the hook."

"Well...you did overstep there, don't you think? Doling out punishment like that?"

"A few push-ups won't kill him. Does he always talk to you like that? Did *Scott* let him talk to you like that?"

Ronni sighed. "Nick was only twelve when Scott shipped to Iraq. I don't think he was quite this mouthy then. Speaking of Scott..." She glanced at her watch, then at her son, struggling with push-up number six. "How long do you think this is going to take?"

"Go. Put your fire out. I'll take him to school for you."

"Really?"

"Why do you sound so surprised?"

"Well, let's see. You haven't spoken to me in almost thirteen years. You looked like you wanted to tear my head off when you first walked into that office. You admitted you hate me for what I did to Ian. But you're offering to do a favor for me."

"I said I was going to be here to help you with Nick. I promised Ian I would, and I haven't lived up to that promise. Besides, this will give me a chance to have a chat with him. Mano a mano."

The ominous note made her look at him sharply. "Just mind your step. While I appreciate the help—"

"And can obviously use it."

"What the hell does that mean?"

He raised his hands in mock surrender. "It means what it means. You have a lot going on. Damn, woman, I just want to help."

She narrowed her eyes at him. "You'll forgive me if I'm a tad suspicious. You're not exactly on my 9-1-1 speed dial."

"And you're not exactly on my Christmas card list. But we agreed to be partners for Nick's sake. So go already."

"Okay." She took a step back in her son's direction. "Uncle Hayden's taking you to school, Nick. I'll catch you later."

He grunted, arms trembling as he lowered himself to the ground again.

"Thanks," she said to Hayden. "I appreciate it." But as she turned and darted down the sidewalk in the direction of her car, she couldn't help but wonder...

Did Hayden have ulterior motives?

HAYDEN LET THE FIRST FEW blocks pass in silence. Let the boy sulk for a minute or two before starting the interrogation. The kid's pride had been wounded, and Hayden needed it to at least scab over before he started picking at it again.

Which was why he was driving in the opposite direction of his destination, his brother Greg's house, where Shannon, at least, would be home to get Hayden out of the damn costume.

Then Nick leaned over and turned down the AC.

"Hey. Hands off. Controls belong to the driver." Hayden blasted it back full throttle.

"What's with you? It's not ninety degrees out."

"When you drive, you can set the stuff."

"Great. Pull over. I'll drive."

"Smart-ass." Hayden adjusted the vents so they all blew in his direction. Greg was so dead. At least Hayden had managed the court appointment with no one becoming the wiser about his "underoos."

"Takes one to know one."

"That's the honest-to-God truth. So, now that we've established we're cut from the same cloth, I want you to explain to me exactly how you ended up with a backpack full of spray paint and pot you claim wasn't yours. Just remember, my BS detector is finely honed, so let's skip the crap and cut straight to the truth."

Nick fidgeted in the passenger seat. After another block and a half of silence, he finally muttered, "There's this girl…"

An enormous sense of relief eased the tightness in Hayden's chest. This was familiar ground. He'd had this conversation with numerous students in his capacity as teacher and coach. He grinned over at the kid. "A girl, huh?" Then he chuckled. "Letting the wrong head do the thinking already? As you can see, that just gets you into trouble."

Without warning, Nick slammed his fist into the dashboard, muttering words Hayden hadn't dared use in the presence of an adult until after he'd enlisted in the Marines.

Hayden started, hands gripping the steering wheel harder. "Hey, sport, easy on the car, huh? What's the problem?" While he'd just laid into the kid for disrespecting his mother, these curses clearly meant something big was up with him.

The boy folded his arms across his chest. "I didn't want to ever be one of *those* guys."

"What guys?"

"The ones that let the wrong head do the thinking."

This time the laughter burst forth fully, causing Nick to glare at him. "You don't know it, but I'm laughing *with* you. Nick, we're all *that guy* at numerous points in our lives."

"Well…I wasn't going to be."

"Welcome to manhood." Hayden swallowed hard. It should have been Ian having this conversation with his son. "At least tell me you're smart enough to use protection. You need condoms?" He reached over, popped open the glove box. "There's a few in here."

"Damn, Unk…" The kid slammed the compartment shut, once more rattling the entire dash. "You're as bad as Mom. 'Here are some condoms, Nick. If you need them, use them,'" he mimicked.

"Your *mom* offered you condoms?" Hayden knew what too many fourteen-year-olds were doing these days—hell, he taught sex ed, although sometimes he wasn't sure who was educating who. He liked sex just as much as the next guy, probably more, but even he had to marvel at some of the stories and problems his kids came to him with. But he hadn't expected Ronni to offer her fourteen-year-old son protection.

Nick shifted in the seat. "Hello? Teen mom?" He snorted. "She's been preaching condoms since I turned twelve. Makes me feel like I was one giant mistake she's horrified I'll repeat."

Hayden steered to the side of the residential neighborhood street, which was mostly empty at this time of day. He popped the stick shift into Neutral and unbuckled his seat belt, turning to face the boy. "I know that's not the case. In fact, it would break your mother's heart to hear you believed that. No, they didn't plan on you. But once she found out you were on the way, both of your parents were thrilled. Much to the dismay of their own parents. Look, Nick, parents want the best for their kids. Your mom's had a tough row to hoe." Holy crap, was he actually saying these things? Had he suffered heatstroke from the suit?

But it was the truth. He'd been present for moral support the day Ian and Ronni had told their parents, one set at a time. What the kid didn't need to know was how hard Ronni's parents had lobbied for her not to have him. And then threw her out of the house when she'd defied them and continued the pregnancy. "She wanted you more than anything. She just wants your life to be easier. Which means waiting to have kids. Which means making sure you do the thinking with the head on your shoulders."

"You ever let the wrong one do the thinking?"

He laughed again. "Yes. I speak from experience."

"I figured that, what with all the girls you date."

"Hey, hey, watch it there. There's a time and place for everything. Keep that in mind. No point in getting too serious yet. The world is filled with women, Nick. Don't let one tie you down too soon. Especially not one who's already getting you into trouble."

"Wasn't there ever a girl you liked enough not to care if you got into trouble?"

Hayden refastened his seat belt, then pulled the car from the curb. They still had a few more blocks to go to reach Greg's house.

"Uncle Hayden?"

"What?"

"I asked if there was ever a girl who made you not care about getting into trouble."

"Yeah," he finally said. "There was a girl like that once."

"What happened?"

"One of my brothers asked her out first."

"Which one?"

"Never mind. Ancient history."

"What did you like about her?"

Hayden sighed. Dangerous territory, given how his morning had gone. And yet the memories stormed him. Hazel eyes that twinkled when she smiled. How excited she could get over the simplest things. The way she'd chide him and Ian when they'd dared to do things she considered bad or risky. A lump swelled in his throat when he compared those memories to the pale woman he'd seen that morning, with dead, haunted eyes. He forced it down, forced himself to answer. "When she laughed, I thought I could just float on it. Even better if I was the one who made her laugh."

The boy scowled at him. "Lame."

"Okay, she was damn cute, too."

"How did it work out for your brother?"

"In the end, badly. Let it be a lesson to you." It sure as hell had been for Hayden.

CHAPTER THREE

A LANDSCAPER RAKED FRESH mulch across the flower beds in front of Walnut Creek Manor as Ronni crossed the parking lot and headed for the building. Outside the automatic double doors, she paused to take a deep breath. Her shoulders slumped. The place was a prison of sorts. For her, as well. But she came every morning. This made today's second trip. After a moment, she drew in another breath, straightened up and strode on in.

In the waiting area, Vera launched herself from one of the chairs. A young woman hunched over a notepad, and a ponytailed man holding a camera plastered with the WEGL logo sat in chairs beside the one Vera had vacated.

"Ronni! I'm glad you're here. The staff won't let us go back to Scott's room. These folks—" she waved at the two newspeople "—are here to tell his story for a special Memorial Day feature they're doing at the end of the month."

"I know, Vera." She took the woman by the elbow. "Excuse us," she said to the news crew. "We need a moment to talk."

She steered Scott's mother toward the hall, well out

of earshot of the media reps. Willie, the receptionist, offered a sympathetic smile as they passed.

"Look, Vera, I understand that you're proud of Scott and want him honored. But please, think about it. Why don't you invite these folks over to your place, show them Scott's service picture and some of his medals, and just do it that way?"

"But that's the point, Ronni. He's still alive. That would make it seem like he's dead."

Ronni didn't think video footage of Scott in his current state would make him seem alive. She did know he'd hate it. "We've had this argument before, Vera, right after he came home. This isn't how Scott would want people to see him. Please. With everything else that's been taken away from him, don't violate his pride, too. Not any more than it is on a daily basis." And given what a proud man her husband had been, and the indignities he suffered as part of his regular routine, it was probably just as well he didn't know what was going on.

Vera's blue-gray eyes filled. "I just want him remembered on Memorial Day."

"I know." Ronni rubbed Vera's arm, then pulled her into an embrace. "I know. But not this way."

Sniffling, her mother-in-law broke away from her, fishing a tissue from her purse and swiping at her nose. "You're right, Ronni. You usually are. I'll take them home and show them Scott's stuff. Oh, I know. I can show them all his baseball trophies."

"Good. I'm sure that would make him a lot happier."

The pair walked back to the waiting room. The reporter was on her feet when they arrived.

"We're not going to film Scott here," Vera told them. "We're doing the interview at my house. I can show you all his service photos, and some of his medals."

The reporter zeroed in on Ronni, while the cameraman pointed the lens in her direction. "Mrs. Mangano, don't you want your husband's story told?"

"You can do it without exploiting him like a sideshow. What Vera's offering you will let you tell a fine story of a heroic man who served his country honorably." Unfortunately, a lot of Scott's other behavior had been less honorable.

"We'd like to tell your story, too. How much you and your son have also sacrificed. Are still sacrificing."

"Absolutely not. Memorial Day is about those who served." Just what she needed was some reporter grilling Nick, or worse, looking into what they'd sacrificed in the nineteen months since Scott's injury in Iraq, and finding out about Nick's court appearance that morning. She could imagine the lead-in: *And coming up next, a war hero's traumatized stepson runs afoul of the law.*

"Can you tell us the circumstances of your husband's injury?"

"I'd rather not talk about it."

"Didn't it involve a motor vehicle accident?"

The snot-nosed kid had done her homework. "Yes."

"So, your husband went all the way to Iraq and ended up injured, not by an IED or a sniper, but in a motor vehicle crash?"

There was more to the story than that. But… "Yes. Which is just as ironic as stories about vets who come home from Iraq and end up being shot in their own neighborhoods, isn't it? Now, if you'll excuse me…"

The reporter pressed her card into Ronni's hand. "If you change your mind, call me at the station. We'd like to cover all the angles."

After waiting in the reception area long enough to make sure they'd left, Ronni headed for Scott's room, greeting other patients and staff along the way. She paused in the doorway. The drone of the television hummed in the background, some guy talking how-to about fishing. Scott, strapped in his full-support wheelchair, sat in front of it.

But he wasn't watching the screen.

She entered. "Hey, Scott, how's it going? You'll never guess what your mom is up to today. She had plans to make you a TV star. Not to worry, though. I persuaded her to go a different route."

Scott's head jerked in her direction, but his eyes remained fixed on the window.

Not that it mattered where his eyes were aimed.

She crossed to his dresser. A sealed pack of cigarettes and an empty beer bottle had been placed in the middle, just under the wall of photos she'd created. She shook her head. "I see Dan's been by." Dan Abbott was one of Scott's buddies, a long-time friend he'd served with. Not many others found time to visit. The cigs and bottle—empty because Dan always drank it in Scott's honor—were in lieu of flowers, which he said didn't suit Scott.

The photo in the center of her board, Scott in his uniform, always made her nostalgic.

And pissed.

He'd been a handsome man, even more dashing in that damn uniform. But as Babcia, her paternal grandmother, had always said, handsome is as handsome does. And Scott's behavior...well, it hadn't all been pretty.

Ronni grabbed a container of lotion, then dragged a chair to his side. Pouring some of the cream into her palm, she slicked her hands, then began applying it to his forearms.

Forearms that had once been strong, but had withered with disuse over the last nineteen months. "Did you have your physical therapy this morning?" Dry skin and atrophying muscles were only two of the battles waged daily for someone like Scott.

Someone with PVS, permanent vegetative state. Permanent because he'd been this way for more than a year.

She chattered at him like a magpie, saying nothing of substance. Because although he made a great listener—no different, really, than before he'd been injured, where she'd be lucky to get an occasional grunt out of him in response—one never knew who was lingering in the hallway, also listening.

And if there was one thing she'd learned, it was to keep the dirty laundry out of sight.

She worked her way down to his hands. Hands that had once caressed her. Held her. Loved her.

She clenched her teeth, then swallowed hard against the sudden wave of nausea that climbed her throat.

Hands that had caressed and loved other women, as well. Including while he'd been on tour in Iraq.

She had the pictures to prove it.

"Moм!" Nick's voice echoed down the staircase. The boy's lungs apparently hadn't been impacted by his foray into smoking.

Ronni pushed back from the small desk that served as both the reception booth and her office at the salon in the basement of her house. The house she'd moved into when her parents had kicked her out, pregnant with Nick. Babcia had taken her in. When she'd died five years later, she'd willed the house to Ronni.

Leading to another round of her father's wrath. The last time she'd seen her parents had been in the lawyer's office, for the reading of Babcia's will.

"Mom?" Nick yelled again.

No customers on Mondays. Instead, she used that time to catch up on paperwork—or computer work, to be more accurate. And do the major cleaning. Or course, today had also been Nick's courthouse appearance, and she was still drained from dealing with Vera and the reporter at the nursing home.

"Mom!"

She strode around the desk and through the archway to the hall. Going left would take her to the parking lot in the back of the house. Turning right led to the stairs. She stood at the bottom and looked up at her son, silhouetted at the top. "What, Nick? And please don't bellow."

"Uncle Hayden's here. He brought pizza."

Hayden? *Here?* Now?

"I'll be right up." She returned to the computer, saving and backing up data, closing down the programs. What could Hayden want? Why not just call her to deal with scheduling his time with Nick?

At the top of the stairs, she flicked off the basement lights and drew the door closed. The spicy aroma of pepperoni and tomato sauce wafted from the kitchen. Two steps later, she watched Hayden bop Nick on the hand with a paper plate as her son reached into the pizza box on the table.

"Wait for your mother."

"I'm hungry."

"And you can be hungry until she gets here. Won't kill you."

For someone who hadn't spoken to her in years before this morning, and whose first glance had spewed death in her direction, the man was awfully defensive of her.

Or maybe that was just the good manners Lydia Hawkins had drilled into her children.

Ronni sighed. Another point where she'd failed to live up to Hawkins standards. It was probably just as well that they didn't speak to her. Most likely she didn't want to hear what they'd have to say.

Hayden had ditched his court clothes in favor of a pair of faded, well-worn jeans that cupped his butt…in a way she had no right noticing.

Nor should she have noticed his broad shoulders in the skintight turquoise T-shirt that accentuated the sandy highlights in his hair and the muscles in his back.

But then, a woman would have to be dead not to notice those kinds of things about him.

Although most days she felt so numb she wondered if she were dead, or in some other form of living limbo like Scott…apparently she wasn't.

Good to know. But rather surprising.

A cool breeze flowed into the room through the sliding glass door that led to the deck off the dining area, bringing another surge of spicy pizza scent her way.

Hayden turned around. "Hey, there you are." He waved his hand toward the table. "I brought dinner. Thought maybe you could use a break after today."

"That's very…thoughtful of you."

"Saved me from Meat-loaf Monday," Nick said, wrinkling his nose.

"And I can pop it in the oven tomorrow night, and we'll have Meat-loaf Tuesday for a change of pace." Ronni took stock of the table. Napkins, a six-pack of root beer and a four-pack of dark ale rounded things out.

Nick dived into the box, dragging a slice onto his plate and immediately taking a huge bite.

"Brought your favorite," Hayden said to her. "Pepperoni from Two Friends."

"That's not her favorite," Nick said around his half-chewed food.

Ronni mentally head-slapped him. Another demonstration of his fine manners.

"It's not?" Hayden rounded the table. Instead of taking the empty seat at the end, he pulled out the chair opposite Ronni. "Do you know how much of that your mother ate while she was pregnant with you?"

Nick paused midbite, staring at his uncle. He chewed several more times, then swallowed the chunk of pizza in his mouth. "That's Scott's chair."

"Nick—" Ronni began.

Hayden held up his hand. "Not a problem. I can move." He started to head for the chair at the end.

"No. You're fine. It's not like Scott's using it." She glared at Hayden while he wavered, looking back and forth between her and Nick. Finally, he sank down in the original place and warily reached into the white cardboard box.

It had been just over two years since Scott had sat in that chair, the last night before he'd reported to the base for training before deployment.

Nick's eyes narrowed and he shot daggers at Hayden, who squirmed, glancing back at Ronni again for confirmation.

She shook her head. "Stay there. Nick, you don't seem to care when it's one of your friends sitting there. Colton or Andy."

"That's different." He leaned back in his chair and folded his arms across his chest.

"How so?"

"It just is." The boy dragged another piece of pizza onto his plate, laying it on the remainder of the first one. He stood. "I'll be in my room, playing Halo. Thanks for the pizza."

"You're welcome," Hayden called to his back as he fled the kitchen. "Is he always such a charming dinner companion?"

"Sometimes he's almost civilized. Other times…not so much." Ronni picked the pepperoni pieces off her slice, depositing them on the edge of her plate. "But that's the first time I've seen him get bent out of shape about someone sitting in Scott's chair. I'm sorry."

Hayden's shoulders twitched in the tight turquoise cotton. "No big deal. It's been a major day for him. I'll cut him some slack." He watched her peel the last few slices of meat off her dinner. "Seriously? No pepperoni?"

She shrugged. "It bothers my stomach now."

"And here I thought I was getting it right."

"I appreciate the effort. As you can see, it's easy enough to take them off."

The edges of his mouth turned down, and a tiny divot appeared in the center of his forehead as his eyebrows scrunched.

"I'm not the same person I was thirteen years ago, Hayden. At least, I like to think I've changed. In ways that matter more than what I prefer on my pizza. Surely you're not the same as you were then?"

A loud caw saved him from answering. Ronni looked

out on the deck, where a large crow was perched on the railing, flapping its wings. She chuckled. "I swear, that bird has a better sense of smell than any blood-hound." She ripped a section of crust off her slice, then grabbed her plate and root beer. "Wanna finish this on the deck?"

"Why not?"

When she opened the door, the crow flew off to a tree on the far side of the yard. She set the crust on the corner of the railing farthest from the round wrought-iron table and two chairs. When they'd settled in, the crow swooped back down from the tree, landing beside the pizza crust. "Good evening, Mr. Black," Ronni said. "You look dashing tonight, as always."

Wings spread, the crow gripped the crust in one foot, pecking at it.

"I thought those things ate meat. Dead meat."

"They also hunt and eat other things. This one likes pizza crust and bagels."

"Charming. And you learned that how?"

When she laughed for real this time, Hayden fought against the pull in his gut. A spark twinkled in her eyes, and thirteen years faded. For a brief moment, he could see the Ronni he remembered, the young girl she'd been, not the world-weary woman she'd become.

She was right about changing. If only he could tell just how deep those changes in her ran—and if they were for better or worse.

Although he was hard-pressed to imagine how much worse it could get compared to what she'd done to Ian.

"He's a thief, that's how. I like to have breakfast out here. One morning I ran inside to answer the phone, and when I came out again, damned if he hadn't helped himself to my bagel and was eating it right there on the railing."

The bird hopped closer, dragging its prize with it.

"Let's talk about Nick," Hayden said. "I've got some ideas, and I want to get your two cents."

"Okay."

Hayden explained free running, a sport that combined running with strength training and climbing. There was a stuntman, balls-to-the-wall mentality that went with it, but he wisely kept that to himself. He suggested that a fitness routine would not only keep Nick occupied—and potentially tire him to the point that he was too exhausted to get into trouble—but also the fitter he was, the more his self-esteem would improve.

"Did you know Nick thinks you believe having him was a huge mistake?"

"What?" Ronni pushed aside her plate, then leaned back in her chair. She rubbed at the muscle in her neck. "Why would he think that? That's crazy. Some days he's the only reason I get out of bed in the morning."

"Apparently your attempts at sex ed have convinced him you regret having him."

She blew out a long breath, sliding down in the chair, folding in on herself.

"Hey."

She tipped her head up, glancing at him through her long dark eyelashes. The crow shuffled closer, his shadow from the slanting sun's rays falling across her face. The bird bobbed its head, making a low throaty noise.

"It's not your fault. I mean, you've got to teach him these things, right? You can't control how he interprets them."

She shrugged. "I should have known. Been more in tune. Something. I'll talk to him about it. Not tonight, because I want him to feel comfortable talking to you. I mean, that's the whole point of you stepping into the Big Brother role, right?"

"Right."

"Although your family nickname is JabberJaw?"

"Unfortunately, yes."

"Telegraph, telephone, tell Hayden?"

He grinned as light—life—came back into her eyes. She'd been just as good at giving him crap when they were younger as he'd been at dishing it.

"So he should know what he's getting into when he confides in you."

Hayden thumped his chest. "That hurts, right here."

"I'm sure it does." The edges of her mouth twitched, but the smile never materialized. "Well, since you're spilling your guts…did you find out anything else?"

"Just that there's a girl involved somehow. I'd guess the paint was for public declarations of love."

"And the pot?"

"Haven't gotten that far yet. But I don't think it's as bad as you're probably imagining."

"My son was arrested, Hayden. That's pretty bad." She picked a piece of cheese off her pizza, nibbled at it, then set it back on the plate. "Nick's the only thing I have left. Ian's gone, Babcia's gone, Scott's…gone…."

Hayden leaned forward. "Listen, I'm sorry about Scott. From everything Nick's ever said about him, he sounded like a good man."

"Scott was a good stepfather. The jury's still out on whether or not he was a good man." She glanced down at the table.

Interesting.

Even more interesting… He reached across the tiny table, took her left hand in his right. He stroked the base of her ring finger. No indentation, no smooth skin on the inside. His number one rule about women was absolutely no getting involved with a married one. He knew how to identify the signs of a recently removed wedding band, and Ronni didn't exhibit them. "When did you quit wearing your wedding ring?"

"Let go!" She recoiled, trying to yank back her hand, but he held on to her.

"Touchy subject?"

"More like none of your damn business."

"Anything that affects you affects Nick, which as of now makes it my business."

"I've lost weight," she snapped, still tugging on her hand. "It falls off. I didn't want to lose it."

A loud caw sounded. Wings spread wide, the bird landed on the edge of the table. A split second later, pain flashed across the back of Hayden's hand as the crow stabbed him with its beak.

"Damn!" Hayden swatted at it. It launched into the air, returning to the tree in the corner of the yard. "Son of a... I think it likes you, Ronni."

She gathered her plate and bottle, rising from the table. "But not you. And that makes two of us right now. I think it's time for you to go, Hayden."

He rubbed furiously at the red blotch already appearing on the back of his hand. "I didn't mean to upset you. Just trying to understand what's going on. The lack of wedding ring seemed odd to me. I also realized today that at some point Nick stopped calling Scott 'Dad' and switched over to using his first name. You know when that was?"

She shrugged. "Not really. I just chalked it up to him getting too big for his britches."

"Was it before Scott deployed? Or after? Before his accident?"

"Before he deployed, I think. Like I said, I figured it was just Nick getting older. Testing the water with Scott. It annoyed him, but when he didn't make a big deal about it...Nick just kept calling him Scott." She turned her back, heading into the house.

Hayden's gut jumped to high alert. A too-big ring was easily fixed. Something didn't add up.

BY THURSDAY NIGHT, he didn't know much more. He'd spent Tuesday and Wednesday after school with Nick, teaching him the basics of weight training, working out in the school's gym.

And working on the kid for information.

But when the subject of his stepfather came up, the teen shut down. Just as his mother did.

Hayden pulled into the long, tree-lined driveway of his parents' home, the house where he and all his siblings had grown up. He'd called a family meeting. Made it easier to tell the story about Nick just once. Besides, he had something he needed to propose.

They weren't going to be happy.

He edged the Camaro to a halt behind Greg's Tracker. Finn's Explorer was already there, too. Hayden did a quick scan of the rest of the vehicles, and cursed under his breath.

He was the last to arrive. To his own meeting. They weren't going to let him live this one down.

He trotted the rest of the way down the driveway. The final overhead garage door on the three-car bay was open, and he darted through it, weaving his way around several bikes lying on their sides. Some of the kids had obviously been at Grandma and Pop's after school today.

He brushed his palm over the hood of his father's Lexus as he passed. Still warm. Good sign. His dad hadn't been home that long, either.

Hayden jumped the two steps to the landing. The screen door's hinges squeaked as he entered the mudroom. No matter how much WD-40 they used on the thing, it always squeaked—his mother's early warning system, he suspected. Although if the whole gang was gathered, the hinges wouldn't usually cut through the din and chaos.

They weren't gathered around the kitchen table, or milling around the island. Chatter came from the dining room, where everyone had gathered around the table.

Head ducked, shoulders pulled up, he sauntered in. "I'm not late," he announced as he slid into the chair beside Greg. The table's extension leaves had been removed, shortening it to the original length. His father sat at one end, his mother at the other. On one side of the table, seated in birth order—organization was key in a family so large, and they all had assigned seats for this—were Alan, Bethany, Cathy, Derek, Elke and Finn. On Hayden's side of the table were Greg, him, Judy and then the twins, Kyle and Kara. With Kyle just done with law school, it had been a while since they had all gathered like this.

"No one said you were." His father grinned at him. "Guilty conscience, son? Something you need to confess before we get started?"

Hayden arched an eyebrow. "No." He scanned his siblings. Greg twitched next to him. "But maybe Greg…?"

His brother blushed and gazed at the table.

"Greg? Something to tell us?" Mom asked.

Bethany fidgeted in her chair, also staring at the table.

"Holy crap," Hayden said, quickly putting two and two together and getting three. Bethie was an ob-gyn. And if she was in on Greg's secret… "Shannon's pregnant, isn't she, you dog?" He slugged Greg in the shoulder.

"Ow! Hey! She's going to kill me." Greg groaned. "We planned to tell you all at the Memorial Day picnic. She wanted to get into her second trimester before we spilled the news. Congratulations, JabberJaw," he added. "You've done it again."

The next few minutes passed in relative chaos, as everyone left their seats to congratulate Greg, hug him, pound him on the back, offer him tips on dealing with pregnant women. Finn had gone slightly green, not that Hayden could blame him, given his experience with Amelia's high-risk pregnancy last year. She'd spent months on bed rest after coming damn close to losing the baby—a baby she'd conceived to save their older daughter.

Hayden stood off to the side and watched it all unfold, a sense of emptiness growing in his chest. Now, with the exception of the twins, the "babies" of the family, he was the only one who remained without a marriage or child notch on his belt.

And for the first time ever, that bothered him.

"All right, all right. Let's get back to business," Mom said.

Once they were settled, their mother propped her elbows on the table, lacing her fingers together. "We're here tonight to discuss the situation with Nicholas. I know we're all very concerned about him. Hayden?"

He started with that surprising phone call from Ronni,

requesting his help, which earned eye rolls from several members of the family. He covered the meeting at the courthouse, the terms of Nick's probation.

"The kid got in over his head because of a girl he's trying to impress." The brothers exchanged knowing looks around the table. "The situation with his stepfather is putting a strain on both him and Ronni. She's at the nursing home every day, running a business to keep a roof over their heads, and trying to raise a teenage boy all by herself."

"Well, that didn't take long, did it?" Judy piped up from his right elbow.

"Long for what?" He turned to face her.

His sister's eyebrows drew down and her nose wrinkled. She held up her pinkie. "For Ronni to wrap you around her little finger again. Hell, Hayden, I expected you to have more loyalty to Ian."

Hayden leaned closer. "Don't you dare question my loyalty to Ian. Ever. I'm going to do whatever I need to do for Ian's son."

"Including sing the praises of his mother?"

"That's not what I was—"

"Enough," their mom said. "I understand she's having a difficult time right now, Hayden. I'm sure dealing with her husband isn't easy." The lines in Lydia's face softened in sympathy, shocking Hayden. Maybe there was hope.

"Apparently, it's not. Look, I'll be the first to admit, I never thought I'd say this." Exactly when he'd come to his revelation about Ronni, he wasn't sure. But seeing that flat, hollow look in her eyes, knowing just how much the weight of the world was on her shoulders… He'd given Ian his word that he'd look after *both* Nick and Ronni.

He scanned the people around the table, stopping at his mother. If she came on board with his plan, the rest of them would have to fall in line, as well, however grudgingly.

He took a deep breath and braced himself for the chaos he knew would ensue. "It's time to bring Ronni back into the family."

CHAPTER FOUR

OUT OF THE FRYING PAN, into the fire…

Ronni clutched the slow cooker of pierogies made from Babcia's recipe as she meandered down the Hawkinses' driveway. With every step, her feet grew heavier. Nick, seemingly miles ahead of her, carrying the chocolate babka she'd baked, turned around. "Mom. Come on. What's taking you so long?"

"Just trying to…" Avoid the whole thing? Find a reason to turn and run? When Hayden had extended the invitation to the Hawkins Memorial Day picnic, held on Sunday of the holiday weekend, she'd been stunned. Skeptical.

Terrified.

And that hadn't changed over the last two weeks. Except maybe to have intensified. "Uh, just trying not to drop the pierogies."

Nick waited for her to catch up. Then he said, "Mom, don't sweat it. Grandma Lydia's not going to bite you or anything. It's going to be fine."

She pasted on a smile for his sake. He'd been so excited by the idea of her attending the annual barbecue, one he'd gone to every year. Without her.

Why mess with success?

Because it meant so much to her son.

The driveway was packed with cars. She'd intentionally parked at the very end, facing the road.

The knot in her stomach grew. She followed Nick in through an open overhead door...and stopped. A bright blue motorcycle, dulled with a layer of dust, sat in the far corner of the oversize three-car garage.

Ian's motorcycle.

Her nose tingled. She took a step in that direction—

And Nick called from the steps into the house, "Mom? You coming?"

She turned away and followed him inside. So much had remained the same over thirteen years. But in the kitchen, there were new granite countertops and black appliances.

The sliding glass doors that led to the wraparound upper deck were open. A warm breeze drifted in, carrying music and the chatter of numerous people, punctuated with the occasional shriek of a child's laughter.

To her relief, Ronni didn't recognize any of the people milling about the kitchen, so she smiled and nodded at them, then trailed her son into the dining room. "Desserts go in here," he told her, setting the babka on the table, which already held plates of brownies, several pies, peanut-butter-kiss cookies and an ornately carved watermelon basket filled with fruit salad.

Finn's handiwork, no doubt.

"We'll put the pierogies downstairs, Mom." Nick darted out of the dining room and rounded the railing that overlooked the main foyer. He barreled down the first short flight of steps, giving the suit of armor that stood guard in the foyer a high five as he passed.

Ian and Hayden had once mounted Sir Hawkins, as the armor was called, in the back of a pickup truck bed and crashed the Millcreek Fourth of July parade. Hayden drove, Ian stood in the back with the knight and tossed candy to the kids…and sixteen-year-old Ronni had simply gawked from the sidelines, amazed at their audacity.

A week later, she was dating Ian Hawkins.

A year later, she'd already had his son.

Another year later, she'd been closer to losing him than she'd ever imagined possible.

She descended that first set of stairs, giving Sir Hawkins a wistful look as she crossed the slate-tile floor to the set that led to the basement.

The level of noise coming up made her pause. She took a deep breath, then plunged down the final stairs, into the large rec room. Lots of bodies in this room.

Including…Lydia Hawkins.

The hair on Ronni's neck bristled, and her stomach rolled.

For a moment, she was sixteen again. About to face this woman with the news she was pregnant.

At least then she'd had Ian at her side.

The noise volume in the room shifted, and she could sense the stares. She shuffled forward, cleared her throat. "Mrs. Hawkins. Thank you for having me." She shoved the slow cooker in her direction. "I brought pierogies. They're my babcia's recipe. I, uh, I brought a chocolate babka, too. Nick told me to leave it on the table in the dining room."

Lydia took the container from her. "Thank you."

Ronni met her gaze. Lydia's hair had gone completely silver in the intervening years. But her eyes were as blue as ever. Those eyes examined and accused Ronni in one slow sweep.

"I—I'm sorry," Ronni murmured, knowing she'd been measured and found wanting. Again. So many things she needed, wanted to say. But those two words summed up everything.

At Lydia's curt nod, the entire room came back to life, as if everyone had been holding their breath.

But Ian's mother narrowed her eyes. A subtle message flickered there. This had been the public reconciliation. There would be a private come-to-Jesus meeting, just the two of them.

Something to look forward to.

Ronni swallowed hard, glancing around for Nick. Not seeing him, she seized the opportunity. "I, uh, I'm going to go find Nick."

"Okay."

Like a child dismissed from the principal's office, Ronni darted toward the open French doors that led out to the patio, dodging bodies.

Just outside, she misstepped, collided with someone. "S-sorry."

"Where's the fire?" The man held her by the arms to steady her. "Ronni."

She stared up at one of Ian's brothers. "Greg. Hi."

"You're shaking like a leaf. I take it that means you've run into my mother already."

She nodded.

He gave her a once-over. "I don't see any blood. That mean it went well?"

"I think it means she's saving it for later, when there aren't so many witnesses."

"Ah. That could be. Well…it's good to see you again." His tone was even, polite, sounding mostly sincere to her. But he'd been close to Ian, too. He released her arms. "Hey, come with me. There are some people I'd like you to meet."

He led her past the huge, stainless steel grill where Finn stood, spatula in hand. Smoke billowed out, carrying the tantalizing aroma of barbecue. "You already know Finn," Greg said as they passed. "Finn, say hello to Ronni."

"Ronni." He saluted her with the spatula. Finn had already been off to college when she'd started dating Ian, but she'd met him during school breaks and summer vacation.

"Finn." She wanted to ask him how his new family was doing, especially his daughter, Jordan, who was almost the same age as Nick. Jordan had received a cord-blood transfusion from her baby brother back in the fall. But Greg beckoned her forward.

They stopped at one of the picnic tables, where two women sat. One bounced a chubby baby on her knee. The other's face lit up at Greg's approach, leaving no doubt in Ronni's mind as to her identity. "Let me guess. Shannon, right?" Nick kept Ronni updated on all the family activities—and there had also been the wedding invitation Nick had received last summer.

"Right," Greg said. "Ladies, I'd like you to meet Ronni, Nick's mom. Ronni, this is my wife, Shannon, and this is Amelia, Finn's…"

"Don't you dare call me his woman, or some other equally prehistoric term, Greg," the woman with the baby—Amelia—said.

"I was going to say the love of Finn's life. Will that work?"

"You were not going to say that," Shannon said.

"Hey, whose side are you on?" Greg protested.

The camaraderie, the friendly teasing—this was something Ronni had missed about the Hawkins family.

Greg bent over, cupping Shannon's chin in his hand, and kissed her.

The air around them sizzled with the electricity they generated.

Something else she missed…

"Oh, no," a child said. "Not kissing again." The boy groaned. "Uncle Greg…"

Greg broke away from his wife with a chuckle, looking over at the kid. "And this is our boy, Ryan."

Ronni knew that Ryan was actually Shannon's nephew. Shannon had gotten custody of him a few years earlier, after Ryan's father had murdered his mother. In front of the poor child. Greg and Shannon had met and fallen in love because of it, and now were in the process of petitioning the state to terminate Ryan's father's parental rights so they could formally adopt the boy.

"So my work here is done. I've grossed you out—" he pointed at the boy "—and given you something to think about till later." He winked at Shannon, whose face flushed. "I'll leave Ronni in the care of you ladies, okay? Come on, Ry, I think I promised you I'd take you to do some fishing." He extended his hand and the pair wandered down the slope of the large grassy hill, toward the small pond at the bottom.

"It's nice to meet you, Ronni," Amelia said, blowing raspberries on her son's small fingers as he poked at her mouth.

"Same here." Nice to be around newer members of the family who hadn't known Ian and hopefully didn't have the same sharp ax to grind. "So this is Chip?" She nodded toward the baby.

"Yep. The one and only." The baby had saved his big sister's life.

"How is Jordan doing? Nick told me all about her. I think it made him stop and think, to find out he had a cousin who was…" Ronni stopped. Bad form to remind a woman that her child had almost died.

"Dying?"

Ronni grimaced. "Sorry. Wasn't thinking. Open mouth, insert size-eight foot."

Amelia shrugged. "It's true, though. She was. Now… she's somewhere on the upper deck, I think, sulking because I wouldn't let her come unless she promised to keep her mask on." It was needed to protect Jordan's still-fragile immune system from germs. Nick had found the mask kind of cool. Mysterious. Greg had decorated a series of them specially for Jordan, raising them to the level of intriguing for kids who didn't have to wear them.

"Sulking? Sounds like a perfectly normal teenager to me."

"Exactly. Thank heaven."

It certainly put Ronni's problems with Nick into perspective. And also reminded her that Lydia had lost a child. The pain of losing Ian had been great for Ronni, so she could only imagine how Lydia had felt.

Her apology was long overdue. Maybe their private meeting would be a good thing.

The three women chatted awhile longer about children, life in general, the Hawkins family in particular as they watched kids jumping on the trampoline, another group fishing down at the pond under Greg's watchful eye. Playful teasing. Friendly banter. Ronni soaked in the laughter, the connections, the rapport….

A lump swelled in her throat. Her stomach tightened.

Se hadn't just lost Ian. She'd lost all this. All of *them*.

And it had been easy to pretend it hadn't mattered to her. Out of sight, out of mind.

But being here with them, she realized she'd lost even more than she cared to admit to herself.

"Excuse me," she choked out to the two women, who

were now eyeing her apprehensively. "I—I think I'm going to take a walk."

With that, she bolted toward the woods on the side of the house.

Toward a sanctuary she hadn't visited in years.

HAYDEN WAITED for the kids to climb off his back, then stood, handing the football he'd had clutched to his stomach to Derek's son, Jack. He brushed pieces of grass off his jeans. "Okay, that's it for me. I'm done."

"Aww, Uncle Hayden. Come on. Just a little more?"

"Nope." He ruffled Jack's hair. "You guys don't need me to play."

"But it's more fun when you do," Kyle said, grinning at him over the heads of the rest of the kids, from Lila, Derek's youngest, to Nick. It had been Nick and Hayden against Kyle and all the other kids.

"Yeah, great fun. Everyone pile on Uncle Hayden. Well, now you can all pile on Uncle Kyle 'cause Uncle Hayden's going to get something to eat. Nick, you wanna come?"

The boy shook his head. "I'll play."

"Okay, Nick's the new team captain. All you kids against Uncle Kyle." He laughed, cuffing his younger brother on the shoulder. "Good luck."

Hayden trudged up the hill. Spotting Jordan on the upper deck, he waved to her. She waved back, less than enthusiastically.

The above-ground swimming pool was still

covered—Dad never opened it until the first weekend of June—but some of the family sat in chairs on the pool deck.

No sign of Ronni. Hayden skirted the pool and the hot tub, which was also still covered, but the kids would no doubt be in it later on. He found Greg watching over Finn's shoulder at the grill. "You backseat cooking?"

Finn snorted, slipping a thermometer into a piece of chicken on the grill. "He's trying to."

"Smells great."

"Did you have any doubts?" Finn pulled the temperature probe out, set it on the grill's shelf. "Almost done. Make yourself useful, Greg, and bring me the burgers and dogs. Food should be ready in about twenty more minutes."

"Timing is everything," Hayden said. "Do I know how to call it or what?"

"What," Greg said.

"Hey, either of you seen Ronni? Nick's here, and I heard through the grapevine she presented Mom with some food, but I haven't seen her."

Greg jerked his head toward the side of the house. "I left her with Amelia and Shannon at the picnic table by the bonfire pit. Figured they'd be the most welcoming to her, give her a chance to ease back into the family. I know it's not easy for any of us, but the girls in particular, especially Judy, seem hell-bent on continuing to shun her."

"Good idea, Greg." Hayden trotted toward the picnic table, but saw only Shannon, Amelia and the baby. Chip sat in the middle of the table, chewing on a set of plastic keys. He burst into a wide, drooling grin and flung them on the ground when he saw Hayden. The baby held his arms out.

"Heya, Chipster." He grabbed the child off the table, tossing him into the air and catching him. The boy shrieked in delight.

"If he throws up on you, I don't want to hear it," Amelia said. "I just finished feeding him a few minutes ago."

Hayden threw the boy into the air a few more times, until the child laughed so hard he started to hiccup.

"You're making me sick just watching," Shannon said, grabbing at her stomach.

This time when Hayden caught him, he growled like a bear, nuzzling the boy's neck and shoulders. "I'm gonna eat you up, Potato Chip. Num, num, num." He "flew" the baby back to his mother. "Greg said he left Ronni here with you guys. Where'd she go?"

"Last I saw her, she was heading into the woods. Toward the tree house, I think." Amelia pointed with one hand, holding her squirming child with the other.

"Thanks."

The remains of last year's leaves crunched under his feet as he traversed several hundred yards into the woods. The burble of a brook served as a beacon, though the path, constantly traveled by numerous Hawkins kids and grandkids, was well worn.

Ten feet off the ground, nestled between two oaks and a maple tree, the family tree house produced its own special magic. A project two summers in the making for Michael Hawkins, Hayden's dad, *tree house* didn't quite do the structure justice. Yes, it was in the trees. Yes, it was a house.

But it wasn't a few haphazard boards and a canvas roof....

Two stories tall, it had a corner turret containing a spiral staircase that rose to the sleeping loft. The metal roof made rainstorms a real experience. It also had a wraparound deck, and a retractable ladder to ensure privacy.

As he'd expected, the ladder had been drawn up.

"Ahoy in the tree fort! Who's up there?"

When none of the kids responded, he knew he'd found her. "Ronni? The ladder's up. I know you're in there." He circled around to the back of the structure. Standing on the bank of the brook, he looked up at the wide bay window. Sure enough, he could see her silhouette in the corner of the window seat.

Over the gently rushing water and chirping of birds, he caught the sound of sniffling.

"Buzz off, Hayden." Her muffled voice came through the open side window.

"What are you doing up there?"

"Having sex."

"Alone?"

"That's the only kind I've had for a long time. So go away."

"Can I watch?"

A snort of choked laughter mingled with a sob. Both sounds tore at him.

"Come on, Ronni. Lower the ladder."

When she didn't respond, he returned to the front, backed away, then started running. Several feet from the maple tree, he leaped into the air, planting one sneaker on the trunk and pushing off immediately, to hang by his fingers from the edge of the balcony. Swinging his body, he got his leg up on the ledge, moved his hands onto the rails, then pulled himself up, finally climbing over the railing. "Ladders are for wusses, anyway."

At the front of the building, he opened the door. Ronni was curled up on the window seat on the far side of the room. "Hey, you're not having sex."

She glanced out at the brook. "There's just no fooling you, is there?"

"Nope. Not when it comes to sex." He passed the handmade game table with its inlaid chess-checkerboard, then dropped opposite her on the seat. Her brown sandals lay on the floor nearby; her bare feet, sporting turquoise toenails, rested on the cushion. She had her arms crossed over her knees, her chin resting on her wrist.

"You've got a Rudolph nose." And the telltale red-rimmed eyes to go with it.

She lifted her shoulders.

"Thinking about Ian?"

"Among other things."

"Like what?"

"Like…how lucky you are to have such a big family.

If Greg is mad at you, you've got Finn. Or Derek, or any of the rest of them. If your parents are mad at you, you've got all your brothers and sisters."

"Being part of a big family isn't always all it's cracked up to be." Sometimes you got lost in the shuffle. Sometimes your parents were way too busy to deal with your pressing concerns and handed you off to an older sibling.

"Nothing ever is. And yet… My parents put me out years ago, and despite sending them a Christmas card every year at their new home in Arizona, they don't call, they don't write. Email. Text. Something. Anything."

The fact that she still tried to contact them surprised him more than her parents' continued silence. James Davidowski was a hard-core SOB who'd turned his back on his daughter when she'd needed him the most. And his wife, Lisa, had quietly gone along with him.

"I'm an only child. Babcia's long gone, Scott's…long gone, too." She took a deep breath. "Vera's my stand-in mom. I've got her and Nick. So whatever hardships come with your big family…you're lucky."

"That still doesn't explain the tears." He reached out, stroked the top of her foot.

"Being here today made me realize how much I'd lost. More than just Ian. All of you."

Hayden cursed under his breath. Talk about being a hard-core SOB. He and the rest of the family had done the same thing to Ronni that her own parents had.

Abandoned her when she'd needed them the most.

Granted, they'd all been in desperate pain themselves over Ian's loss, but even so...

They'd made a mistake.

He'd promised his brother to take care of Nick and Ronni. Instead, he'd fled, joining the Marines as though that could ease the pain of losing his best friend.

He'd discovered you couldn't outrun pain.

Or guilt.

"I still miss him."

He glanced up to meet her eyes, saw the shimmer there. "Me, too," he said, his voice gruff, thick.

"Sometimes I think about how different life would be if he hadn't gotten sick...."

"Me, too." Hayden lifted his hand, stroked the side of her face.

"He wasn't supposed to die," she whispered. Her lower lip quivered. The tears she'd struggled to hold back spilled down her cheeks, flowing over his thumb. "He was supposed to get the bone marrow transplant and be fine, like Jordan."

"Aw, hell." Hayden grasped her forearms, untangled them, pulling her into an embrace. He shifted them both on the cushion, leaning his back against the wall, cradling her against his chest. The scent of citrus rose from her hair. He stroked the silky smooth strands. "I'm sorry, Ronni."

"For what?" she murmured into his shirt, burying her face in his shoulder.

For not telling his family, or the doctor, about Ian's new symptoms, the pain in his chest and back, the breathing problems. For believing his brother when he'd said he was just upset over losing Ronni.

Hayden tightened his arms around her, rocking her gently. "For not being there for you when you needed me."

"I—I wasn't there for Ian when he needed me."

"No. You weren't. Guess we both screwed up, huh?"

She nodded against him.

"Forgive and forget?" Not that he would ever actually forgive himself. Or forget, either. Nick's lack of a father to help him transition from boy to man only deepened Hayden's sense of guilt.

She nodded again. Her body eased in his embrace, melting into him. He continued to stroke her hair. Having her in his arms felt somehow right. Comfortable.

For a moment, they just sat there, each wrapped up in their memories of Ian. A silent tribute to the young man they'd both loved.

Hayden had held her like this in her parents' driveway, the night she and Ian had told them about her pregnancy. While Ian, hot-tempered, stormed back into her house to confront her father alone, despite Hayden's urging him not to.

He'd come back out with an overnight bag. Ronni had spent the next three days sleeping on the sofa in the Hawkins family room while a truce was negotiated by Hayden's father.

That truce had lasted only until Ronni's parents realized she'd paid them lip service about having an abortion. At which point she'd gone to live with her grandmother.

"After Ian, I've missed you most of all, Hayden."

Not sure what to say to that, he pressed his lips to the top of her head. He was only just beginning to realize that he'd missed her, too.

"Do you know why we broke up before his death?"

His muscles tensed. "Yeah. You said you were too scared to watch him die."

"That's a big part of it. But more because he kept telling me what to do after he died. He wouldn't stop talking about it like it was a done deal. Like his fate was sealed. He'd given up." Her voice trembled. Hayden tightened his grip on her, offering comfort he should have offered years earlier.

"'Love again. Promise me you'll fall in love again.'" She swallowed hard. "I kept telling him he had to be positive. And he'd say he was positive—positive he wasn't going to make it, and I had to prepare myself. I finally told him I couldn't take listening to him like that anymore. That I wasn't going to stand around and watch him just give up. To call me when he decided that Nick and I were worth fighting for." Her voice dropped to a choked whisper thick with emotion. "He never called."

"I had no idea."

"You could have asked. *You* could have called."

"I'm sorry." He'd been too busy blaming her, blaming himself, to face her after his brother's death. "Why didn't you call him?"

"I did. Once. He told me to stay away. To leave him alone. To start getting on with my life. Then he hung up on me." She sighed. "Everything I did was wrong."

"I know the feeling." Hayden rested his chin on her head, snuggling her closer.

And got the jolt of a lifetime when his body reacted, making his snug jeans even tighter.

Oh, hell, no. This was *Ronni*. Off-limits on so many levels.

Trying to appear nonchalant, he eased her backward, breaking contact. Ronni was a pretty woman. His body *liked* pretty women. Responded to pretty women in close proximity. No reason to freak out. Remove the physical stimulus, lose the response. No problem.

Ronni shrugged from his embrace, shifting away from him until her back pressed against the opposite wall again. "Why did your mother invite me here today? Why now?"

"Because you opened the door first by calling me. Asking me for help with Nick."

She groaned.

"You needed help, right?" he pressed.

Her cheeks colored, and she ducked her head. "I suppose."

"Hey." He waited for her to look at him. "There's nothing wrong with needing help from time to time. You've got a lot going on right now."

In the distance, a clanging pierced the tranquillity of the tree house. Dinner bell.

"Chow's on. What say we go get something to eat?"

She shook her head. "Not really hungry. You go ahead."

"No." He rose to his feet, then pulled her up, as well. "Taking care of Nick means you have to take care of yourself, too. You need to eat. And more than that…you need to face the family. Hiding out here is not going to mend the fences. Especially not with my mom."

The color drained from Ronni's cheeks. "I—I…"

"I've got your back," Hayden told her. "I should have had it all along. You're not in this alone now. Okay?"

"Oh, hell…"

He grinned. "That's the spirit."

TRUE TO HIS WORD, Hayden stayed at her back. Or her side. They shuffled through the buffet line together, him occasionally slipping foods onto her plate. "Try this. Shannon makes awesome mac and cheese."

Unwilling to offend Shannon, who'd made an effort to reach out to her today, Ronni accepted the spoonful of creamy pasta.

Not that Hayden gave her much of a choice.

He didn't give her a choice in their seating, either, guiding her to a spot at the end of a picnic table that included Finn, Greg and their immediate families. Jordan plunked herself down at the table across from Amelia, folding her arms over her chest with a heavy huff. "This is a load of fun. When do I get to eat?" The mask muffled her words, but didn't hide the teenage attitude Ronni was intimately familiar with.

"You know the rules, Jordan. If you want to eat, I'll take a plate somewhere with you, just the two of us," Amelia said.

"What about the tree house?" Ronni offered. "We just came from there. There's nobody else out there. If she can't take the mask off around a crowd...no crowd there. Make it a picnic."

The girl's eyes lit up and she clapped. "Oh, yes. Can we, Mom?"

Amelia looked at Finn, who nodded. "I don't see why not."

Finn climbed from the table, their son in his arms. He placed the baby in Amelia's lap. "I'll put the food together so it's easy to carry. Jordan, come pick out what you want."

Jordan jumped from the table and headed for the doors to the basement. Elke, with a plate of food in one hand, baby monitor in the other, paused at the spot Jordan had just vacated. "Is she coming back?"

"No," Finn said. "Park it." As he passed Ronni, he leaned down. "Great idea. Thanks."

"Would that I could solve my own teenager problems so easily."

He gave her a pat on the shoulder. "They do make life interesting, don't they?"

"Understatement of the year. Speaking of which..." She glanced at the nearby tables. "Where's Nick?"

"Last time I saw him he was down at the pond, helping Jack and Katie fish," Greg said. "But nobody's down there now."

"Oh." She pulled her cell phone from her pocket, shot him a text asking where he was. "He loves to fish." She turned to Hayden. "Maybe you can take him one of these nights? Scott used to take him fishing all the time."

"I could probably manage that. I'd have to get a license…."

"Plenty of Scott's poles are collecting dust in our garage. You can use one of those."

The table fell strangely silent, with everyone suddenly interested in the food on their plates, or with full mouths.

The elephant in the room no one wanted to talk about. So she did. "It's not like Scott's going to mind, right?"

No one answered. Finally, Elke spoke up. "Nick's told us your husband's PVS?"

"Yes."

"How long now?"

"Nineteen months."

"That's really hard. When I did my nursing practicums, I cared for some PVS patients. Rough stuff for the families. I'm sorry."

"Thank you."

"Sitting at the bedside of someone you love, waiting for them to die, *is* very hard." Lydia's voice coming from behind her made Ronni jump. She twisted her head to look at Ian's mother. "We have some experience with that, don't we?"

Lydia gazed down at her, face unreadable in the sunlight. "Ronni, when you're done eating, I'd like a word with you. We'll use Michael's office."

CHAPTER FIVE

THE GHOST WAS BACK. The second his mother had left, old Ronni vanished and new-but-definitely-not-improved Ronni returned.

She'd wilted, withered, right in front of him.

"Mom's bark is way worse than her bite," Hayden assured her, watching Ronni push mac and cheese around on her plate. "Why are you so scared of her?"

Ronni shrugged. "Oh, maybe because I got knocked up when I was sixteen, then had a hand in her son's death. And now I've managed to screw up her grandson."

"Ian's death was not your fault. We blamed you for part of it because we were all hurting. Watching him, so sick, and so sad over you for the last few weeks of his life… You were an easy scapegoat. A target for our pain. We were wrong to do that." Hayden said it loudly enough to carry to the whole table, giving Greg and Elke long, pointed stares. Too bad more of his siblings weren't around to hear him. He'd be repeating himself numerous times. "And Nick's not screwed up. He made a mistake. We all do."

"Some of us make more than others." She shoved her plate aside. Her cell phone, lying on the table, vibrated, and she picked it up. "Nick's in the kitchen, eating with Derek and his kids."

Hayden nudged her plate back in front of her. "Finish your food."

"No. I didn't have much of an appetite to start with. And now…" She climbed from the table. "This conversation has been put off for thirteen years. It's way past time."

Hayden hastily untangled his long legs from the bench and strode after her as she headed toward the basement doors. Without faltering, she plowed through the throng that had gathered around the food-laden buffet table in the game room, oblivious to or ignoring the looks she was getting. Hayden slowed down long enough to glare at Judy, who despite having a toddler in her arms and a preschooler tugging at her pant leg, had managed to spare an evil glare for Ronni as she'd passed through.

Hayden got to the paneled hallway just in time to see her pause outside his father's home office. "Ronni!" he called. "Wait for me."

He caught her just as she opened the door.

She placed her palm on his chest. "No, Hayden. I appreciate the thought. I really do. But this is between your mom and me." She stole a peek over her shoulder, to where Lydia perched on the edge of the oversize cherry desk.

"You're sure?"

Ronni nodded. "Just…don't go too far, okay?"

"You got it."

Mrs. Hawkins set out a chair for her in front of the desk and gestured to it. "Have a seat."

The padding of the folding chair squished as Ronni did as she was told. There were no extra "real" chairs in the office because Michael Hawkins didn't usually hold meetings here. And if, as a Hawkins child, you were summoned to this room, you stood.

She knew because Ian had told her numerous stories of being brought before the family judge. More often than not, he'd stood here with Hayden at his side, the pair of them in trouble for one incident or another.

The Sir Hawkins escapade, for example.

She bit back a smile.

"Something amusing I missed about this?"

Ronni raised her head, met Lydia's frank blue eyes. "I was just thinking about Ian. About the Sir Hawkins incident at the Fourth of July parade."

The corner of Lydia's mouth twitched, and she shook her head. "If it wasn't one thing, it was another with those two. And yet..." her expression sobered "...somehow, neither of them ever got arrested. *None* of my children ever got arrested."

Ronni sighed, lowering her gaze to Lydia's beige mocs. "I'm sorry." And yet she knew some of the Hawkins kids, Ian included, had done things that, had they been caught, could have resulted in arrest. The thought buoyed her. Maybe Lydia wasn't Perfect Supermom after all.

"Sorry for what?"

"For everything. For what's going on with Nick, for—for Ian…"

The soft tick of a clock on the bookshelf punctuated the silence that grew and grew until Ronni was afraid it would strangle her.

Finally, she glanced up at Lydia, whose blue eyes shimmered. The muscle along the edge of the older woman's jaw twitched. "Why? I've waited years to know why you abandoned my son when he needed you most."

"Because I was afraid. Because watching him fade inch by inch hurt more than I'd expected." Ronni shook her head, offering a wry half smile. "Ian was larger than life. A force of nature."

Lydia nodded. "He was that."

Ronni swallowed hard. "I—I couldn't stand to see him like that. I'm sorry. I was only eighteen…."

"And he was only nineteen," Lydia asserted.

"I know. If I could go back and change it, I would." For one thing, she'd marry Ian when he asked the first time. But she'd stubbornly wanted to be sure he loved her for her, not because they were having a baby together. Then he'd gotten the cancer diagnosis—and when she'd asked him to marry her at that point, he'd refused. He had promised that after he'd beaten the cancer, they could revisit the marriage issue, but he wasn't going to marry her just to make her a widow. When he'd become convinced he wasn't going to make it, she'd stormed out….

And then it was too late.

"How much would you change?"

"W-what?"

"Would you change...getting pregnant?"

Ronni shook her head. "No way. Nick might be making me crazy right now—"

"Which is what teenagers do."

"But I wouldn't give up having him. I wouldn't miss out on any part of my life with Ian...except the part I did miss out on. The end. I'd do that differently."

Lydia's mouth flattened. After a moment, she nodded. "I'd do it differently, too. After Ian died... Hayden was right, what he said outside. You were an easy scapegoat. Watching your child die... If you thought you hurt, know that I hurt even more."

"I'm sure you did," Ronni said softly.

"You hurt my son. Badly. I wanted to make you pay for that. I was so angry at you for making his last few weeks even more miserable. He had enough to deal with. He didn't need a broken heart on top of it. I'm sorry. I didn't consider how young you were, or how much you were aching, too."

"Mrs. Hawkins, I was trying to make him fight. He'd given up. Resigned himself to dying."

The woman looked stricken. "What? No. Ian was a fighter. He didn't give up until after you..."

"Maybe he didn't tell you how he really felt?"

A knock sounded on the door. Lydia scowled. "Not *now*."

The door opened, and Alan, her oldest son, popped his head in. Hayden peered over his shoulder.

"Sorry, Mom, but this… Ronni, there's something you're going to want to see. Right now."

Her cell phone vibrated in her pocket. Ronni pulled it out as she rose to her feet. A call from Vera. She stabbed Ignore. "Is Nick all right?"

"Nick's fine," Alan assured her. "Nothing to do with him. Well, not directly." He crooked a finger. "Follow me."

Grateful for the interruption, but apprehensive at the same time, she headed out the door on his heels, Hayden on hers, and Lydia bringing up the rear. "What's going on?" she asked Hayden.

He shrugged. "Not sure."

By the time they'd made it up the long flight of stairs to the foyer, their unusual parade had picked up a few more people. On the main floor, Alan bypassed the living room, the dining room, and headed down the main hallway. At the base of the stairs that led upstairs to the bedrooms, he turned into the family room.

"Mom," Nick called from the kitchen, "what's up?"

Alan stopped in the doorway, shaking his head while furtively pointing at her son.

Ronni popped into the kitchen. "Nothing." She glanced at the two plates in front of him. The end of a hot dog in a shred of bun smeared with mustard were the only things that remained. "You get enough to eat?" Sometimes the kid was a bottomless pit. And when his friends stayed over, she needed a full freezer just to keep up with their teenage appetites.

Derek, sitting at the end of the kitchen table, sawing up a hot dog for the little girl next to him, rolled his eyes. "Unbelievable what he just put away. I don't think I ever ate that much. Something to look forward to with Jack, I suppose."

Jack stuck out his tongue in his father's direction. Then he turned to Nick. "You wanna go play some more football?"

"Sure." They both jumped from their seats.

"Clean up after yourselves first," Ronni said.

They skidded to a stop, raced back to the table, grabbing up their plates and napkins, which were promptly stuffed into the oversize garbage can by the pantry before they resumed their race outside. The screen door squeaked, then slammed.

Ronni headed back to the family room. Hayden waited just inside the doorway, as did Alan, who held the television remote in his hand. The big TV in the entertainment center had been paused.

Lydia sat next to her husband on the blue-and-white sofa along the front wall. Judy had joined them, as had Elke, both sisters minus their children, though Elke clutched the baby monitor in her hand.

"Shut the door, Hayden," Alan said.

He arched an eyebrow, but did so.

Ronni's phone vibrated in her pocket again. She pulled it out. Another call from Vera. Once more she stabbed Ignore. She would connect with Scott's mother after Alan unveiled his mystery.

Her stomach knotted. Oh, please, God, don't let him

have gotten his hands on some kind of video surveillance that showed Nick creating graffiti with the spray paints he'd been caught with.

Just what she needed. Graphic evidence of her ineptness at motherhood.

"Dad and I were catching the news. As soon as we saw it, we figured you needed to see it, too." Alan pointed the remote at the set, and the picture jerked back into motion.

"Tonight as part of our special Memorial Day weekend coverage, we've got a story that will deeply touch you. A veteran who came home, not missing a limb, but in limbo." The male anchor at WEGL shuffled several papers, then addressed the young female reporter who'd joined him at the news desk. "Some of you may remember about a year and a half ago, when Sergeant Scott Mangano—"

Ronni's chest tightened. She pressed her hand over her heart.

"—was injured in Iraq. He spent time in Walter Reed before being transferred to a care facility here in Erie. Tonight we bring you the full story of a war hero whose condition raises thought-provoking questions. Sergeant Mangano, soldier, son, husband, stepfather... But what really happened that fateful day in Iraq? Was it a deployed man's worst nightmare? His body, a mere shell, clings to the remnants of life. His mother holds out hope for a recovery that, according to medical experts, will never come. Tonight, we remember and honor this man."

The screen showed Scott's military photo as they cut to a commercial.

Ronni's hand slid to her stomach. The two bites of mac and cheese she'd eaten threatened a return trip. Her knees trembled.

Alan fast-forwarded the commercials. The silence in the room made the whoosh of her pulse in her ears sound even louder.

Hayden laid his hand on her shoulder. "Sit down, Ronni. You've gone white as a..." He hesitated a moment. "A ghost."

Somehow he steered her over to the other sofa, getting her seated. As he perched on the arm of it at her side, her phone vibrated again.

Alan stopped the playback as she pulled it out. This time when she saw read the display, she flipped it open. "Vera?"

Hysterical tears and incoherent babbling came through the speaker. The only things Ronni could make out were "news," "I'm sorry," and "true?"

"Vera, I haven't seen the whole thing yet. We'll talk about this later, okay? I'm sorry, I have to go." She clicked the phone shut.

The door to the family room flew open and Nick barreled through, his phone in hand. "Mom! Andy texted me and said there was a piece on the news about Scott and..." The boy paused, taking in the television, and the somber expressions on the adults' faces. "Nobody thought I should see this? I'm not a baby!"

"Then sit down next to your mother and don't act like one," Hayden said.

Nick threw himself onto the sofa on the other side of her, crossing his arms over his chest.

"L-let's get this over with, please." Ronni looked at Alan, who nodded and started the playback again.

The woman reporter provided the narration this time. "This was Sergeant Mangano before his deployment." Scott's service photo flashed again on the screen, followed by a series of other pictures. "He was a son." Scott hugging Vera. "A husband." A picture from their wedding day of Scott feeding Ronni cake. "A stepfather." A photo of Scott with Nick, each of them with a fishing pole. Vera had been very generous with access to her family photos. "He worked in the shop at General Electric. This is Sergeant Mangano now."

Ronni sucked in a deep breath as a shot of Scott in his wheelchair, vacant eyes staring into the distance, filled the screen. "Oh, God. No. How did they get that footage?" Her fingernails dug into her palms.

"Living in the limbo known as persistent vegetative state—"

"Permanent," Elke corrected from across the room.

"According to medical experts, there's little chance of change." The story cut to a neurologist from one of the local hospitals, talking about PVS in general terms.

Then they showed Vera, holding Scott's picture. "I still have hope. You can't give up hope. Miracles happen."

Ronni's eyes misted over. Bless Vera's heart, she still couldn't accept that her son wasn't going to recover.

"The cause of Sergeant Mangano's injury wasn't an IED." They went into the details of Scott's accident, the crash and rollover of the truck he'd been driving on duty. "We spoke to some of the other members of the unit to get their take on how something like that could happen."

Ronni shifted toward the edge of the sofa as her stomach twisted again.

Dan, Scott's buddy, shrugged his shoulders. "Accidents happen, man. No matter where you are, *bleep*—" they blurred his mouth and bleeped out his chosen curse word "—happens. The roads over there ain't exactly I-90, you know?"

"Any possibility he was impaired in some way? Had he been drinking? Had some sort of emotional distress?" the reporter asked.

"He wasn't DUI. And he seemed fine to me. Like I said, *bleep* happens."

"Another member who served with Sergeant Mangano has a different theory."

"Distracted?" said another female voice as they showed the footage of Scott in his wheelchair again. "Yeah, I think he had his *bleep*in' head up his *bleep* that day." There wasn't a note of sympathy in her response.

Ronni went dead still when they showed the woman's face, a brunette with a medium-length shag and pouty lips coated with a glossy sheen. For a moment, Ronni's lungs couldn't expand past the band of steel encircling her ribs. Her heart pounded. She'd seen that face before. Those pouty lips and dirty mouth had been doing dirty things…to her husband.

Bile rose in her throat.

The next question the reporter asked went unheard, but the response…

"A Dear John Skype. That's what he told me."

The air in the family room changed. The weight of the stares from the Hawkinses made the hair on the back of Ronni's neck stand up. Hayden, eyes widening as he looked at her, shifted away.

The explanation sat on the tip of her tongue, the urge to blurt it all out almost unbearable. But a glance at her son's befuddled expression showed he hadn't understood the woman's claim.

And Ronni refused to taint Nick's memories of the only father he'd ever known. She forced herself to breathe through her nose slowly, keeping her teeth clenched.

"Technology has changed how our troops communicate with their loved ones while deployed. Internet-based phone calls let soldiers read bedtime stories to their kids. In this case, it may have contributed to the accident that changed Sergeant Mangano's life." They showed the original series of pictures again, Scott as son, husband, stepfather. "When we asked Mrs. Mangano about the circumstances of her husband's accident, she had this to say."

"I'd rather not talk about it."

Ronni winced at her clipped tone in the nursing home's reception area. Editing could certainly make an innocent comment seem a hell of a lot worse.

The rest of the so-called news report blurred. Something about the sacrifices made by military personnel. About honoring those who'd served. And remembering those like Scott who'd made it home, but not in the same condition he'd left.

Alan clicked the television to a stop again.

A fuzzy spot appeared in Ronni's field of vision, a sparkling haze that remained even when she closed her eyes tight.

Fabulous. Just what she needed.

She opened her eyes. Everyone—or at least the ones she could see—stared at her expectantly.

She jumped from the sofa, stumbled toward the door as the flickering spot expanded to blot out more of her vision. "I—I need to use the bathroom." Arms outstretched, she bolted.

Hayden watched her stagger from the room, then turned back to face his family. She'd Dear Johned an active military man while he was deployed to a war zone?

It didn't get much lower than that. Except maybe for leaving a dying man.

Hayden had been willing to finally forgive her for the situation with Ian. Especially after learning how his brother had been resigned to his death, and she'd tried to make him fight. But this latest revelation...

"Same old Ronni," Judy quipped. "Man in trouble? No problem. Bail."

"What's a Dear John Skype?" Nick asked. "I mean, I get Skype. It's how we talked to Scott in the field. But Dear John?"

Judy, eyes blazing, leaned forward. "It means your mother told Scott she was going to divorce him while he was in the middle of a war."

Nick jumped to his feet, sending Hayden into full alert mode. His muscles tensed as the boy glared at Judy.

"Well...maybe she should have." He ran out the door, calling for his mom.

Not the reaction Hayden had anticipated from his nephew. The rest of the family looked equally surprised.

"In the interest of fairness," Alan said, "the media likes to sensationalize things. People have agendas. We don't know what that woman's agenda is."

"Ronni didn't deny it," Judy pointed out. "Isn't that the sign of a guilty person?"

"The news also glossed over the fact she's at the nursing home *every day*. Caring for someone who's completely incapacitated," Elke said. "I can't see a woman who'd intended to divorce a man sitting by his bedside, wiping drool from the corners of his mouth and dealing with everything else that goes with PVS."

"We blamed her for abandoning Ian," Hayden said, torn between the urge to defend her and the sick feeling in his gut that the Dear John thing was indefensible.

"There was more to the story than we knew." Most of the family still didn't know what Ronni had told him about her breakup with Ian. "And Nick's reaction…"

Mom sighed. "Nick's reaction, indeed. There's more going on here than meets the eye. Hayden?"

"Yes?"

"Find out what it is."

They all filed out of the room, Alan lagging behind the others. He handed the remote control to Hayden. "Listen, little brother…"

"Yes, much older and therefore thinks he's much wiser brother?"

"This has to be tough on you. So if you need someone to talk to… I know you head for Greg or Finn first, but they might be caught up with their own stuff now."

"Yeah. Thanks."

Alan nodded, then left.

Alone in the empty room, Hayden rewound the news program. He stopped on the picture of Ronni and Scott's wedding. There had still been light in her eyes that day.

Exactly when, and why, had the sparkle gone out?

That had to be the key. Perhaps the key to Nick's turmoil, too.

Secrets. Dear God, how Hayden detested secrets.

"Unk?" Nick reappeared in the doorway. Nearly as tall as his mother, he held her by the elbow, keeping her upright.

Hayden fumbled with the remote, jabbing the power button. The television faded to black. "Yeah, Nick?"

"We need your help. Mom's sick."

Ronni's face was no longer white, it was pasty gray. Small beads of sweat covered her forehead.

Hayden leaped from the arm of the sofa. "What's wrong?"

"Aura," Ronni said. "Which means I've got about twenty minutes before my head explodes. I'd really rather it didn't explode here. Way too much noise, not to mention some people might take too much pleasure in seeing me writhe in pain. I need to get home."

"But she can't see to drive," Nick explained.

"You still get those migraines?"

She nodded.

"All right. Let's go." He slid alongside her, wrapped her arm around his waist, his around her shoulders. "I've got her, Nick."

The boy reluctantly stepped away. This protectiveness of his mother was a side of him Hayden hadn't seen in the two weeks since the courthouse meeting.

He steered Ronni across the corner of the kitchen and through the mudroom, carefully guiding her down the stairs into the garage.

"Nick, honey…you stay. I don't want you to miss any of the fun. The bonfire. The fireworks. You always look forward to those." Ronni stopped moving as they approached the open garage door.

"It's okay, Mom. I'll come home and take care of you."

"That's sweet. But I'm going to take my meds and pass out, anyway. Please…"

If Hayden took Ronni home, and she passed out, it would give him a chance to snoop. Plus, once the migraine broke, he wanted answers about the news program tonight. He jumped on the bandwagon. "S'okay, sport. I'll get her home and take care of her. No worries. Somebody else can give you a ride home later."

The kid tilted his head, both eyebrows rising.

"What?" Hayden asked.

"Five minutes ago you were with the rest of them, ready to post her head on a pike or something. Now I'm supposed to believe you want to take care of her?"

"Right now, knowing how my head's going to feel, I'd prefer it on a pike," Ronni muttered. "Nick, I don't have time to argue with you. Please. I love that you want to take care of me. I do. But stay and have fun. I'm supposed to take care of *you*."

"You're sure?"

"Yes."

"Okay."

"Good." She started forward again. When they exited the garage, she turned her face into Hayden's shoulder, using her free hand to cover her eyes. They headed down the driveway.

"You still throw up when you get migraines?" he asked.

"Sometimes."

"We'll take your car."

CHAPTER SIX

FIVE MINUTES FROM her house, she moaned, pressing her hand to her head.

"Do I need to pull over?" he asked softly.

"No."

"Good. 'Cause you know how some guys will hold your hair back while you puke? FYI, I'm not that guy."

"Shh. Don't talk," she whispered harshly.

He pulled her Jetta into the short driveway at her place, the one that led to the one-car attached garage. Another longer one ran alongside the house, down the hill to the back, where the salon customers parked.

She used both hands to hold her head when he closed the car door. "Sorry."

By the time he made it to the passenger side, she'd hauled herself out. Rocking on her feet, she reached for him.

He steadied her, guiding her through the door to the left of the garage. They entered into her narrow laundry. The appliances had seen better days. The hooks on the wall were all empty.

Eyes closed, arms outstretched, Ronni groped her way to the hall. He glanced over her shoulder to be sure the door to the basement was shut. If she tumbled down those, a migraine—or the news report—would be the least of her worries.

"Thanks," she murmured as she staggered toward the kitchen. "Going to bed."

He continued to follow her. As they entered the kitchen, the house phone rang. Ronni flinched at the noise, covering her ears. Hayden glanced at the base on the counter. The message indicator showed eleven messages for her. The answering machine picked up as they crossed into the living room, Ronni trailing her hand along the wall of the hallway.

"Mrs. Mangano, this is Eric Hanover. I'm a reporter from the *Erie Gazette*. I'd like to interview you about your husband and the story that ran on WEGL tonight. Please call me back. You can reach me at…" The man left his contact information.

Ronni groaned as she turned into her bedroom. She dropped onto the queen-size bed without turning down the quilted spread. Mostly white with some brown and pink, it was feminine, but not fussy. Just like Ronni.

Lying back, she draped her arm across her face and didn't move.

Hayden went to the bottom of the bed, slid off her tan sandals. As he did, something on the inside of her left ankle caught his eye. A small tattoo? He couldn't quite make it out.

"Close shades?"

Without a word, he pulled the shades on the two windows in the room, one that overlooked the parking lot in the back, and one on the side of the house. Then he went into the bathroom. The ranch-style home had only one bathroom, but it could be accessed from either the master bedroom or the hallway. Hayden rummaged in the linen closet for towels, in the process finding the box of condoms Nick had mentioned during their first mano a mano chat, right next to Ronni's "personal" supplies. He'd have to talk to her about the idea that a fourteen-year-old boy might help himself to condoms, but it was far less likely if they were sitting right next to feminine hygiene products.

Retrieving two blue hand towels, Hayden laid one next to the sink, then ran the other under hot water until steam billowed. After wringing it out, he quietly returned to the bedroom. "I brought you a hot towel."

She reached for it.

"Careful," he murmured.

Ronni held it in the air for a moment, testing the heat, then draped it across her face from one ear to the other, covering her eyes.

She sighed. "You remembered. Thanks."

How could he have forgotten? He'd helped Ian run hot towels for her when she'd been pregnant with Nick and having migraine attacks. She'd refused to take any kind of drugs for the pain then.

"Shh. Let the medicine work." He'd retrieve the pills from her purse first thing when they'd gotten into her car. "Any other way I can help?"

"Yes." She panted a few moments, wrestling with the

pain. "Lie down and stick your hand under my head. Under my neck. I'll show you."

Hayden glanced around the room—looking for what, he wasn't sure. It just seemed odd. Still, it wasn't as if he hadn't climbed onto a bed with plenty of women. She wasn't precisely inviting him *into* her bed.

Images of being there stormed him—of Ronni, naked in the moonlight and candlelight, panting not from pain, but from pleasure....

Son of a— What in the hell was he doing, fantasizing about *her* like that? He'd broken up with Piper three and a half weeks ago. It wasn't as if he'd been deprived for an extended period of time.

Careful not to jounce the springs too much, he stretched out on his side and eased his hand under her neck as she'd asked.

She grunted. "Stick your thumb here." She indicated the spot where her skull joined her neck on the left side.

He applied pressure.

"Harder."

Ironic word choice on her part, Hayden mused. Usually when he was sprawled on a mattress with a woman and she said that, she didn't have a headache. But since one of his cardinal rules was always oblige a lady in bed, he pressed harder.

"Mmm."

That sounded near enough to satisfaction, so he maintained the position.

Then the phone on her bedside table rang. She

groaned. He withdrew his hand and rolled from the bed, rounding it to grab the handset and jab the off button. In the distance, the kitchen extension continued ringing. "Be right back," he told her.

A soft length of fabric tangled around his shoe as he hurried from the room. He kicked his foot up, catching the material and slinging it across his shoulder.

In the kitchen, the answering machine took the call. "Ronni Mangano? Heartless bitch. You should be ashamed of yourself." Just as Hayden reached for the photo to give the woman caller a piece of *his* mind, she hung up.

Now the blinking light read thirteen messages. On the off chance one of them might have actually been important, he listened to them all. A few were from Scott's mother, complaining that Ronni wasn't answering her cell, and requesting she call back. Several were from media people besides the *Erie Gazette*, and the rest were like the one he'd just heard—strangers who didn't have anything better to do than attack someone they didn't know over a story they didn't have all the facts on.

Facts he wanted.

Hayden—hell, his entire family—had condemned Ronni once. No more rushing to judgment when it came to her.

He left the messages on the machine, but turned off the ringer. She had enough to deal with right now.

The material he'd slung over his shoulder slipped. He caught it, holding it out. Navy blue, worn from repeated washings to the point of being tissue thin, the thing looked familiar. He could barely make out a figure on the front.

And then it hit him. It was the oversize nightshirt featuring the Tazmanian Devil from the Bugs Bunny cartoons that Ian had given Ronni for Christmas the year she'd been pregnant with Nick.

That she still had it, still obviously wore it… Hayden cleared his throat and draped it over his shoulder again.

On the return trip, he cut through the bathroom, heating the second towel and taking it with him. "Fresh towel," he whispered, dropping the nightshirt back on the floor near the bedside table.

She held out the now-cool terry cloth, exchanging it. He tossed it onto the bathroom counter from the door, then eased back onto the bed. When he pushed his thumb into her neck, she rewarded his efforts with another soft sigh of relief.

He lay that way for a long while, getting up to bring a hot towel several times. Eventually her breathing evened out, and she didn't stir when he quietly asked if she wanted a reheat.

Stretched out beside her, watching the gentle rise and fall of her chest by the light that slanted in from the bathroom window, Hayden was filled with a feeling of peace.

Of belonging.

Which made no sense at all, given the questions

he had for her, and the "recon mission" he needed to complete.

Not to mention the husband who belonged on this side of the mattress.

Chastising himself, he climbed from the bed without disturbing her—another skill he'd honed to an art form.

Using his cell phone as a flashlight, he started his investigation with the tat on her ankle, because it intrigued him. Body art reflected very personal things.

As he knew from experience.

He pushed the hem of her jeans up. In the glow from the phone screen, he could make out a broken heart superimposed on the Liberty Bell, with the cracks lining up. Amazing artwork. He turned the phone around, snapped a picture of it. Greg was the expert at art interpretation. Hayden fired off a copy to him, asking for his thoughts.

Though curious about Ronni, he wanted to know more about her husband. She'd married Mangano about a year after Hayden had returned home from his enlistment. Nick had been around seven.

A tall chest of drawers butted against the wall near the bathroom door. The top, where most men kept watches, cell phones and other odds and ends, was bare. He carefully opened the top drawer. Nothing inside.

The same held for each of the other drawers, with the exception of the bottom, where he discovered a collection of Ronni's sweaters, tucked away for next fall.

Not a stitch of Scott's clothing.

Odd.

He moved toward the closet next. Same thing. One side clearly held Ronni's things, while the other was empty save for a few strays of hers that had invaded.

Maybe Scott had used the closet in the guest room.

But across the hallway in the spare room, the only sign of Scott Hayden found was his dress uniform, still covered in plastic from the dry cleaners. On the shelf above it, a shoe box held his ribbons and other small uniform necessities.

Where were his cammies? His sea bag holding all the stuff he'd deployed with? And what about his civvies?

The Dear John scenario looked more and more plausible.

Although maybe she'd erased him from the house sometime after his accident? As a way of accepting the finality of his injury?

In the living room, one picture of Scott sat smackdab in the middle of the mantel. Over the years, Hayden hadn't paid much attention to the man his brother's son had called Dad. Not after an initial check by the family into the guy's background had revealed nothing of concern. Interrogating Nick from time to time hadn't revealed anything to worry about, either. Hayden vaguely recalled Scott dropping the boy off at his parents' once or twice. But that was the closest he'd ever come to meeting him.

Hayden studied Scott's military photo. The dark blue eyes had a hard edge to them. Hell, the whole face had a hard look, as if he was a guy who got what he wanted—or took it.

Finally, Hayden headed to Nick's bedroom. Opening the door, he stepped over dirty clothes scattered on the floor.

The corner desk boasted a computer with dual monitors, three empty energy drink cans and assorted snack wrappers. A flat-screen television perched on top of Nick's dresser. World of Warcraft and Halo posters graced the walls, along with several bikini babes.

Hayden checked those out carefully, his grin growing. From these examples, the boy had good taste in women.

Over the twin bed, framed photo collages celebrated different periods in Nick's life. One picture jumped out at Hayden immediately—baby Nick slumbering on Ian's chest. Others also demanded his attention: Hayden's parents with Nick, and one of him and Judy, the proud godparents, with the baby on Nick's christening day.

There were pictures of Nick with the family from more recent gatherings, including Greg and Shannon's wedding last summer. How had Ronni gotten her hands on those? Although given that all the kids ran around with camera-equipped cell phones these days, in all likelihood, the pictures had come from one of his cousins— or from Nick's own phone.

Despite the grudge they'd held against Ronni, she'd done her damnedest to make sure Nick remained a part of the Hawkins family, and remembered Ian.

Another collage featured pictures of Nick with Scott.

So apparently Ronni hadn't completely erased him from the whole house—just from their bedroom.

Curiouser and curiouser.

In the closet, Hayden shoved his fingers into a baseball glove that had been buried under some shoes in a corner.

Nothing. He searched the kid's socks, every other nook and cranny he could think of. All he found worth noting was a battered copy of *Playboy*, which he tucked back into its hiding place. Compared to some of the things the kid could find on the internet these days, *Playboy* was tame and classy.

Hayden crept back into Ronni's bedroom. At some point she'd removed the towel from across her eyes and tossed it on the floor. Sleep had smoothed the pain and anxiety of the day from her face.

He reached down, brushed the hair from her forehead, stroked the skin over her eyebrows.

Life had given her enough lemons to start a factory, never mind a lemonade stand. Gut instinct told him she had other lemons he didn't know about—yet.

Once again he had the urge to wrap her in his arms and shelter her. Tell her it was all going to work out.

He turned on his heel and bolted.

SEVERAL HOURS LATER, as he sprawled on Ronni's sofa, television remote in hand, sound turned way down,

Hayden's cell phone vibrated. Nick's number showed on the caller ID. "Yeah, Nick, what's up?"

"How's my mom?"

"Sleeping it off."

"Oh. Good." There was a pause. "So what are you doing?"

"Watching TV." Hayden cut the next pause short. "Spill it, Nick. What do you want?"

"Well…Pop's having a sleepover in the tree house. I want to stay, but I didn't want to call Mom because of the migraine."

"So you're looking for *my* permission?"

"Well…you can at least let her know. Leave a note or something. That way she won't worry."

"Nick, all she does is worry about you right now." Among other things. "Yeah, stay. I'm sure your mom will be fine with it. Speaking of Pop, is he around?"

"Yeah."

"Good, put him on."

"Hayden?" his father's deep voice came onto the connection. "How's Ronni?"

"Okay. Sleeping now. Listen, Dad…if you get a chance tonight, at the sleepover, see if you can't get Nick to talk to you. Maybe you'll have better luck than I have. After all, you've got a hell of a lot more experience at it than I do."

"That's true. But then, there's really only one way to get experience at being a father."

"Yeah, well, so far I don't seem to be cut out for the job. Probably best that I haven't procreated."

"One never knows what the future holds."

Hayden laughed. "Not for me, thanks, Dad. I'm pretty content with my life the way it is." And yet…he *had* felt a pang of longing at the family meeting.

"Don't close doors to the possibility, that's all I ask."

Hayden shook his head. Parents. Did they ever stop? "Tell Finn or Greg to call me. I'll need them to bring my car over here."

"Get any answers yet?"

"No. She wasn't in any shape to talk to me. But I'll find out before I leave."

Or he wouldn't leave…

RONNI BLINKED to bring the red numbers on the clock into focus: 11:37 p.m. Noise from a car door had pulled her from sleep.

The sickening pain of the migraine had broken, thank God. She pushed herself upright, swinging her legs off the bed.

Her foot encountered a cold, damp towel on the floor, and she recoiled, stifling a yelp. Leaving it there, she headed for the living room. Through the picture window, she saw Hayden and two other men in the glint of the streetlight. Three cars, her Jetta, Hayden's Camaro and a Tracker, filled the driveway. After some low conversation, one of the others—Finn, maybe?—cuffed Hayden on the arm. Finn and the other man, most likely Greg, but hard to tell in the dim light, got in the Tracker at the end of the driveway and took off.

So where was her son?

She met Hayden in the kitchen.

"Ronni," he said. "You're up. How's the head?"

"Okay. Just the hangover now." Migraines tended to leave her feeling sort of fuzzy, out of it, when they'd broken. A lovely leftover. She flipped off the dining area light, leaving the space lit only by the fluorescent bulb over the sink. "Where's Nick?"

"He wanted to stay. Dad decided to do a sleepover in the tree house with the grandkids."

Ronni slid into a chair at the kitchen table, shaking her head. "My son, who's on *probation,* wanted to do a sleepover with his grandfather and the younger kids in the tree house? What's wrong with this picture? Or am I just being too suspicious?"

"That's the problem with being fourteen. There are moments when you're on the cusp of manhood, and other moments when you're still more kid."

Ronni snorted. "Let's be honest. All men are always still part kid. It's why they have kids of their own—to give them excuses to keep playing with toys."

"I don't need any excuses." Hayden stood over her, shifting back and forth on the balls of his feet. "Can I get you something to drink or anything?"

"No, thanks."

"Good. Then let's not beat around the bush, okay?" He dropped into the chair next to her. "Did you Dear John your husband while he was in a war zone?"

At first she stared at the edge of the table. But something made her lift her head and look him right in the eye. She took a deep breath. "Yes. I did."

Lips pressed tightly together, he shook his head, his disapproval plain. "For the love of God, why? When a man's in action…whatever problems you have, you suck them up and wait for him to come home. Otherwise…"

"He ends up like Scott." She lowered her gaze, rubbing her forehead with her fingertips. "Believe me, I get that I'm responsible for his condition."

"I didn't say that."

"You didn't have to."

"Ronni…" Hayden waited in silence until she looked at him again. "Why? That turned out to be the important question about you and Ian. I understand that situation a lot better now. Were you afraid he'd die, too? Wanted to get out before that happened?"

She recoiled, leaning away from him. "No. That's not it at all."

"Well…that's how it looks. Like whenever your man is in the most trouble, you get while the getting's good. Before it all goes to shit."

She shoved back her chair, ignoring the pang in her head when she jumped to her feet. "That's *not* how it is. I'll be right back."

She stormed down the hallway to her bedroom, her pulse thudding in her temples, warning her to calm down or risk reactivating her migraine. Laptop clutched to her chest, she returned to the kitchen. She placed it on the table in front of Hayden, powering it up and logging in.

"What's this?" he asked.

"I'm going to show you *why*. You know how they say a picture's worth a thousand words?"

He nodded while she opened a password protected file.

"Video's worth even more." She walked away, leaned her head against the cool glass of the patio door. No way would she watch it again. But then, she didn't have to. The images were seared into her memory. Sometimes she saw versions of it in her sleep. Not so much recently, but at first… "Go ahead. Start it."

Keys clicked as Hayden did as she asked.

"Oh, yeah, baby, suck it." Her husband's voice drifted from the built-in speakers of the laptop.

"That's Scott," she pointed out. "Since I doubt you recognize his voice."

"No," Hayden said, clearing his throat. "But I recognize that face looking up at him from the news."

Ronni's heart pounded. She closed her eyes, but like the aura from the migraine, could still see the images… desert cammies and boxers down around his thighs, G.I. Jane on her knees in front of him.

"You like it, don't you?" Jane asked.

Scott groaned in reply.

"Better than what you get at home, right? Say it. Say I'm better than your frumpy wife at home."

"Finish me, baby. Stop talking and use that wicked mouth to get me off."

"Tell me I'm better."

"You're better. Way better. Now finish me, or I'll ram—"

The sound halted abruptly. "I, uh…I get the picture," Hayden said.

"Oh, no, not yet. But I can provide more pictures until you do." Hot tears leaked from her tightly scrunched eyes, and her stomach ached, as if someone had punched her in the gut. Finding out your husband had betrayed you was bad enough. Seeing the deed done, right in front of your very eyes, was something else entirely.

She hadn't realized it could still hurt this much after nineteen months.

Hayden's chair scuffed on the floor. A moment later he stood beside her.

She turned her face away, pressing her right cheek against the glass. Her tears made it slick. "Don't touch me," she whispered.

"Okay," he said gently, his breath warm on her shoulder. "Not touching."

"T-this—" she had to swallow hard as a huge lump filled her throat "—wasn't the first time."

"Shit." Hayden's curse held a note of apology.

"I caught him a few months before he deployed. Kicked him out then. We told Nick he was starting training early. Fortunately, he did have training to go through that took him out of here."

"But…" Hayden prodded.

"But he promised me…" She silently cursed the tears she couldn't control. "Said he needed me and Nick to come home to. Couldn't deploy without knowing he had us waiting for him. He swore it wouldn't ever happen again. Like a fool, I believed him. Gave him another chance. You can see what it got me."

"Combat does funny things to some people. They find ways to blow off the stress."

She jerked her head around, shifting to face him. "Like blowing someone else's *husband?* Are you making *excuses* for them?"

"No. I'm just saying—"

"Do you have any idea how it makes a woman feel when she finds out her husband has betrayed her? Cheated on her?"

"Can't say I do."

"It makes her feel not good enough. D-defective." Ronni's jaw quivered.

Hayden couldn't stand her tears another second. He grabbed her and pulled her into his arms, pressing her face into his shoulder. "The only one who's not good enough is him, sweetheart. He's the defective one, not you."

Suddenly her dead eyes made sense. The bastard who'd professed to love her had killed her spirit.

Ian had to be rolling over in his grave. Hell, Hayden was shocked his brother hadn't become a zombie and clawed his way from the earth to avenge her.

"I'm sorry, Ronni." He stroked her hair until she stopped shaking against him. "Does Nick know about this?" he asked gently.

"What?" She shoved away from him. "Are you *crazy?*

Of course he doesn't know. Why in the world would I burden my son with *my* problems? Screw with the memories of the only father he's ever known?"

Hayden shrugged. "Just wondering, because of his response to the news today. He asked what a Dear John was." And then there had been his comment weeks ago about not wanting to be the kind of man who let the wrong head do the thinking.

"And you *told* him?"

"Judy did. When she'd explained it meant you told Scott you were divorcing him, Nick said, 'Maybe she should have.' Are you sure he didn't find this file on your computer?"

"Absolutely not. The entire computer is password protected, and the file has another separate password."

Hayden held up his hands. "Okay, okay, take it easy. Just asking. Who else does know?"

"You mean besides G.I. Jane, the slut bitch whore?" Ronni's hands fisted and a spark of anger glinted in her eyes.

He bit back a grin. *That's the spirit.* "Yeah. Besides her."

"Just my best friend, Tamara."

"Nobody else? You're sure?"

She nodded.

"So who sent you the video?"

"It came from a generic Yahoo address. If I had to guess, I think it was G.I. Jane."

"Why?"

"Because she wanted my husband. War zone sex

wasn't enough. She wanted him free to be with her when they came back stateside."

"Makes sense, I suppose."

"Either way, it doesn't matter. Somebody who wanted me to know sent me the file."

"She couldn't have sent it in-country." If either Scott or his mistress had gotten caught in a Middle Eastern country with a pornographic file, they'd have been in huge trouble. Not just for breaking the fraternization rules. Porn, or even something as mild as some romance novel covers, could get you into a huge jam in the Middle East. The armed forces took complying with the local norms seriously.

"Easy enough to send a file by snail mail to a girl-friend, and have her email it. There are ways."

"True."

"So…am I forgiven for my Dear John to a lying cheater in a war zone?"

"I don't know. Are you?"

She ducked her head against his scrutiny. No, she hadn't forgiven herself, that much was plain.

"Listen, Ronni…I know you don't want Nick to find out about this. But you're going to have to brace yourself. You're in for a shit storm. And your only defense is to put the truth out there."

"What do you mean?"

Hayden crossed to the counter, where the answering machine's blinking number now read twenty-seven messages.

And pressed Play.

CHAPTER SEVEN

HAYDEN'S SNEAKERS POUNDED the pavement of the multipurpose trail along the edge of Presque Isle. Dawn had broken only an hour ago. Early morning sunlight reflected off the bay as he burst into the clearing by the ferry dock. Veering off the paved path, he headed toward one of the picnic tables. Just as he reached it, he leaped and dived forward, placing his hands on the middle of the table, vaulting over it. Between his location and the path, an empty park bench stood beneath the trees. He did a simple vault over that one.

If only he could clear life's obstacles as easily.

The gentle lap of the water along the shoreline accompanied the slap of his feet. Every now and then he encountered another runner or a biker.

As he ran behind the ranger station, his iPhone, strapped to his biceps, vibrated. He slowed his pace, twisting his arm to see who was calling.

Ronni. He stopped on the bridge by the pond, leaning against the railing. The Velcro straps grated as he yanked the phone out. "Ronni?" He blew out several times, trying to get his breathing under control. "What's up?"

"I, uh, I need some help. Damn, I seem to be saying that far too often lately."

"What's wrong? Another migraine?" She'd seemed fine when he'd left sometime after midnight. At least as far as the migraine went. As far as the emotional fallout from yesterday, she'd still been unsteady.

"No. News crews."

He bent over, put his hand on his knee, sucking in another deep breath. Abruptly stopping a run like that played havoc on the body. "Calling you?"

"No. On the street out front of the house. There's a minor swarm of them."

"Damn."

"My thoughts exactly. Don't they have Memorial Day parades and stuff to cover today?"

"Guess not." He straightened, then bent backward over the railing, stretching his abs.

"Some of them rang my doorbell earlier. I threatened to call the cops if they didn't get off the property." Panic made her words tumble over each other. "They just kept hollering questions through the door. They finally moved to the street when a squad car drove by. I need to go see Scott, then head over to your parents to pick up Nick. But I don't want to get ambushed when I walk out of here."

"Sit tight. I'm on the peninsula. I've got about another mile to get back to my car. I'll pick up the pace and be there as soon as I can."

Her sigh carried a note of relief. "Thanks."

He hung up the phone, strapping it on his arm again.

Just as he'd feared after listening to her messages last night, the vultures had landed.

And knowing the media, they wouldn't be satisfied until they'd picked Ronni's bones clean. Nick would be caught in the cross fire, which was the last thing the kid needed right now.

Hayden glanced at his watch, gathered himself and sprinted like hell for the parking lot.

Six minutes later, sweat running down the sides of his face and tank top plastered to his chest, he pulled up at the Camaro. He reached into the backseat, grabbed a towel. After mopping his face with it, he draped it across the seat so his sweaty legs wouldn't stick. The car roared to life. The twenty-five miles per hour speed limit drove him crazy as he headed for the park exit. The thundering beat of DragonForce music blared from the speakers, only emphasizing the crawl of the car.

Eighth Street, with all its traffic lights, didn't help, either.

On the street in front of Ronni's house, he passed a car labeled *Erie Gazette*; apparently Eric Hanover had decided not to wait for her to get back to him. Other media vehicles, from the three local television stations, were also parked on the berm. Then there were un-marked cars that had to belong to the photographers hoisting cameras with big, intrusive lenses.

How the hell had word spread so damn fast? Did the media tweet each other or what?

"Who's that?" one of them called as he climbed from the car. Shutters clicked in chorus. "Sir, sir! Can we speak to you?" a woman yelled. "Who are you? What's your relationship to Ronni Mangano?"

He resisted the urge to flip them off, and slipped in through the laundry room door. Ronni stood at the kitchen counter, a black bag in front of her, cup of coffee cradled in one hand. Dim sunlight filtered through the curtains she'd drawn across the window over the sink. The vertical blinds over the sliding glass door to the deck were also drawn. "Good. I see you've battened down the hatches."

"Best I can. Unfortunately, the picture window in the living room doesn't have either blinds or curtains."

"You're probably going to want to do something about that."

She set the mug in the sink. "Seriously? I mean, they'll be gone by tomorrow, right?"

He lifted one shoulder. "Juicy story. Depends on how the public responds, I guess. Ratings rule. Let's roll. I don't want to hang here any longer than necessary."

She hefted the black bag. In the laundry room, she hesitated. Started to backpedal. Fold up.

"Ronni." He waited for her to look at him. "Listen to me. When we walk out that door, it's critical that you hold your head high. You have nothing to apologize for or feel guilty about. You are the wronged party here. So you freakin' square your shoulders and hold your head up."

Uncertainly flitted in her eyes.

"The people out there are sharks. If they smell even a hint of blood in the water, you're done for. Do you get me?"

Lips pressed together, she nodded.

He shook his head. "Not convincing at all. I don't care if you don't feel it. You fake it till you make it, okay? Think how much satisfaction Scott's bitch is getting from this."

That got a glint of anger from her. She snapped to, jaw set.

"Better. Let's move." He opened the door, placing his body between her and the photographers. Taking her elbow, he escorted her to the car, holding her back with a slight shake of his head when she tried to rush. Cameras snapped and the people across the street jostled each other for a better view. They called her name, shouting instructions, asking questions.

"Mrs. Mangano, tell us more about your husband!"

"Ronni, Ronni, look over here!"

"Did you tell your husband you were divorcing him?"

"That's right," Hayden murmured to her as the color drained from her face. "Head up. You're doing great. Ignore them." Once she was in the Camaro, he circled around the front. Seeing some of them heading for their own vehicles, he backed onto the street and stomped on the gas.

Three blocks later, he made an abrupt right turn onto a side road, and started weaving through neighborhoods. Ronni braced herself against the dash. "Easy,

Speed Racer. Let's get to the nursing home in one piece, huh?"

Hayden made another turn. "Yeah, we will. First, though…" He gestured to his tank top and running shorts. "I need a quick shower and change."

She wrinkled her nose. "Thought it was some dirty gym clothes in the back that smelled so ripe."

"That's the smell of man, babe. I know it's been a while, so I understand why you don't recognize it."

She snorted, a small smile playing on her lips.

Immensely satisfied by what felt like a huge victory, Hayden checked the rearview mirror. From what he could see, no one had followed them.

Which was good, because he certainly didn't need them finding his place.

THEY PULLED INTO A CONDO complex near the mall. Ronni stared at the maze of cookie-cutter brown buildings. They drove around to the back. Hayden jabbed a button on the visor, and the garage door of a unit toward the end went up. He steered the car into it. "Don't get out until the door closes. I don't think anyone followed us, but still…"

"Okay."

Once the door shut out the morning sunlight, they both climbed from the car. In the forward right corner of the basement garage, Hayden's white-and-silver motorcycle glistened under the overhead light. A far cry from Ian's dusty bike she'd seen in the garage at the Hawkinses' yesterday. Several empty storage racks stretched across the front wall, along with a washing machine and dryer. Hayden yanked his tank top over his head and dropped it on the floor beside the washing machine, then immediately started up the stairs.

Leaving her to follow, staring gape-mouthed at the muscles in his back. Not to mention the play of his glutes in the formfitting spandex running shorts.

Not an ounce of fat on him. The devilish urge to pinch his butt had her reaching forward. At the last second, she controlled it, pulling back. The door at the top of the stairs spilled them out into his kitchen. He leaned into the fridge, grabbing a bottle. Guzzling the blue contents, he turned to face her.

A black band encircled his left biceps, accentuating the ripped muscles there. Prominent veins ran down his arms.

A bead of sweat broke loose from his collarbone and traveled south over an eight-pack washboard stomach so fine women undoubtedly wept at his feet.

Reasonably fit as a teenager, he still hadn't looked like *that* the last time she'd seen him shirtless. "The Marines really agreed with you, huh?"

He looked confused, followed her gaze down. A slow, predatory smile made the dimples on either side of his mouth appear. "Think so?" He flexed, making his pecs jump.

She shook her head. Oh, yeah, he personified the boy your mother had warned you about. Her mother had, anyway. Had warned her about both rowdy, good-looking Hawkins boys. She'd reminded Ronni of that repeatedly after the pregnancy confession.

And while Ronni might change how it had turned out, especially losing her relationship with her parents, she wouldn't give up getting involved with Ian for the world.

"Make yourself at home," Hayden said. "Give me ten minutes." He strode from the kitchen, his feet pounding up another set of stairs. A minute later, running water gurgled through pipes overhead.

Curious, and with nothing better to do, she opened cabinet doors. He apparently owned dishes only for two—two white bowls, two square plates, two rocks glasses. The silverware was the same, thrown loose in a drawer. Not a pot, not a pan…

The refrigerator held mostly bottles—sports drinks, orange juice, water and dark ale. Foam containers bearing Finn's restaurant name, Fresh, sat side by side with Tupperware bowls.

Other than the packaged leftovers—not junk food by any means, but various veggie and meat combos—little resembling actual food besides a jar of all-natural peanut butter and a loaf of whole wheat bread appeared in the kitchen.

A small square table, its surface marred with scratches, occupied the far wall. Neither chair matched its dark wood—or each other.

The water stopped running overhead as she wandered into the living room, which featured a gas fireplace in the corner. As for the rest of the room… "You've got to be kidding me."

His "furniture" consisted of a wall mounted wide-screen television, a zero-gravity lawn chair and a rickety TV tray that held the remote control and an empty dark brown bottle.

Stereo speakers perched in each corner of the room near the ceiling. Beneath the television, a small black shelving unit held the cable box and stereo.

This wasn't a condo. It was a man cave all the way.

She was still standing in stunned amazement when he barreled down the stairs, dragging a polo shirt over his head. She swung her attention to him. He pulled to an abrupt stop halfway to the kitchen. "What?" he asked, looking down at his clothes. "Is my fly open?"

Which, of course, made her check the zipper on the snug, faded jeans. Her cheeks warmed. She snapped her gaze upward. "I love what you've done with the place. Please tell me you're not sleeping on a mattress on the floor."

For a split second, his expression grew somber. Then he gave her a half grin, shrugging. "Hey, I've only been here a month. And no, I'm not sleeping on a mattress on the floor. I have a bed and everything." He raised both eyebrows, leaned toward her. "You wanna see?"

A wave of warmth flowed over her. *Idiot. Don't be flattered. Mr. Flirt would say that to any female.* "Pass, thanks."

"Your loss. If there's one room in a house I know my

way around, it's the bedroom." His blue eyes sparkled mischievously.

She shook her head. "You're so bad." And yet he'd managed to make her forget all her problems if only for a few moments.

"Bad boys have more fun."

"Bad boys get into more trouble." And she had enough of that. She checked her watch. "Let's get going, okay?"

"Sure."

Her husband and son were both waiting for her.

"I'VE NEVER LIVED by myself before," he found himself blurting to her halfway to the nursing home. They'd spent the rest of the time in silence. He'd mulled over a variety of topics, but that hadn't been one of them.

"Which means what, exactly?"

"Just that…" The quiet made him crazy? Being alone had turned out to be something he wasn't very good at? A month in his own place and he was seriously considering asking Kyle to move into the second bedroom now that the squirt had finished law school. But did Hayden really want to confess those things to her? "I never had to furnish a place before. My sisters offered to swoop in and take care of things, but I didn't want to end up with pink curtains and crap, you know?"

"Pink curtains would definitely clash with your TV tray."

"Yeah. It's just…" He twitched one shoulder. "I guess

I don't spend a lot of time there. Not so far, anyway. It serves its purpose."

"It looks like a college kid lives there. Actually, college kids usually have more furniture than that."

"A college kid couldn't afford my electronics." Hayden turned the Camaro onto the road leading to the nursing home.

She lifted the oversize black bag from the floor, cradling it on her lap as she stared out the window. Then groaned, slumping down in the seat.

"What's— Son of a…" He tightened his grip on the wheel as they cruised by the line of media people now camped outside the nursing home.

Hayden pulled into the parking lot, bypassing the driveway that led to the portico at the front entrance, and whipped around the back of the building. When he found a green door near a Dumpster, he stopped alongside it, underneath the No Parking sign. "Call them," he ordered. "Get someone to open this door for us."

"Us? You're coming in?"

It hadn't been on his to-do list that morning, but now… "Yes. I'm coming in."

Her eyes widened. She looked down at her hands, laced together over her bag. Then she glanced back at him, offering him a tiny smile that seemed more sad than happy. "Thank you."

Once again he realized just how alone she was. He might be officially living alone, but he had his entire family at a moment's notice. Sometimes when he didn't want them, but still…

He cupped the side of her face in his palm, brushed his thumb across her cheek, which flushed beneath his caress. "You're welcome."

When she shifted her face to look down again, he removed his hand, let her go. "The call?"

"Oh, right." She rummaged in the purse—how the hell could she find anything in there?—finally retrieving her cell. After a short conversation with the staff, they slipped into the nursing home.

Hayden followed Ronni down the hall. She greeted people by name: Joe, an old man in a ratty blue bathrobe, shuffling down the corridor in his slippers; Helen, a woman with sunken lips, indicating she hadn't put on her dentures yet that morning; Chris, a staff member pushing a cart laden with covered breakfast trays.

Beneath the scents of coffee and institutional scrambled eggs, he caught whiffs of cleaning solution.

He followed Ronni farther into the maze of hallways. The one-story building sprawled in several directions. They crossed through the main foyer, heading down a westward wing.

He damn near barreled into Ronni when she hesitated outside a door. Her shoulders raised a fraction and her head leveled. She sucked in a deep breath and entered the room. He stayed on her heels.

"Morning, Scott," she chirped, dumping her bag on the bed.

The man strapped into the wheelchair bore only a passing resemblance to the military photo Hayden had studied last night. The eyes no longer carried a hard edge.

Ronni ruffled Scott's hair. Not exactly the caress of a lover or a wife. Something more perfunctory. Professional. Detached. But then who could blame her for that?

"I brought my clippers. You really need a haircut, don't you? Guess I haven't been paying close enough attention to it." She rummaged in the bag, pulling out an assortment of stuff.

Hayden continued to study her husband. The wide shoulders had shrunk, as had the rest of him. Interesting how they'd *both* shrunk from their former selves. Scott held his head on an angle, his mouth gaped open at one side. Morning shadow stubbled his chin and jawline.

And that was where Ronni started. She flicked a button on a battery-powered razor, using one hand to tighten Scott's skin while she buzzed away his whiskers. Once in a while he made throaty noises, or moved. Not purposefully. More like involuntary muscle contractions, like a twitch.

Hayden folded his arms over his chest and leaned against the wall, feeling like a voyeur. When she'd finished the shave, she lifted a bottle from the small dresser, dousing her palms with aftershave. The application turned more into a caress this time.

"There. Now you're smooth and smell nice. The nurses will appreciate that."

Bits of hair fell into the sink in the corner of the room as she shook out the razor's screen.

"Why didn't you go ahead and divorce him, Ronni? I mean…"

She gestured at Scott. "You have to ask? Look at him. What kind of a woman divorces a man who can't shave himself? Who can't even hold the pen to sign the divorce papers? Doesn't have a clue what planet he's on, let alone what's going on in his personal life?"

Hayden snorted. "Probably a good many of them, especially in your situation."

"I'm trying to set a proper example for my son, Hayden."

"And prove something to yourself, as well?"

She shrugged, unfolding a black plastic cape and shaking it in the air. "Maybe."

"Doing penance. For Ian."

She froze, then turned stricken eyes in Hayden's direction. Several heartbeats passed. "Maybe." Fastening the cape behind Scott's neck, she draped it over his form, hiding the palsied arms, the thin frame. She tucked the edges around his shoulders, then straightened, facing Hayden again. "I'm just trying to do the right thing. After all, he *is* my husband. I made vows."

"Vows he broke. Repeatedly."

She shrugged. "For better or worse."

"Doesn't get much worse than this, does it?"

She shook her head. "No. I don't suppose it does."

"If he hadn't been incapacitated?"

"We'd be long divorced by now." She ran a comb through Scott's hair, then picked up her clippers. The tool hummed to life with the flick of her finger, and she

raked it over the hair in the comb. In a few short minutes, she'd completed his cut. Wordlessly, she cleaned
up her supplies, shaking the cape over a small garbage
can, scooping up strands from the floor with her fingers.
She washed her hands, then returned to Scott, evaluating
her work. "You want to know another 'worse' thing?"

There was more? "Sure."

"The only reason I can be sure he's not cheating on
me now is that he's not capable. Even if he were in this
chair because he was paralyzed from the waist down,
he'd still find a way to cheat on me. Or at least, I'd sus-
pect it. When trust is broken…"

"It's damn hard to repair."

A man in blue medical scrubs appeared in the doorway. "Ronni? I'm going to close the door here. Apparently one of those media people got into the building.
Mrs. Bernard saw him skulking in the hallway and hit
him with her purse. We're searching for the guy now.
We'll let you know when he's been removed."

"Thanks, Tony."

"No problem." He closed the door.

Ronni sighed, sinking onto the edge of Scott's bed.

"You're not going to be able to keep avoiding them,
Ronni. You're going to have to make a statement or
something. Hopefully that will get rid of them."

"What am I going to say?"

"How about the truth? The public sympathizes with a
wronged woman. You're in good company. And Scott's
in lousy company. Seems like there's a new celebrity

cheating husband crawling out of the woodwork every damn day."

She shook her head. "No. I can't. I *won't*."

Hayden pushed himself off the wall. "Why not? I'm damn near certain that if the tables were turned, this guy—" he gestured at Scott "—or at least, the guy he used to be, wouldn't hesitate a split second to throw you under the bus."

"For Nick. My son loves and looks up to this man. I won't tarnish that. That's not what I want him to learn about love and marriage."

"Protecting him to protect Nick?"

She nodded. "You can't tell him, Hayden. He lost Ian. He's lost Scott. I don't want him to lose his respect for the memories he has of Scott, too."

"I'm not crazy about keeping secrets, Ronni."

"So I hear."

"They always come back to bite you in the ass." But how could he not honor her request to spare her son further pain? Hayden strode around the wheelchair and its occupant to sit on the bed beside her, so close their thighs touched. He took her hand, laced her fingers with his. "Just in case no one's told you lately—and I'm pretty sure they haven't—you're an amazing woman." Every ill thought he'd had about her since Ian's death had proved to be wrong.

"Thanks." She squeezed his hand.

"Scott doesn't know it now, and obviously never did, but he's one hell of a lucky man. But you deserve better than this, sweetheart."

Her thumb slid over Hayden's, caressing him. Her lower lip quivered, and she looked down.

"You do."

"I don't fold anymore," she said. "I stay in the game."

"I can see that."

"That includes dealing with the newly introduced jokers." She gripped his hand again, then disentangled their fingers. "Fasten your seat belt. I think it's about to get a little bumpy."

"A *little* bumpy? What the hell do you call the insane turbulence in your life already?"

"Oh, it's going to get worse before it gets better."

"Why's that?"

She grimaced. "Because I'm about to invoke a Hawkins Family Emergency Meeting."

CHAPTER EIGHT

FIVE DAYS LATER, all the details worked out and everything and everyone in place, Ronni paced the waiting area of the nursing home. Saturday morning. She should have been elbow deep in Mary Martinez's foils, but no, instead she was here. The week had been just as bumpy as she'd predicted. A number of her regular clients had canceled appointments with her, while other new clients had taken those open slots just to get a look at her.

She'd caught one woman, who'd turned out to be a reporter, wearing a wire, for crying out loud.

The temptation to snip her hair just a little too short had been overwhelming. Ronni had settled for kicking her out with a half-finished cut. Served the woman right.

After getting his probation officer's permission, but over her son's considerable protests, she'd sent Nick to stay with Lydia and Michael, trying to keep him out of range of the cameras. It had been his final week of school before summer break, and his grandparents had been more than happy to haul him back and forth for his finals.

For this morning, Nick had been farmed out to Finn's

place, where he intended to spend time with Jordan working on some sort of video project.

Vera leaned against the reception desk, toying with the straps on her purse. Hayden's family, from Alan to Kyle, along with Lydia and Michael, all perched on various seats in the waiting room. From the far side of the space, Judy cast anxious glances Ronni's way.

Judy had taken the most convincing, but with her background in PR, had been the most important piece of the plan. After hearing all the gory details, she'd been the one to arrange the press conference for Ronni, and had helped her write the speech.

Traditional media had started the mess, but it had exploded over the internet, as well. Blogs for military wives were roasting her. Blogs for right-to-die advocates were slugging it out with right-to-life advocates over Scott's situation. The gossip sites were all over the story.

Today was about trying to take back some control.

Ronni cleared her throat. "Thank you all for being here," she said to the Hawkins clan. "It…it means a lot to me." She blinked back the mist forming in her eyes.

"No. Oh, no." Judy rushed over to her. "You are not going out there with red eyes to start with. Stop it. Right now."

"Sorry." Ronni ran the tip of her finger under her eyes, careful not to smudge her makeup.

"Remember what I told you. In the media, you're either a sinner or a saint. You're a sinner turned saint.

If there's anything the public loves, it's a reformed sinner."

Ronni nodded.

Judy checked her watch. "Okay, folks, it's five minutes till. Let's get this show on the road."

As Hayden moved to Ronni's side, Judy snapped, "You, back off. I want you standing several people behind her. They're already having a field day with you." Photos had surfaced of her with Hayden, including one of him with his hand on her elbow, protectively putting her into the car on Memorial Day.

"Foxtrot uniform," he growled at his sister—his politically correct military euphemism for *eff you* when his mother was in earshot. "I'll be standing right behind or beside her. If you try to stash me in the back, they'll assume we have something to hide. Which we don't."

The papers in Ronni's fingers rattled as they walked through the automatic double doors. A podium had been set up next to the flagpole beyond the entrance portico. She hesitated when she saw the throng of people and cameras. "I can do this," she murmured. "Show no fear, right?"

"Right," Hayden agreed.

She kept walking. Shutters clicked. Cameramen adjusted lenses as she set her notes on the podium. Judy stood off to the side, but in front so she could offer covert coaching tips. Vera took a position at her left, while the Hawkins family closed in a semicircle behind her.

Hayden radiated reassurance and support from just behind her right shoulder.

"Good morning. Thank you for coming. As you all know, I'm Ronni Mangano. I have a brief statement to make." She gestured at the building. "My husband, Sergeant Scott Mangano, resides here. Scott was injured in Iraq nineteen months ago while serving with his National Guard unit. He came home severely brain damaged. His condition is now classified as permanent vegetative state. My husband was a proud man. He wouldn't want people gawking at him. This is not a circus. We're not celebrities, and we really don't want all this attention. Such as it is, this is our life. We just want to be left alone to live it."

Ronni swallowed hard. "Everyone wants to know if I told my husband I wanted a divorce while he was in the field. The ugly truth is yes. I did."

Murmurs circulated through the crowd of media people, and more shutters clicked.

She ducked her head.

Hayden cleared his throat softly.

Ronni raised her chin to look out at her judges through a shimmering haze. She blinked rapidly. "I live with that truth every day. With the guilt and the anguish of knowing I may have contributed to my husband's condition." Tears escaped, cascading down her cheeks. She swiped at them with the back of her hand, doing her best to stifle them. "It's certainly not how I wanted things to turn out."

"Why?" someone shouted. "Why'd you want a divorce?"

"I'm not going to answer that. I have a teenage son who doesn't need the messy details about our relationship circulated all over the internet. And if you have any decency at all, you'll honor my request for privacy in that matter."

Judy waved her hand, shaking her head, pointing at the paper. *Get back on the message and don't antagonize the press* came through loud and clear.

"My husband deserves the respect that all our men and women who serve this country in the armed forces deserve. Are they perfect? No. Are their families perfect? No. We're just regular human beings, like everyone else. I'm not the first wife to Dear John an active military man. I won't be the last. I had my reasons. But I'm standing by Scott now. Please let me do so in peace. Thank you." She folded the paper.

The crowd surged to life, all shouting questions at the same time.

"Have you considered withholding medical care from him?"

"Are you staying with him just to continue getting his service benefits?"

"Scott's mom, Vera! Vera! What do you think about your daughter-in-law asking your son for a divorce, possibly leading to his injury?"

Vera leaned in to the microphone. "Are you married, young man?"

The reporter shook his head. "No."

"Have you ever *been* married?"

"No."

"Then you don't have a clue, do you? Marriage can be trying. It's hard work. Ronni has explained to me what happened, and I'm satisfied with her explanation." Vera took Ronni's hand, squeezed it. Scott's mother hadn't been exactly surprised to find out her son had been cheating. She'd suspected it for years. Turned out Vera had her own experience with cheating husbands. Apparently Ed, Scott's father, had stepped out on her more than once. Vera, however, had chosen to ignore it, and had stayed with him until his death, five years ago.

Relief that she hadn't shattered Vera's image of her son had tempered Ronni's aggravation that Vera had suspected Scott and never even dropped a hint to her. But it had reinforced her desire to shelter Nick from the unvarnished truth about his stepfather.

"Didn't you walk out on your son's father while he was dying?" another reporter shouted. "What makes Scott different?"

Every last Hawkins behind her bristled at that question. Ronni could feel the electricity in the air. When they'd been given the full story about what had happened with her and Ian, there'd been a lot of chagrin on everyone's part. They'd agreed to let bygones be bygones, although Ronni still wasn't certain she'd completely convinced Judy.

Hayden stepped up to the podium. Judy's eyes bugged out, and she frantically shook her head.

Hayden ignored her, yanking on the microphone to reposition it. "The people you see standing here, surrounding Ronni in this difficult time? We're the family of her son's father. Ronni Mangano has our full support. That should tell you something."

That had been the point of invoking the Hawkins Family Emergency Meeting. Even if she hadn't been a Hawkins family member in good standing at the time.

There was something comforting about having them around her. About having Hayden back in her life, willing to tilt at windmills for her.

"Don't you have something better to do?" Hayden continued. "Isn't some star getting out of rehab today? Didn't some celebrity forget to wear her panties? Shouldn't you all be covering that kind of stuff and leaving this poor family in peace?"

"Are you involved with Mrs. Mangano?" one of the women reporters asked.

"Yes."

Judy rushed forward.

The clicking of cameras crescendoed, and Ronni's stomach tensed. What was he thinking, baiting them like that?

"I'm her son's uncle, and her friend."

A pack of wolves circling prey, they all started clamoring, shouting out their questions again.

"What kind of friend?"

"Mr. Hawkins, are you the reason she wanted a divorce?"

"Tell us more!"

Elbowing Hayden out of the way at the podium, Judy leaned in to the mic. "Thank for you coming." Then she turned, spreading her arms wide and herding Ronni into the midst of the Hawkinses. "Get her inside. Crap, Hayden, you just don't know when to keep that big mouth shut, do you? Good going."

"YOUR MOM LOOKS really happy there," Jordan said. She was sprawled on her stomach across her bed, watching him work on her computer at the desk in the corner of her bedroom.

Nick studied his grinning mother on the monitor as the video clip played. She laid her finger over her lips, telling the cameraman—he suspected Uncle Hayden— to be quiet. Then she crooked that same finger in a "follow me" gesture. The camera did, bobbing behind her as she crept down a hallway. The camera panned down to his mom's butt in a pair of tight jeans, then back up again. That was *so wrong* in so many ways. Yeah, Uncle Hayden, for sure.

In the arch of a doorway, she motioned him closer. "My boys," she whispered, jerking her head toward the room. "Don't wake them."

His father slumbered in a rocking chair, head tipped back, mouth open. Baby Nick slept on his father's chest, Ian's hand sprawled protectively over his back.

"Yeah," Nick said to his cousin. "She looks happy." He jabbed the stop button.

"Why'd you stop it?"

He shrugged. "I want to look through more clips. You can help me decide which ones should go onto the special DVD I'm making."

"What's this for again?"

"It's a present."

"For your mom?" Jordan rolled over to sit on the side of the bed, leaning forward. "For her birthday?"

"Sort of. Not exactly." Actually, it was for his father's birthday. An occasion his mother celebrated every year, although he only ever got to participate in the chocolate-cake-for-breakfast ritual that day. What else she did was a mystery because he always spent the day with his grandparents. It became a tradition, because on his father's last birthday, Grandma had babysat Nick while his parents had gone out to celebrate. And ever since then, Mom believed that having Nick with them on Ian's birthday compensated in some way for his dad not being there.

Nick didn't think he'd ever understand the adult thought process.

"Do you ever think what it would be like to know your dad? I used to do it all the time."

Nick scowled over his shoulder at her. "All those drugs they gave you for the chemo scrambled your brains. My father is dead. Yours…you just didn't know yours."

"In your head, silly. Imagine it." She shrugged. "I imagined it a lot before I actually met him. I just wondered if you did the same."

Sometimes when no one was around, he talked to Ian. Especially after Scott had shipped out. And then checked out. But to admit it… "Don't be dumb."

Jordan sighed, then rose from the bed to glance out the window at the front of the house. Great. He'd hurt her feelings. "Sorry. Guess I'm just in a bad mood today. Every time I turn around right now, my mom's pawning me off. First to Pop and Grandma's for the week, now here. Not that I don't want to be here," he added hastily when she turned to look at him. He shrugged. "Whatever."

"What do you think she's telling the newspeople?"

"Hopefully to mind their own damn business." First getting caught holding the bag—literally—had put a major crimp in his life, and now this thing with the media and Scott had added a new layer of crap he didn't need.

Although it had gotten Megan to start texting him again. She'd seen the news and starting asking him all sorts of questions. So at least it wasn't a total bust.

For him, anyway. For his mother…

He turned back toward the computer, scrolling through a list of other clips he'd imported from the old family videos.

The door to Jordan's room opened. Aunt Amelia bustled in, leaving Aunt Shannon standing in the open door.

"Mom!" Jordan protested. "You don't knock?"

"Umm…no." Aunt Amelia toyed with the ends of a tape measure draped around her neck.

"Aren't you supposed to be studying for your boards?" Jordan asked.

"I am. But I need some help. I'm doing some stuff on skeletal dimensions and body composition as related to age. Nick, can I ask you a favor?"

He pushed the chair back. "I guess."

"Just need to get some measurements. Shannon, you have the notebook, right?"

Aunt Shannon held up a tiny blue spiral notebook. "Right here." She flipped it open, clicked a pen. "Ready when you are."

"Since when does Aunt Shannon help you with research?" Jordan asked.

Aunt Amelia scowled at her. "Since now."

"I thought she was supposed to be filling in as a prep cook while Dad's at the press conference thing?"

"Jordan, enough questions. She's helping me for a minute because I asked her to." Amelia gestured at him. "Come stand over here, Nick. I promise you, this will be quick and painless."

Warily, he stood, then advanced to the middle of the rug at the foot of Jordan's bed.

"Great. Hold your arms straight out." She grabbed the end of the tape measure. Nick extended his arms.

Jordan's mom pressed the metal tab to his shoulder, then measured the length to his wrist, calling out the number to Aunt Shannon, who dutifully wrote it down.

The process was repeated for the length of his spine from the base of his neck to his tailbone, from his hip to his heel, and other assorted measurements.

"Thanks. Got what I need. We're good, right, Shannon?"

Aunt Shannon tapped the notebook with the pen. "Got it all here."

"Okay." Aunt Amelia held out her hand for the pad. "You can head back to your chopping or whatever you were doing down in the kitchen. And you two can get back to what you were doing." She paused in the doorway. "What *were* you doing?"

"Mo-om," Jordan said. "What do you *think* we were doing?" She blew out an exasperated breath. "Smoking dope and having sex?"

Nick winced. While the adults in the family had been enlightened about his probation, his cousins hadn't. And Aunt Amelia's scrunched eyebrows said she considered the former an actual possibility.

A guy made one stupid mistake and it messed up everything, including the way people looked at you.

"Not funny, Jordan."

"Oh, lighten up, Mom, would you? A year ago you didn't think I'd live long enough to torment you with thoughts of sex, drugs and rock 'n' roll."

"A year ago, you were plotting behind my back to run away to Erie to meet your father."

Jordan beamed an innocent smile. "And look how well that's turned out. Now we live in Erie with Dad and Chip, and we're really a family. I think you owe me and my plotting a great big thank-you."

Aunt Amelia wagged a finger. "If I recall correctly, you're supposed to still be grounded for that adventure. Don't make me rethink it."

Jordan keeled over on the bed as if she'd passed out. Her voice floated up faintly. "Right. Sorry. Never mind. Carry on. Go study for your test!"

Aunt Amelia left the door partially opened behind her.

"'Rents," Jordan said, sitting back up on the bed. "They think we're totally stupid or something. Like after all I've been through, I'm going to be dumb enough to smoke dope. Or anything else for that matter. No, thanks. I've had enough drugs in my system already."

"Remember that the first time some guy you think is totally cute asks you to try it." Admittedly, it hadn't just been because of Megan. Curiosity played a part.

Jordan cocked her head, studying him. "Oh, man, Nick. You didn't?"

He lifted his shoulders. "Not for a cute guy."

She giggled. "Didn't mean that part."

"You're not supposed to know this."

"Ooh." The bed frame squeaked as she jumped off

it and scurried to his side. "A secret. I love secrets. Spill it."

Given the media blitz, Nick wondered if he shouldn't spill his *biggest* secret to his mother. But when she'd sat down to explain that she had asked Scott for a divorce while he was in Iraq, she'd refused to give Nick the reasons, saying only that it was an adult issue, and something she didn't want to saddle him with. That it wouldn't be fair.

What wasn't fair was what Scott had done to his mother. Nick picked at the edge of the pink mouse pad on Jordan's desk. His mom deserved to know. But it would hurt her. Make her feel even more horrible.

As horrible as Nick had felt when he'd found out Scott had been using their fishing trips as a cover story to his mother for screwing around on her.

Nick didn't want to hurt her.

For now, he'd just keep his—and Scott's—secret a bit longer.

"WHATCHA LOOKIN' AT?"

The slats on the blinds snapped back into place as Ronni whirled from the picture window in the shop. "Tamara." She extended her arms to hug her friend, whose salon, A Cut Above, was also closed on Mondays, making it their preferred day to get together. "I didn't hear you come in."

"I got that. Especially when you didn't respond to my

report that there were only two lone photogs lurking out there today."

That was welcome news. Slowly but surely, interest in her story was easing, at least in the traditional media. Ronni had gotten invitations to appear on several talk shows. She'd politely declined.

Tamara squeezed her, then stuck her fingers in the blinds, widening the gap so she could look. "And now I get why."

"Why? I was just checking on Nick." Ronni looked out again herself. In the blazing sunshine, Hayden and Nick leaned over a pair of sawhorses, repairing one of the house screens. The rest of the frames were stacked on the ground alongside the driveway. Part of Hayden's plan to keep Nick occupied and doing useful things involved catching up on the household chores that had gone neglected since Scott had shipped out. Some of them had actually been neglected since before he'd left for Iraq.

Hayden was shirtless and his muscles glistened with sweat. His cutoff jeans hugged his rear, the frayed edges caressing rock-hard thighs.

Tamara sighed. "Poetry in motion. Checking on Nick, my ass. More like checking out the pretty man-candy. He could park his boots under my bed anytime. Please tell me his boots have been under your bed, and then give me all the details so I can live vicariously through you."

"Um, hello? I'm *married*. Hayden's boots haven't

been under my bed." Though Ronni had to admit to herself that the more time she spent with Hayden—and he'd been way more than fulfilling his court-appointed obligations to Nick since school had let out last week— the more drawn to his looks she became. That was how bad boys sucked you in. They looked damn good. They made you laugh. They made you feel…special. Protected. And before you knew it, you were lusting after them.

Which only led to trouble later on.

"You're married, not dead."

"And neither is my husband."

"You're a widow-in-waiting to a cheating son of a bitch."

"Hey. Vera's not a bitch. Be nice."

"A lot of media types have already decided you're involved with Hayden. When's the last time you had real sex?"

"It's been so long I forget." Ronni sighed, watching the ripple of Hayden's back as he stretched, then picked up the repaired screen, setting it with the others completed.

Then he said something to Nick—the in-wall air-conditioning unit hummed too loudly for Ronni to hear what—and dragged the sawhorses closer together. He placed one hand on each, then eased himself into a handstand between them.

Upside-down now, facing them, Hayden bent his arms, dipping lower between the boards, then pushing himself back up, his legs shaking, his abs contracting with the effort.

Making Ronni's stomach tighten, too.

"Ohmygod," Tamara whispered. "I think I just had a mini-orgasm." She closed her eyes, drew in a deep breath, then slowly let it out, humming in pleasure. "No wonder women wait in line for thirty days with Hayden Hawkins. And then do nothing but sing his praises after he moves on."

Ronni tore her attention from the window. Pursing her lips and narrowing her eyes, she glared at her friend.

"What? I hear the same girl talk in my salon chairs as you do in yours, sister. And the talk around town about that man… If you don't want to take a number and get in line, maybe I will. Just imagine the things he could do with that body."

Turning back to the glass, Ronni shivered.

Tamara laughed. "I see you *are* imagining it. That's my girl."

Outside, Hayden swung himself off the sawhorses and moved to the grass, gesturing for Nick to follow him. Her son shook his head.

Hayden crooked a finger, then pointed to the lawn at his feet.

Shoulders slouched, Nick slunk to the spot Hayden indicated. Hayden stepped back. He held his hands up and rocked forward on his feet, demonstrating how to plant palms on the ground.

Once more Nick shook his head. Hayden cocked his,

propping his fists on his hips. His mouth moved, but Ronni had no clue what he said. Finally, Nick tentatively leaned over, placing his hands on the ground and kicking his legs up.

His uncle caught his ankles and gripped them, not just helping the boy balance, but, judging by the way Hayden's biceps popped, supporting his weight, as well.

Nick's entire body shook. He bent his arms as Hayden had on the boards, dipping lower. Then he struggled to push himself upright again.

Hayden called encouragement; that was easy to read through the window. And he slowly coaxed Nick into a full-arm extension.

At which point Nick gave up, leaving Hayden holding him fully. He lowered the boy to the ground, laughing.

Nick laughed, too.

Ronni smiled.

It had been a long time since she'd seen her son laugh like that.

"All kidding aside, he seems like a good man, Ron."

"Yeah. If you overlook that whole can't-stick-with-one-woman thing." She shook her head. "Why is it men can't keep it in their pants if they're supposedly committed to someone?"

"Hey, I've never heard anyone say Hayden's a cheater. And we'd have heard if he was." Tamara had actually been the one to come to her with suspicions about Scott based on tidbits she'd heard in her salon. Which proved exactly how good a friend she was. When someone came to you, terrified of hurting of you, but not willing to let someone else keep doing so, that was a friend.

"He doesn't have to cheat," Ronni stated. "He doesn't have time to get bored with a woman. Thirty days and she's history."

"Maybe he hasn't met the right woman yet. Until then, you can't really hold it against him. He's up-front about it. Women go into it with eyes wide open."

Ronni shrugged. It really wasn't any of her business how Hayden ran his love life.

Footsteps pounded on the concrete sidewalk. The door in the entryway burst open.

Peals of Nick's hysterical laughter echoed through the confined space of the hallway, bouncing into the salon. He staggered into the room, clutching his stomach. "Mom! Mom!" He laughed again. "You won't believe it. It's too freakin' funny!"

"Yeah. Hysterical." Hayden appeared in the archway, shirt balled up in his hand. "I need to borrow your shower, Ronni."

"Heat getting to you?" Tam asked.

Nick straightened, wrestling for control. "You know that crow? Mr. Black?"

"Yes," Ronni said.

"Well he…he…he…" Stifled guffaws made him stutter.

"He dive-bombed me," Hayden said. "So can I use your shower or are you going to make me drive home like this?"

"Dive-bombed?"

"He pooped on Uncle Hayden's head!" Nick collapsed on the floor, laughing again.

Ronni struggled to keep a straight face.

"Damn bird. I told you that thing hated me, Ronni."

"Surely you don't think he did it on purpose, do you?"

"Hell, yes, I do. That thing has the accuracy of a smart bomb."

Tam made sympathetic noises. "Now, you don't want to get in a shower with bird poop in your hair. Why, that's just going to make it run down your head, and…" she paused, giving his torso a long once-over "… your whole body. You don't want that. Come here." She crooked her finger at him, just as he had with Nick. Then she strode to the shampooing station and caressed the yellow chair like a model on a game show demonstrating a product. "You just sit right here and we'll get you all fixed up."

Hayden glanced warily at Ronni.

"She's right. We can wash it a lot easier here. Shampoo in the eyes is one thing. You don't want to risk—" she cleared her throat to silence the giggles "—bird droppings. Ick."

Nick finally settled down enough to climb to his feet.

He wiped his eyes. "I'm going upstairs to play Halo. You know where to find me if you need me for more chores. Or, you know, to protect you from birds."

"You've done a lousy job so far!" Hayden called after him as the teen headed up the stairs. "And keep laughing. I'm telling you, payback's a bitch. Soon, kid, real soon."

"Come on, big boy." Tam patted the chair again. "Have a seat and Ronni will get you cleaned up." She glanced at her watch. "Because much as I'd love to get my fingers in your hair, I simply have to run." She retrieved her purse from Ronni's desk, slinging it over her shoulder. "You get the chance, you hit it for both of us," she whispered as she hugged Ronni.

"The only thing I'm hitting is you," Ronni murmured back, slapping Tam's arm. "Thanks for coming. Even if you are ditching me already."

"Forgot I have a meeting with a product salesperson over lunch. My bad. Later!"

When she got behind Hayden, she paused just long enough to make groping motions near his butt.

Ronni shook her head. Tam grinned, offering her a thumbs-up before heading for the stairs.

"You sure about this?" Hayden asked. "'Cause I can just get in the shower and be done with it."

"Frankly, I'm not crazy about the idea of bird poop in my shower. I'd rather sanitize my sink here."

"Okay." Ever since coming inside, Hayden hadn't been able to take his eyes off Ronni. Not even for the friend, who as a curvy, buxom platinum blonde, should have been registering on his radar. She'd certainly been sending off enough signals.

Instead, it was Ronni who captured his attention. She wore a powder-blue baby doll type blouse with a plunging V-neck. The flouncy hem featured lacy details. "You look really pretty today. That shirt suits you." The words were out of his mouth before he realized what a bad idea they were.

What a bad idea thinking about Ronni that way was.

But he'd never controlled his flirting. And apparently couldn't start now.

Her cheeks flushed and she ducked her head. "Thanks."

Hayden once more cursed Scott Mangano for what he'd done to her. For making her feel so...how had she put it? Defective.

He parked himself in the shampoo chair, his clammy skin sticking to the yellow vinyl.

Ronni pulled a towel from an overhead cabinet, wrapping it around his neck. "Okay, lean back."

The chair reclined, a footrest rising to support his legs. Water hissed behind his head. Ronni splashed it over her hand, adjusting the temperature. "Too hot," she said.

She leaned over him, presenting him with a delectable peek down the V of her shirt. A pale pink, push-up demi bra—Victoria's Secret, if he wasn't mistaken, and he wasn't often when it came to lingerie—offered up the creamy swell of her breasts. "Oh, I'll say," he agreed.

"I'm sorry!" The handles squeaked as she adjusted the water further.

"No problem." Actually, it was a big problem.

And growing bigger by the moment. He shifted in the chair, trying to adjust the lazy half-mast he sported. He should close his eyes, or look at the ceiling, and yet the view was beautiful.

Had it been any woman other than Ronni, he'd be exploring the option of peeling the baby-doll shirt and low-rise jeans from her to see if the panties matched the bra.

She blasted his head full-force with water, momentarily distracting him, and he shut his eyes tightly as spray misted his face.

"Just want to do a really good rinse before I get my hands in there," she explained.

He'd like to get his hands in there, too. And his mouth and—

Ronni. Ronni. This is Ronni *you're fantasizing about, sport. Ian's girl. Nick's mom. Scott's wife.*

Hayden conjured up the image of Ronni and Scott's wedding picture from the newscast, then recalled Scott, secured in a wheelchair at the nursing home.

That did the trick, short-circuiting his trip to Fantasyland faster than a cold shower.

The spray shut off. Two quick squishes were followed by the unmistakable sound of hands working a lather.

The scent of coconut filled the air. Then she plunged her fingers into his hair. She followed the first wash quickly with a rinse and another lather. This time she rotated her fingertips across his scalp, massaging deeply.

He sighed. While he'd had his hair washed by a woman before, it had never felt quite like this.

Soothing, yet stimulating…

Far more intimate than the way he'd seen her touch her husband's hair. More caressing, more exploring…

More erotic.

Was she feeling it, too?

Fighting a losing battle, he decided to just go with it. Purge it from his system. Envision the pair of them naked in a shower, her lathered hands massaging a lot more than his scalp. His own soaped-up palms caressing every last inch of her.

If she had any clue what was running through his hopelessly dirty mind, she'd give him a frigid cold rinse.

Or would she?

He damn near choked when she asked, "You want me to blow it?" while running a towel over his hair.

"No. No, that's quite all right." He grabbed the cloth from her, bolting upright and out of the chair. "Thanks." He turned his back on her, making a production of drying his hair, at the same time willing his now full erection to vanish. In a hurry.

Which wasn't happening.

So he dried slower. The scent of cleaning solution

flooded the room as she scoured the sink. His cell phone chirped from his pocket. "What should I do with this?" he asked, holding out the yellow terry cloth.

She held her hands up like a catcher over the plate and he tossed it to her, then pulled out his phone, reading the text.

He chuckled, snapping it closed.

"Oh, that was a dirty laugh if ever I heard one," she said, putting the towel into a hamper drawer she'd pulled from the oak-colored cabinet near the shampoo station. "What's up?"

He grinned at her. "Remember that payback I keep promising Nick? For laughing at me the day of his probation hearing, when I got stuck in the Captain Chemo suit?" He'd told her the story of what had happened, along with Nick's reaction when they'd gotten to Greg's house.

"Yeah."

"It's time."

CHAPTER NINE

"COME ON, NICK. Let us see," Uncle Hayden said through the wooden slats on the dressing room door.

"No freakin' way! I'm not coming out there like this." Another glance in the mirror made Nick shudder. No way in hell he was even going out the door into the seamstress's shop, let alone appear in public in this getup. There were other ways of doing community service.

He'd rather pick up rotten garbage on the side of a highway.

Aunt Amelia and Aunt Shannon had sold him up the river. Those measurements hadn't been about skeletal size. They'd been sizing him up for this suit.

"Did you put on the mask like I told you?"

"What difference is a mask going to make?" He stared at his reflection. Skintight purple spandex with green trim. Green...*briefs* was the best word he could come up with to describe them. A yellow triangle with the radiation warning symbol plastered the middle of his chest. The green cape intended to fasten at his shoulders was draped over the back of a chair in the enormous dressing room that usually held brides, judging from the magazine clippings taped to the wall-size mirror.

"Trust me on this. I know what I'm talking about." The doorknob rattled. "Look, let me in, okay?"

"No. Tell Uncle Greg I'm sorry. I can't do it." He reached around the back of his neck and started to unzip the thing, but couldn't reach it once he'd lowered it an inch or two.

Metal rasped. The push-button lock on the door popped, and Unk, clad in his own ridiculous costume, which now sported a new zipper, slipped in. He relocked the door behind him.

"Good. Get me the hell out of this!" Nick presented his back to his uncle.

"Nope. Not yet." He yanked the zipper to the top, attached the cape, then put his hands on Nick's shoulders and turned him on the platform to face the mirror again. "Tell me what you see."

"An idiot."

"Fair enough." He lowered the purple mask over Nick's eyes, securing it in place. "And now?"

"An unidentifiable idiot?"

Uncle Hayden laughed. "There is that. Nobody has to know who's behind the mask but you."

"And the whole rest of the family, including you, and you have a big mouth."

"Good thing I'm well adjusted or I'd get a complex." Unk settled his own mask into place and stood beside him, draping his arm around Nick's shoulders. "Wanna know what I see?"

"*Two* idiots?"

"I see Captain Chemo and his sidekick, Radiation

Boy. Two characters who can bring smiles and laughter to people who need it."

"Exactly my point. I don't want people laughing at me."

Uncle Hayden sighed. "Nick, do you remember seeing the videos of Jordan when she was in the bone marrow transplant unit? With sores in her mouth so bad she could barely speak? Hair falling out?"

Nick glanced down at his bare feet. "Yeah."

"Now imagine you could make her feel a tiny bit better, even for just a minute. Would you do it?"

He dragged his toes back and forth across the carpet. "I suppose."

Unk slapped him on the back. "Look in the mirror."

Nick tried not to grimace as he did.

"Besides chemo and radiation, there are two powerful tools in the fight against cancer. Laughter and hope. That's what we represent, Nick. We don't just stand for chemo and radiation. We're hope."

Nick let that sink in for a minute. "Is that why my dad died? 'Cause without my mom, he didn't have hope anymore?"

Uncle Hayden stepped off the platform, standing between him and the mirror. He bent his knees, sinking lower until they were eye-to-eye. "I used to believe that. But now..." Unk shrugged. "For some reason, he thought he was fated to die. Why, I don't know. But it wasn't your mom's fault."

"What do you think he'd say if he saw me in this getup?"

A twinkle appeared in Unk's eyes, behind his red mask. "I think he'd say, 'The two of you get in the back of the pickup and let's crash a parade.'"

"Really?"

Unk nodded. Then his smile faded and he gripped Nick's shoulder. "And I think he'd tell you how proud he is of you."

"I'm—I'm on…" Nick's throat tightened, making it hard to speak. He averted his gaze. "Probation."

"Hey…" Unk's fingers tightened. "You made one lousy judgment call. And got caught. Your dad raised a lot of hell in his short life. He just never got caught. Nick…"

He lifted his head, met Unk's eyes again.

"He's proud of you."

Nick blinked a few times, cheeks growing warm beneath the edges of the mask. Superheroes—or their sidekicks—didn't cry.

Unk cleared his throat, then poked him in the ribs. "Now you know why I've been so tough on you in our workouts. We gotta get more muscle on you. Trust me, women love superheroes."

He snorted. "Women love vampires. Or werewolves. Not men in capes."

A slow smile curved Unk's mouth. "You'll see."

Someone rapped hard on the door. "What's going on in there? Is something wrong with the costume? I want to see how it looks!"

"Chill, Greg," Hayden yelled. "We'll be out when we're ready. Superhero bonding with his sidekick, here." In a flash, he'd jumped back onto the platform and grabbed Nick in a headlock, bending him over. He gave him a noogie, rubbing his knuckles on the top of his head. "So what do you say, kid? You gonna be my sidekick or do I have to get rough with you?"

"I suppose."

"Ooh, try not to overwhelm me with your enthusiasm." Uncle Hayden let him go, moving for the door.

Nick rubbed his head, straightening up. "Unk?"

Hayden stopped, turned. "Yeah?"

"My dad…"

"What about him?"

"He'd…he'd want me to protect my mom, right?"

"Protect her from what?" Unk returned to the edge of the platform.

Nick shrugged. "Being hurt."

"By who?"

"Doesn't matter. That person can't hurt her anymore. But…I mean…ah, hell, I don't know what I mean." Holding Scott's secret was driving him crazy. If he told Uncle Hayden, most likely he'd tell his mother.

Problem solved. Except for the part where Mom would get mad at him for not telling her years ago, when he'd first found out. And it would still hurt her. "Never mind. Let's go show everyone how the costume looks."

Unk pulled off his red mask, reached forward and

yanked off Nick's mask. He stared at him for a moment. "Who can't hurt her anymore, Nick?"

"S-Scott."

A muscle on the side of Unk's jaw twitched. "Tell me."

The soft whir of the ceiling fan seemed ten times louder as they stood there in silence. Nick stared at his feet in the mirror, flexing his big toe.

"Nicholas, spill it. I'm not screwing around here."

He jerked his head up. "Scott was." Nick drew in a deep breath and let it out slowly, tension in his chest easing.

Unk's eyebrows climbed his forehead. "Scott was...?"

"Screwing around."

"Son of a bitch. You knew about that?"

"Yeah. He used to tell Mom we were going fishing. He'd get me set up by the ferry dock, and then tell me he had an errand to run. Sometimes he'd be gone for an hour or two. One day I had to go to the bathroom. I was coming out when I saw a woman drop him off in the parking lot. He kissed her before he got out of the car. Not like a peck on the cheek, either. After that, I'd always watch. Caught him with a few different ones."

"Did he know that you saw him?"

"The first time."

"What did he say?"

"He said I'd understand when I was older. That he loved my mom, but men had needs. And that if I told her, it would break her heart and make her cry, and I didn't want that, right?"

Hayden clenched his teeth so hard he could hear the muscles straining. The urge to go to the nursing home and shake the shit out of Scott Mangano subsided only because it wouldn't satisfy. The man—and he used the term lightly—had used a son's love for his mother to hide his infidelity. "How old were you, Nick?"

"Ten."

"So you've been carrying this for four years?"

The boy nodded.

"Maybe you understand now why I don't keep secrets?"

He bobbed his head again.

"Good." Hayden strode to the door, yanking it open. "Ronni? Come in here, please."

A stifled squeak made him return his attention to Nick. The kid shook his head frantically, backing away. He stumbled off the raised platform, kept moving until he'd pressed himself into a corner.

"Don't do that," Hayden chided. "Man up. She already knows. She's been going out of her mind to protect you, and you've been doing the same thing for her. Time for both of you to come clean."

Ronni appeared in the doorway, Greg peering over her shoulder. Hayden pulled her into the dressing room, slamming the door in his brother's face.

"Hey!" Greg protested, banging on the wooden slats. "I'm the creator! I should get to see."

"You're going to break my door," said Mrs. Bagley, the seamstress. "You boys need to settle down."

"Foxtrot off, Greg. Family emergency here. You can see in a few minutes. Go draw something." Hayden leaned against the door frame, crossing his arms over his chest, facing into the room. Nobody else was getting in here until mother and son had aired their dirty laundry.

Ronni glanced from him to her son. "What's going on? Nick, do you hate the costume that much? Can you just try to do it for Uncle Greg and Jordan?"

"It's got nothing to do with the costume," Hayden said. "Tell your mother what you just told me."

The boy looked down at his feet again.

"I'm not doing it for you, Nick. You're not a little kid. You can do this."

"Umm…"

Ronni skirted the platform, went over to him. She lowered herself into a chair, took his hand. "Nick?"

"I'm sorry, Mom," he choked out. "I should have told you when it happened the first time. 'Cause it was way before he deployed. You could have divorced him then, and maybe he wouldn't have gotten hurt. But I didn't want to hurt *you*." He dropped to his knees in front of the chair, leaning in to wrap his arms around his mother's waist, pressing his face into her belly.

Ronni stroked his hair, casting a wide-eyed, concerned look over his head at Hayden. He jerked his chin in the boy's direction.

"Told me what, sweetheart?" she prodded.

"That...that Scott was cheating on you."

Ronni took Nick's arms, pushed him back so she could see his face. "You knew about it?"

He nodded. "Scott met women when we were supposed to be fishing together."

Fire flared in her eyes. "He used *you* to cover his affairs?"

"Sometimes, yeah."

She cupped her son's face with one hand. "I'm sorry, baby. I had no idea. He had no right to put something that heavy on you. No right at all." On the side of her leg, out of sight from Nick, her other hand curled into a fist.

Looked like momma lion had the same urge to shake the snot out of Scott as Hayden had. Good for her. Feeling mad at the bastard beat feeling...defective. Unworthy.

"You knew, too?"

"Remember before Scott deployed? He had to go to training at the army base first?"

Nick nodded.

"I found out just before then. That was the first time I asked him for a divorce."

"So why didn't you divorce him then?"

"Because I believed him when he said he loved me. And you. That he wanted to make it work. That he needed to have us to come home to. That it wouldn't happen again."

"So then why...oh."

Hayden could see understanding dawn in the boy's

eyes. A mask of maturity slid into place over his features. For a split second, Hayden would have sworn he was looking at his younger brother, he resembled Ian so strongly.

"It happened again, didn't it?"

"Yes."

"Got it. So you told him you wanted a divorce while he was in the field…"

"Then he got hurt."

"And you didn't want to divorce him?"

"It wouldn't have been right." She sniffled.

"Mom." Nick rose to his feet, pulling Ronni out of the chair. He wrapped his arms around her, this time offering comfort instead of seeking it.

Hayden took a step in their direction, then froze, resisting the damn near overwhelming impulse to envelop both of them in a group embrace.

Ian would definitely be proud of his son.

Hayden sure as hell was.

And yet a sense of emptiness clung to him like the red cape of his costume.

Maybe he wasn't as content with his life as he'd thought. Maybe he needed something more from a woman than thirty days.

RONNI KEPT HER ANGER carefully in check for the rest of the afternoon. Nick modeled the costume for Greg, for the costume designer and even Jordan, who'd been invited along because of her plans to make a special video version of Captain Chemo. She'd wrangled Nick's grudging agreement to participate provided she didn't list his name in the credits.

Nick asked to go home with Jordan so they could work on several projects, including planning for the Captain Chemo movie. A quick call to Amelia, who was rapidly becoming one of Ronni's favorite new Hawkinses, even if she hadn't married Finn—or maybe because she hadn't—brought permission.

Greg took off with the kids, leaving Ronni with Hayden.

"I should have driven my own car," she griped as they pulled away from the seamstress's shop.

"You got somewhere else you want to go besides home? Name it. I'm happy to oblige."

Ronni wrapped the straps of her purse around her hand. "I'd like to go to the nursing home and tell Scott exactly what I think of him. Damn him for doing that to Nick. You know, the one thing I thought he had in his favor was that he was always a good stepfather. Now he's ruined that, too. Bastard. And I can't yell at him, or smack him silly, because what would be the point? Not to mention the nursing home would probably call the cops on me, and that would bring the press running again, and…"

Hayden grinned at her.

"What the hell are you smiling about?"

"I have just the thing to make you feel better." He whipped the Camaro into a Country Fair parking lot, then pulled right out again, heading in the opposite direction.

"Where are we going?"

"You'll see."

"I'm not in the mood for games, Hayden. I'm in the mood to tear someone a new one."

"Exactly."

She settled back in the seat. Let him be cryptic. *Men. Can't live with them, can't...divorce them when you'd really, really like to.*

A heavy dose of guilt followed hot on the heels of that thought.

A few minutes later, they pulled into Hayden's condo community. "We're going to your place?"

"Yep." He parked the car outside the garage this time. After escorting her in, he flipped on the lights and closed the door. Leaving her standing in the middle of his basement garage.

"Okay, now what?"

"Give me a second." He rummaged in the corner near the storage shelves, then staggered out with a heavy blue punching bag in his arms, fastening it to a chain dangling from an overhead beam.

"You've got to be kidding me."

"No. You said you wanted to rip someone a new one. You want to smack Scott silly and can't. Here. Pretend this is him. Tell him what you think."

She rolled her eyes.

"Bottled up emotions aren't any healthier than keeping secrets." He squared his shoulder against the bag, then slapped the front of it with his palm. "Come on. Take a jab at it. At him."

"I don't know how."

"Sure you do. Make a fist and sock him."

"I feel stupid."

"Okay, let me demonstrate." Hayden slid from behind the bag. Fists raised in front of his body, he bounced on the balls of his feet. "Mangano, you're a worthless piece of scum. This is for Nick." Hayden threw a punch with his right hand, then left, then right again. "And this is for Ronni." He kicked it so hard the chain rattled with the force.

She winced.

Hayden stepped back, swept his arm toward the bag. "Go on. You'll feel better. At least tell him what you think."

"I—I hate you for what you did to my son." She balled up her hand, poked the bag halfheartedly.

"That's *hate?* Your babcia could hit harder than that." He circled around behind the punching bag again. "This so-called man used your son to cover up his cheating on you."

She slammed the side of her fist into it hard enough to make it move this time. "Bastard."

"Better." When she didn't continue, he did. "He slept with other women, then came home to you."

She kicked the bottom of the bag. Her sneaker jammed into the top of her foot but that barely registered.

"Yeah, that's the spirit. I know where that kick was aimed."

She repeated the motion. *Bam.* "I'd like to kick him in the nuts so hard, he has to spit them out."

"Yeah, babe, now you're talking."

"You stole my son's innocence." Punch. "Betrayed my trust." Kick. "Abused my love for you." Double punch.

Her knuckles stung and her foot throbbed in time with the rapid beat of her heart. She continued assaulting Scott-by-proxy. "You made me feel worthless. Ugly." The vibrations from that punch traveled up her arm to the shoulder. "And just when I thought I'd freed myself, you had to be stupid."

Her only previous boxing experience had been on the Wii gaming console in her living room. Actually hitting something satisfied her a hell of a lot more.

"You came home a turnip!" Whap. "And now I'm stuck with you." Kick, punch. "Stuck with you, dammit!"

Chest tight, she unleashed a final flurry of kicks and punches that made every cell in her body vibrate. Her chest tightened as the impact of her words solidified.

Words she'd never spoken aloud before.

Knees giving way underneath her, she sank to the concrete floor. Tears spilled down her face.

Hayden quickly abandoned the bag. The exercise had been even more successful than he'd expected.

What he hadn't expected was a meltdown. He dropped to the ground behind her, extending his legs around her. His chest pressed against her spine and he wrapped his arms around her. "That's telling him," he murmured into her hair.

Deep, gut-wrenching sobs, punctuated with gasps

for air, shook her body. He rocked forward and back in time with the swaying punching bag. Holding her while the anguish ran its course.

Her pain made him hurt. Made him wish he could somehow ease it. But a hot towel wasn't going to make this feel any better.

Eventually the creaking of the chain stopped. The bag stilled. Ronni sagged against him. "I didn't mean it," she whispered.

"You did." He rested his chin on the top of her head, tightened his grip on her. "And that's okay. You're allowed. It's just us." He forced a lighter note into his voice. "And if you say, 'Yeah, but you have a big mouth, Hayden,' I'm never letting you use my punching bag again."

She didn't respond. He shifted, placing his mouth closer to her ear. "Ron?"

Not being able to see the expression on her face made it a lot harder to figure out exactly what was going on with her. He leaned forward, snaked his arm under her thighs and lifted her. With a few minor maneuvers, he positioned her so she sat at his side, facing him.

He cradled her cheeks in both hands, raising her head. Tear tracks marred her makeup. He brushed at them with his thumbs. "It's okay, Ronni."

"No. It's not."

The woman he'd spent thirteen years condemning as a walk-away, who'd unknowingly shaped his own perceptions of commitment and trust, had actually taken stand-by-your-man to a whole new level.

Her lower lip quivered. He grazed his thumb over it. Once. Twice.

The temperature in the garage climbed.

Her eyes widened.

His heart pounded. With anticipation, desire… Normally he would just move in, claim her lips. But with her…he needed to get control of this before it got away from them. Needed to scare her off before he did something they'd both regret. "I want to kiss you."

His declaration hung between them. He braced himself.

Her pupils grew larger. The edges of her mouth curled. "I want to let you."

Sucker punched. For a moment he couldn't breathe. Not the response he'd expected.

CHAPTER TEN

RIGHT THERE IN THE MIDDLE of his basement floor.

She'd damn near given in to temptation. But... she hadn't. And now she'd spent the past few weeks imagining.

The warmth of his mouth on hers. On her skin. The sandpapery caress of his five o'clock shadow on her belly. The weight of his body pressed against hers.

"Earth to Ronni. Come in, Ronni."

"Hmm?" Shaken from her lovely reverie, she found Amelia staring at her from across the wooden table in the picnic pavilion near the ferry docks on Presque Isle. Jordan had selected several locations at the park for scenes in her Captain Chemo video. But the moms had been banished to the picnic pavilion, where dinner was in the process of being prepared, after interrupting the process one too many times with their gasps of dismay over some of the "stunts" Hayden pulled.

The final straw for Ronni had been when Nick had stepped into Hayden's cupped hands—and Hayden had tossed him into the air. Her son had executed and landed a perfect backflip. And she'd just plain flipped.

Getting her and all the moms tossed off "the set." After all, it wasn't as if Nick had been hurt. And Hayden was responsible for himself. But director Jordan and her cast didn't want to keep reshooting scenes. The little kids, dressed in white to symbolize the "good guys," the body's defense systems, didn't take direction well to start with.

The big kids—the grown Hawkins brothers among them—wore black. They were the cancer cells, the invaders. They took direction only marginally better than the little ones.

If Nick ended up with even a scratch, she'd threatened Hayden with serious bodily harm.

And still here she was, fantasizing about him….

It was okay, as long as it stayed in her head, right? And who better to fantasize about than Hayden? Because even if she were free, Mr. Thirty Days wasn't what she'd want in a guy.

"You're so far off in space, I don't think the Hubble telescope could find you. What are you thinking?"

Ronni refocused on the woman across the table. "Um…" Her face warmed. "Beating Hayden if anything happens to my son."

"Uh-huh." Skepticism tinted Amelia's response. "Might have been about Hayden, but that dreamy expression didn't seem to indicate beating. Unless you're into that sort of thing. And I don't think he is."

The flush intensified. "It's not like that."

"But it could be."

Ronni shook her head.

"Because of Scott?"

"Pretty darn good reason, don't you think?"

Amelia raised one shoulder. "You don't wear a wedding ring."

Ronni rubbed the bottom of her left ring finger. Once the skin had been smooth where the gold band had rubbed against it. "I took it off before Scott got hurt."

"And yet you never put it back on again. Think about why you're still with him. Obligation—"

"I prefer the term *responsibility.*"

"Okay. Still, not really a fabulous reason. I mean, I think love can grow out of a sense of obligation. Finn didn't want me in his house last summer any more than I wanted to be there. He took me in because of obligation. Or, as you prefer, a sense of responsibility toward Jordan, Chip and me. But love grew out of that. Is your love for Scott going to grow? Or has that gone the other way?"

"I wouldn't have married him if I hadn't loved him."

"But…?"

"But every time I found he'd lied to me, some of that love died. The pain over his cheating killed it—killed me—more every day."

"And now?"

"When I found out what he'd done to Nick, using him, maybe the last piece vanished. I still care what happens to Scott. There were good moments."

"Of course there were. But is that enough for now? For tomorrow? The next day? Where does your obligation to him end and your obligation to yourself begin?"

Ronni dropped her hands into her lap, continuing to

caress the spot where her wedding ring had once circled her finger. Amelia's probing question hit hard.

"And what about your obligation to Nick? What kind of example are you setting for him?"

Ronni jerked her head up. "What? I'm setting an excellent example. You don't cut and run. You see things through." She'd cut and run with Ian. The biggest mistake of her life. She wasn't going to be that weak again.

"You let people walk all over you, break your heart, hurt you, and you stick around to take care of them. And you wonder why Nick is still trying to get the attention of the girl who got him into trouble?"

Ronni leaned back, stunned into silence. Was that the lesson her son had inadvertently learned?

"I should probably confess I'm not the world's biggest advocate of marriage," Amelia admitted. "Especially where jerks are concerned. So take that into account."

A parade of cars began pulling into the dirt parking lot yards from the shelter. Doors slammed and the boisterous voices of children filled the air. White-clad little ones swarmed the area, demanding food. The bigger ones, men included, followed.

Jordan, with her best friend—her "BFF"—Shelby, who'd come down from Maine for a two-week summer visit on her way to her father's, charged over to the table.

Today Jordan's medical mask featured a mouth with a large director's horn coming from it.

Ronni smiled. "That's a great mask. I think Greg

needs to start a sideline business. If the swine flu ever takes off next year, he could make a killing selling those."

Jordan's eyes flickered briefly at her mother, shooting daggers her way. "I suppose," the girl said. "Mom, Dad says we're going to eat at one of the picnic tables over by the water, away from the group. He said Shelby can come."

"Of course Shelby can come."

Shelby inched closer to Jordan, elbowing her in the side.

"And Nick?" Jordan asked. "Can he eat with us, too?"

"I suppose that's fine with me if it's okay with Ronni."

"Fine by me, too. Just don't be appalled by his table manners. And don't get between him and the food. That can be dangerous."

Shelby giggled.

"So, how's the movie coming?"

"Great. We moved a lot faster once you guys left. There's only one more scene I want to shoot, and we can't do that until later. Let's go get something to eat, Shelby." The pair turned in unison.

"Wait," Ronni called. "Where's Nick?"

"He and Uncle Hayden are changing in the bathroom by the parking lot. Uncle Greg said absolutely no eating in the costumes," Jordan yelled over her shoulder. The girls trotted off toward the long table at the front of the pavilion where the food, everything from baked beans to ziti, had been set out.

"How long does she have to wear the mask? If looks could kill—"

"I'd have been dead a long time ago." Amelia offered a wry smile while shaking her head. "I wanted to go with a full year, which would be October. We've compromised with the beginning of the new school year at the end of August. She's been on cyberschool for so long, she's really looking forward to going back to classes, and insists on doing it without the mask. As long as her blood counts are good, and there are no big outbreaks of anything contagious, then I'm going to have to live with it."

Amelia leaned forward, propping her elbows on the wooden table. "Listen, Ronni, about Hayden…"

Ronni sighed. "Amelia, I know you mean well. But…" She shook her head. "Even if I wasn't still married to Scott, I don't think Hayden is what I'd want in a new guy. If I ever get involved again, I'm looking for a lot more than a love-'em-and-leave-'em lothario."

"Is that all you see? Surely you've already realized there's a lot more to Hayden than that. He helped take care of me last summer when I was on bed rest with Chip. If I needed something, he was there. He came up with thoughtful solutions to some of the problems I was having. He rubbed his pregnant sister's feet. How many guys do you know who'd do that? I mean, you can get them to do something like that if they might get sex, but this was just because her feet hurt."

"I know he can be nurturing." He'd certainly proved that when Ronni had had her headache.

"He's protective of his family. He warned me against hurting Finn." Amelia chuckled. "He scared the life out of the boy who gave Jordan her first kiss." Her expression sobered. "He came home from Shannon and Greg's wedding covered in Jordan's blood, and never batted an eyelash. The stuff that's got you scared? The way he goes through women like other people go through shoes? That's how he protects himself. I think Hayden's so afraid of getting hurt himself, he makes sure it can't happen. I also think that when he falls, he's going to be a forever guy. Just like his father."

When Ronni didn't respond, Amelia added, "Did you know he hasn't had a single date since he started hanging out with you and Nick?"

"He hasn't?"

Amelia shook her head.

"And you're telling me all this why? It's not like he's going to fall for me." Ronni glanced over Amelia's shoulder to find Hayden and Nick approaching. Hayden had his arm draped around her son's shoulders. Nick broke away and rushed toward the food table.

Hayden looked her way, meeting her gaze. And smiled at her.

Her stomach went to mush, and a warm tingle spread through her body.

Amelia cleared her throat. "Hayden's here, huh?"

"What?" Ronni returned her glance to the woman across from her.

Amelia stole a peek over her shoulder. "I rest my case. Everything about you just brightened like someone replaced a forty-watt bulb with a hundred-watt." She rose from the table. "Obligation to yourself, Ronni. See you later."

Where did obligation to self begin or end, compared with plain old selfishness? Was it horrible and wrong to even imagine something more than the tedious existence her life had become?

Ronni pondered all Amelia had said and more as the Hawkins crew bustled around her, the cheerful cacophony a balm for her spirits.

A plate nearly overflowing with a hamburger, potato salad, baked beans and coleslaw appeared in front of her. A matching plate, two bottles of water, and plastic utensils wrapped in napkins joined it.

Hayden sat down beside her, close enough that his arm brushed hers. "Hey. Brought you something to eat."

"So I see. Why do you keep trying to feed me?"

"Someone has to. Besides, I heard the way to a woman's heart is through her stomach." His smile reached his eyes.

"Since when do *you* care about a woman's *heart?*"

Hayden's mouth engaged before his brain did. "Since now."

Holy crap, had he actually said that to her out loud? Even more startling, he realized it was true. Ever since that moment in his garage when she'd confessed to wanting his kiss, and had then pulled back, he'd been on edge. Wrestling with the desire that flared the moment she neared. But he'd also found himself more and more enmeshed in Ronni and Nick's daily lives.

Found himself at home there.

Almost as if they were a family.

Almost as if he belonged.

Ronni stared at him with rising eyebrows. On unfamiliar ground, he opted to revert to the familiar. He leaned his head lower, closer to her ear. "Not just your heart. I'm interested in other parts of you, too. When you look at me like you did a few minutes ago, I want you. I seem to spend half my days hard with wanting you."

She turned her head away, cheeks flaming. Embarrassment, or desire?

He took her hand, tucked it under the table palm-up on his thigh, caressing it with his fingertip.

"What are you doing?" she muttered, trying to pull her hand back. He pressed down, keeping it captive.

"Touching you. Holding your hand like a guilty teenager in the high school cafeteria."

"And you don't think anyone's going to notice?"

"They'll notice it a lot more with the fuss you're making."

"You're not supposed to touch me. We can't—"

"I know." He traced along the edge of her hand, then around each finger. "This is controlled touching. An escape valve. To release some of the tension building between us."

"I—I—" she stuttered as he moved to her wrist, and

then up the smooth skin of her forearm "—I can't eat without my hand."

"True." He sighed, brought his own onto the table to pick up his napkin-wrapped utensils. "I won't interfere with that." A moment later, as he chomped into his burger, the hair on his neck prickled. He glanced around and found Greg staring at him with a frown. He shook his head at Hayden.

His brother had seen. And knew what was going on under the table. Probably figured it had been even worse than it had.

Hayden scanned the pavilion to locate their mother, who fortunately had her back turned, then flipped off his brother. Greg pulled out his cell phone, thumbs moving rapidly.

Hayden's back pocket vibrated. He ignored it, taking another bite of his burger.

Greg waved his phone in the air. He took one step in Hayden's direction, now scowling. Meaning *read my text and answer it, or I'm coming over there, and you won't like it.*

Reluctantly, Hayden dug his cell from his pocket. "How's the potato salad?" he asked Ronni as she picked at her food. "I made it."

She jerked her head up. "You did not. You don't even own a pot, let alone a potato peeler."

"Okay, so I bought it at Wegmans. You gonna tattle to my mom on me?"

A small smile quirked her mouth. "Pretty sure she

already knows. At least you didn't bring the leftovers in the takeout containers in your fridge."

"Hey, there's some good stuff there. Finn's been experimenting with new recipes now that he's got Fresh back up and running." Hayden finally glanced at Greg's text message.

Beers tonight my lair. 9. Finn 2. Be there or we'll come looking for u.

Shit. It wasn't just sharing beers his brother had in mind.

HAYDEN TREADED LIGHTLY upon reaching the second floor of Greg's house that evening. He'd been forewarned via text that Ryan and Shannon, both exhausted from the day's events, had turned in early. As Hayden passed the room that had been the upstairs theater when he'd lived in the house with Finn and Greg, a scant few years ago, the sharp scent of fresh paint drew his attention.

He swung the door partway open and clicked on the overhead light. All the old furniture had been removed. Fresh white walls bore faint pencil marks. Greg undoubtedly had an elaborate mural planned for this room. The future nursery.

Hayden's ribs constricted. Greg now had a stepkid, and a baby of his own on the way. Finn had a teenager of his own through a twist of fate, and an almost-year-old son.

Both had women they intended to spend the rest of their lives with.

Hayden had…an empty place of his own.

He flicked off the light. Stood in the doorway for a few moments.

Finally, he moved on. Ignoring the waist-high stop sign on another door down the hall, he opened it. Climbed the five steps to what once had been the attic, but was now Greg's work space and sanctuary. A window air conditioner hummed away, cooling the area to a bearable temperature.

As he passed Greg's drawing board, he glanced at the sketches there—preliminary panels for Greg's latest Y-Men comic book.

Superhero memorabilia decorated the walls. Greg and Finn were already sprawled on the futon in the sitting area of the studio. The wall behind them featured a mural Greg had done of his various brothers, each as a superhero. The two oversize chairs that faced the futon were empty. Four dark bottles, condensation already sliding down the sides, graced the small coffee table.

Four.

"Ian's birthday's not for a while yet," Hayden pointed out, dropping into one of the chairs. It was only the end of June. Ian's birthday fell on July 21. The last non-birthday time one of them had seen fit to invoke their missing brother had been the night of Chip's birth, when Finn had been drowning his sorrows over Amelia banning him from the delivery room.

"We know that," Greg said. "But since he's part of this…"

Shit. That confirmed it. They wanted to hammer Hayden about Ronni.

Each brother grabbed an ale, twisting off the cap and tossing it on the table, where they collided like hockey pucks on ice. Then each man set his beer down without drinking.

"You do the honors tonight, Hay," Finn said.

With a sigh, Hayden grabbed the fourth bottle, opening it and holding it aloft. "Ian," he intoned. "All for one and one for all." He took a swig, then passed it to Greg.

"Ian." Greg and Finn repeated the ritual they'd instituted in their younger brother's memory. His bottle got parked on the fourth corner of the table, in front of the empty chair.

"Okay," Hayden said. "Let's just get this over with, huh? I've got places to go and things to do."

"Guilty conscience? What makes you think we wanted anything more than to share a beer with our brother? The one who's been so busy lately we've barely seen him?" Finn reclined against the futon's pillow, bottle resting on his chest. "But I'm with you. I've got to pick up Jordan from the roller skating rink in—" he checked his watch "—about an hour. Amelia's home, pacing the floor, counting the minutes. It's the first time she's let Jordan do something like this."

"What about you, Hayden? You got a hot date tonight?" Greg asked.

"Nope."

"A cold date? One of your check-'em-out, see-if-you-want-to-even-give-'em-thirty-days dates?"

"Nope."

"Have you had any dates of any kind since you started hanging out at Ronni's?"

Hayden lifted one shoulder. "I dunno. I've been busy with Nick."

"You don't know?" Finn's tone suggested incredulity. "Check your calendar. *We* want to know."

"Screw off. My personal life is none of your business."

Greg and Finn exchanged glances. "Told you," Greg said. He turned to Hayden. "Are you sleeping with Ronni?"

They stared him down until he finally caved. He needed to talk about it. About her. "No." He slumped against the back of the chair.

"But you're thinking about it?"

He sighed. "Every other minute of every damn day."

"But…she's Ian's girl." Finn set his beer on the table.

"You know, I think if we'd kept her in the family all along, I'd still think of her as Ian's girl. But we didn't. We pushed her out. She hasn't been Ian's girl for more than thirteen years. I don't think he'd mind. I think he'd tell me to go for it." If Hayden could truly live up to the promise he'd made, and take care of Ian's family, he knew his younger brother would cheer him on.

"Maybe. Maybe not. But in either case, now she's Scott's *wife,*" Greg said gently, leaning forward. "What the hell are you thinking, Hay? That's a line you don't cross."

"I know. We haven't." He slid farther down in the chair, stomach tightening. "I want…"

"Her?" Finn said. "We get that. Greg said you nearly burned down the picnic pavilion today just by sitting next to her."

Hayden shook his head. A lump formed in his throat. What the foxtrot was wrong with him? "More," he croaked. "I want…more. With her. Them. Nick, too."

Both his brothers cursed at the same time—though their word choices varied. Then they both stared at him, wide-eyed.

"Say something," Hayden finally begged.

"I'm so sorry, man. I had no idea…." Finn shook his head. "I never thought you'd give it up. But to give it up to a woman you totally can't have, at least right now…" His brother sighed. "Sucks, bud."

"Give what up?"

"Your heart, you big lunkhead," Greg said. "You're in love with her!"

"What?" He bolted upright. "No. No way. It hasn't even been two months since the meeting at the courthouse with Nick's probation officer. I haven't slept with her, for God's sake!"

Finn chuckled. "Yeah, well…I didn't sleep with Amelia before I fell, either."

"Only because you couldn't. Chip's life—hell, Jordan's life—was at stake."

"And…you can't, either," Greg pointed out. "What's the first thing you think about when you wake up?"

"Ronni."

"Last thing before you fall asleep?"

"Ronni." Those bedtime thoughts were usually X-rated, though. He'd had those about plenty of women.

"When you say you want more, what exactly does more look like? If you were going to draw a picture…"

"What you have with Shannon and Ryan. With Amelia and Jordan. They had empty spaces in their lives, empty spaces that you guys filled. It was like there was a hole there just waiting for you. Ronni and Nick have an empty space, too. And…"

"And you want to be the man who fits into that empty space?"

"Yeah. Does that sound as corny as I think it does?"

Finn and Greg exchanged grins.

"Totally."

"Absofreakin'lutely."

"Still…" Greg's expression grew serious. "Not sure what you're going to do about it. She was going to divorce Scott before the accident. What do you think the chances are she'll do it now? Clear the way for you?"

Hayden shrugged. "Not good. She's got major guilt. Obligation issues." His cell phone rang, Rick

Springfield's "Jessie's Girl" spilling from the speakers. His face warmed. "Ronni," he said to his brothers, who both burst into laughter.

"I rest my case, Your Honor," said Greg.

Finn's phone rang a moment later. Hayden rose from the chair, wandering over to Greg's computer table, which featured a high-end printer and a massive flat-bed scanner. The wheeled chair squeaked as he sat on it. "Yeah, Ronni, what's up?"

"The police just called. They want me to come down to the roller rink. They've got Nick in custody. Something about him assaulting someone." Her voice cracked. "Hayden…"

The anguish in her voice tore at him. He was already on his feet. "I'll be right there. We'll go together." He snapped his phone shut, rammed into Finn at the top of the stairs. "Sorry, guys, I've gotta go."

"Me, too," Finn said. "That was Amelia. Jordan called her from the roller rink. Something about a boy bugging her all night, and he ripped her mask off, and Nick let the kid have it, and now the police—"

"Have Nick." Hayden sighed. "Ronni didn't have that information about the other kid and Jordan. Guess I'll see you at the roller rink."

"Welcome to parenthood," Finn said. "Fun stuff, huh?"

Greg followed them down the stairs. "Not an activity for the fainthearted, that's for damn sure."

NICK'S SHOULDERS ACHED. Cold metal bit into the tender flesh around his wrists. His right cheek throbbed in time with his pulse and his knuckles burned. He struggled against the stupid moisture welling in his eyes. His mom was going to have a total fit. And what the hell would happen to him? Already on probation, he wasn't supposed to be getting into trouble.

Still…the jerk had it coming. When he'd ripped Jordan's mask off, and she'd started crying, Nick had lost it.

The crowd of people outside the squad car had grown larger and larger, but he still didn't see his mom.

A short blonde woman cut through the crowd.

Nick groaned. Mandy Curtis, his probation officer. Well, she'd wasted no time getting down here. She corralled one of the officers and headed for the car.

The door he was leaning against opened, and Nick tilted, almost falling out. Mandy grabbed his elbow, which made pain shoot from his wrist to his shoulder. She helped him gain his balance.

"Nicholas," she scolded. "You've been doing so great. What the hell is going on?"

He ducked his head, studied the scuffed tips of his sneakers in the light from the streetlamp in the roller rink parking lot. "Wasn't my fault," he mumbled. "That jerk started it. Put his hands on my cousin. If her blood counts aren't good, she could *die* if she gets an infection."

"Really?"

"Yeah, really. She had a transplant last fall. She wasn't wearing the damn mask as a fashion statement."

"Nick? Nick!" His mother's voice cut through the chaos. With Unk at her side, she made her way over to him. She took one look at him, at his hands secured behind his back, and bit her lower lip.

"Don't," Unk warned her quietly.

She looked away for a minute, taking a deep breath. Then she glanced back. "Are those cuffs really necessary?" she demanded of the nearest cop.

"Until I find out if assault charges are being filed, they are," he said.

Uncle Finn, towing Jordan and her friend Shelby, joined the throng. "There better not be charges. If there are, we're pressing charges against the other kid, too. The one who assaulted my daughter."

All the adults started talking at once, until the cop held up his hands. Then Uncle Alan showed up. Suit, tie, the whole deputy district attorney nine yards. "Let's get to the bottom of this, shall we?"

Ten minutes later, after discussions and negotiations with both sets of parents, the roller rink owners and the cops, it was agreed that no charges would be filed against either of them. The jerk was made to apologize to Jordan, who turned her nose up at him until Uncle Finn poked her in the back and forced her to accept his weak-ass apology.

The boys had to shake hands. Nick, just getting circulation back in his arms, probably squeezed too hard, but neither of them showed it in their faces.

After they separated to opposite sides of the parking lot, Shelby threw her arms around Nick's neck and soundly kissed him on the lips. "You're a hero, Nick."

His face burned. Megan had dumped him again,

calling him a loser, since he didn't want to do anything that could mess up his probation. Part of him thought he'd never get another girl to look his way. Shelby's attention had him hoping otherwise.

Jordan groaned behind the new medical mask, undoubtedly supplied by her father on his arrival. "Like his ego needs encouragement."

"All right, I've got to get Jordan home. Amelia didn't want to wake Chip, and she's texted me eight times already." Uncle Finn held out his hand. "Nick. Thank you for defending my daughter."

"Uh, sure. No problem." He shook his uncle's hand, feeling ten feet tall.

Unk hooked his arm around Nick's neck. "Let's get you home, huh, sport?"

As they headed for Unk's Camaro—Nick spent more and more time riding in Unk's car than his mother's Jetta, which was cool because Unk's was an attention magnet, while his mom's was boring—he turned to glance behind them. "Mom?"

"Yeah, baby?"

"You mad at me?" Nick shrugged off Unk's arm, took a step toward his mother.

"No, sweetheart." She gathered him into a brief hug. "I was terrified for you. For me." She cupped his face in her hands. "You're my life, Nicky. I was scared to death they were going to take you away from me."

Ronni brushed Nick's hair back from his forehead. She tried to hide her dismay at the angry red splotch on his cheek where he'd taken a punch from the other boy. The body-numbing fear had finally begun to fade.

Nick glanced down. "Aww, Mom. Sorry."

"I'm not. I wish it hadn't come to physical blows, but...sometimes you do what you have to do." She glanced up at Hayden, who jerked his head in a quick nod of acknowledgment. He'd coached her during the whole ride over on how not to embarrass the life out of a teenage boy who'd gotten into a fistfight for a damn good reason, and didn't need his mother making things worse.

"I need ice cream," she declared, as she held the seat for Nick to squeeze into the back of the sports car.

Hayden laughed. "I'll swing by the grocery store on our way home."

On our way home...

The words resonated through Ronni. The second she'd hung up from the police, her instinct had been to call Hayden.

And just like that, he'd been there.

Just as she'd known he would be.

Back at the house, while Hayden and Nick created ice cream sundaes in the kitchen, she wandered into the living room. Stood staring at Scott's picture on the mantel.

Tomorrow morning, as always, she would return to the nursing home. Wash him, shave him, comb his hair...do the things she could. The medical stuff—dealing with his feeding tube, things like that, she couldn't handle. So she did what she could for his care. He still wouldn't know her from Angelina Jolie, or G.I. Jane. Wouldn't know day from night, marriage from divorce… or, she suspected, life from death.

Still, *she* knew the difference. Which was what had her tied in knots. She knew the right thing, but dear God, how she was tempted.

Hayden wasn't just an apple.

He was a chocolate-coated, caramel-drizzled, giant apple on a stick.

And she wanted a bite in the worst way.

CHAPTER ELEVEN

THE BIRDS AWOKE even before the sky began to lighten. A chirrup here, a peep there. Then the black became gray. The morning stars faded. The gray turned to pink, revealing tall, puffy clouds across the sky.

Ronni sat on her deck, coffee mug cradled in her hands, and pondered the possibilities. An entire new day wide open before her. As yet unspoiled. So much potential.

"Happy birthday, Ian." She saluted the dawn with lukewarm java and a stifled yawn.

She tried to imagine what he'd be like today, as a thirty-three-year-old man, instead of the nineteen-year-old boy. Would he have filled out, like Hayden? Or still be more lean, wiry?

One thing she didn't doubt. He'd still be a firecracker who urged her to test her limits. Who convinced her, with a grin, to try it, 'cause she just might like it.

With a throaty caw-caw, Mr. Black swooped down from the tree, landing on the railing.

"You're the early bird today. No breakfast yet, only coffee. And I'm not sharing that. Or the devil's food cake I'm eating today." Devil's food had been Ian's favorite cake. Appropriately so. Every year on his birthday, she ate it for breakfast in his honor.

Scott hadn't appreciated that, but she hadn't given any ground on how she spent Ian's birthdays. Her line in the sand.

And since it was her day to do with as she pleased—after tossing a slice of bread to Mr. Black—she hacked into the cake she'd frosted last night before bed, poured skim milk into a fluted wineglass, and drew herself a bath complete with scented Dead Sea salts.

By candlelight, she soaked in the steaming water, eating chocolate cake and sipping milk from crystal. A fine start.

When her fingertips had shriveled, the water cooled, and there was nothing left but smears of icing on the plate, she climbed from the tub. Time for some serious primping.

Two hours later, shaved, plucked, and sporting a new pair of low-riding jeans, she stood in the driveway, while Nick threw some "essentials" into his overnight bag—his Xbox and controllers. Teenage boys had a seriously warped sense of essentials. While Lydia waited for him in her car, Ronni chatted with her once almost mother-in-law.

Wonders, apparently, never ceased.

"I left something for you on the kitchen table, Mom," Nick said as he bounded past.

"Okay, sweetheart. See you tomorrow." Ronni turned to go into the house.

Lydia leaned out the window, calling her back to

the car while Nick loaded his bag in the backseat. "Ronni?"

"Yes?"

"Thank you. All these years, having Nick on Ian's birthday…" Lydia's blue eyes got shiny. "Well…it's meant a lot. Makes the day…easier."

"Good. I'm glad." And she was. The loss of a child had to be the most difficult thing a woman could experience. Ronni hoped never to know for sure.

Back in the kitchen, she found a DVD and a note on the table. "Mom," the note read, "thought you might like this. I converted old home videos to DVD. This is a special one I put together for you. Happy Dad's Birthday. Love, Nick."

Pleased, Ronni took the disk into the living room. Which was where Hayden found her sometime later, laughing and crying at the same time, a stack of crumpled tissues on the end table next to her, more in her hand.

Three weeks had passed since he'd come to her rescue, the night the police had taken Nick into custody. Three weeks during which he'd spent more and more time with them. Feeling more like a family.

More time with her feeling like…something she really wanted. The attraction between them had become damn hard to ignore. When she'd invited him to spend Ian's birthday with her—and her alone—he'd jumped at the chance.

Hayden sank to the sofa beside her. "What's going on?"

She blew her nose. "I'm mad. There's no crying on Ian's birthday. And Nick made me cry. He made this DVD of Ian and me, and Nick as a baby…."

"Horrible child. I'll beat him immediately." Hayden turned his attention to the screen—just in time to see the camera pan down to her butt.

She slapped him on the shoulder. "And who filmed that? Nice close-up of my ass."

"Exactly. It was a nice ass. *Is,*" he amended, before she could smack him again. "What can I say? It caught my attention."

Ignoring the flirtation, even though it made her heart beat faster, Ronni clicked off the television and stood up. "This wasn't on the agenda today. Especially not the crying. But I'm glad Nick made it for me. Getting to see Ian again… So vibrant, so full of life. And that's what we're going to do today."

Hayden jumped to his feet. "What, exactly?"

"Live. One hundred and ten percent. Full throttle."

His Adam's apple bobbed as he swallowed. "Full throttle?"

"Yep. You brought your bike, right?"

"Yes. Didn't you hear me pull in?"

"I was sort of focused…" She gestured at the TV.

"When you said full throttle, I didn't think you meant the bike." He stepped toward her, consuming the space between them.

Despite the central air, the heat in the room spiked to match the heat wave outside. Breathing became difficult.

She glanced up, meeting Hayden's deep blue eyes. The meaning—and invitation—was clear.

"I, uh…" Though the day *was* about living to the fullest, enjoying every moment, she wasn't sure she was prepared to cross that particular line. What the heck had she been thinking, inviting him to be with her today? It was like inviting a match-wielding arsonist into a fireworks warehouse.

"Am I making you uncomfortable?"

"What makes me uncomfortable is we're obviously both considering it."

"I'm fighting it…have been fighting it." He slid his hand along the side of her face, caressing her cheek with his thumb. "But I've never wanted anyone like I want you."

Her heart jumped. This handsome rogue of a man, who could have any woman he wanted, wanted *her*. Defective Ronni Mangano, who couldn't keep her husband happy enough to keep him home. "If you kiss me now," she murmured, "I'm done for. And I don't think I'm ready."

A muscle in his jaw twitched. He closed his eyes, groaning. "Woman, do you have any idea how much strength it's going to take *not* to kiss you now?"

"Good thing you're a superhero."

For a few long heartbeats, he didn't move, leaving her wrestling with her own impulses. Was he going to kiss her?

Or accede to her request?

And did she really want him to stop?

She stroked down his shoulder to his biceps. "And very strong."

"*Not* helping." He shrugged off her fingers, then dropped his arm and clenched both hands into fists at his sides. Opening his eyes, he took a determined step backward, drawing in a huge breath and slowly blowing it out. "Okay. Okay." Another breath. "Well…if that's not on the agenda for today, what is? A visit to Ian's grave?" His brows drew together.

She shook her head. "No. Today is about life, not death. We'll start with a cruise on your bike."

EVERY TIME HAYDEN THOUGHT he had a handle on her, she surprised him. And every time he thought he couldn't be more attracted, he was. Riding on his motorcycle, the incredible sense of freedom, the heightened sense of being in the open air—all of it was better with Ronni on the back. Every time he opened the bike up, she squeezed his ass and legs with her thighs. Which had him looking for routes specifically so he could go faster.

Just for the arousal factor.

He'd had plenty of other women on the back of the bike.

Plenty of other women in and out of his life.

So what was this *thing* between him and Ronni? Since his brothers had labeled it love, he'd been determined to prove them wrong. He'd gone on several exploratory dates over the last two weeks. Given the obligatory good-night kisses. And not a spark. Not even a hint of a spark.

He'd never kissed Ronni, and they were a powder keg.

She consumed his thoughts. Did she remember to eat? Had she had another migraine? How was business going?

Was there a snowball's chance in hell for them?

And was he headed to hell himself for wondering? If his mother found out he was involved—or wanted to be—with a married woman, a much more personal hell awaited him. His earlobe throbbed in anticipation of her dragging him somewhere private for a scathing Mom lecture.

Ronni leaned against him, positioning her head near his ear to shout over the roar of the wind. "Head to Waldameer. I want to play Skee-Ball!"

Twenty minutes later, at Erie's local amusement park, nine wooden balls clunked into the tray of his lane beside hers. "I don't remember the last time I played Skee-Ball," he confessed as she picked up the first ball. "No, wait. I think I might have played a round a few months ago at Chuck E. Cheese's for Ryan's birthday party."

She grinned at him, merriment dancing in her eyes.

"What?"

"I'm just picturing you at Chuck E. Cheese's, surrounded by screaming kids. I don't think most single men who don't have kids would be caught dead in that chaos. Actually, most men who *have* kids would rather die than enter the place."

Hayden twitched his shoulders. "Probably helps that I'm still just a big kid at heart."

"You haven't ever wanted one of your own?"

He leaned over to pick up one of the balls. "Let's make this interesting, huh?"

"Way to change the subject." She tilted her head, one eyebrow quirking.

"Okay, the short answer, which is all you're getting. I've never thought about having a kid of my own, or a family of my own, until recently." He hefted the wooden sphere in his hand. "Now, about that bet..."

"Until recently? Biological clock finally start ticking?"

Crap, she was like a terrier with a bone. "If I win, I get to kiss you. Time, place and duration of my choosing."

Mouth slightly agape, cheeks turning pink, she stared at him. "Uh..."

Perfect. Mission accomplished. "Just kidding."

Finally regaining the power of speech, she said, "Oh, no. Bet's on the table, buddy. And if I win?"

"Seriously?" Again she was totally surprising him. "Yes."

A lesser man would have squirmed under her now-frank appraisal. He just flashed a cocky grin. "Whatever you want."

"*Whatever* I want?" Innuendo laced her voice, and her eyes twinkled again.

Flirting. His element. "Anything goes, babe."

"You may regret giving me a free pass."

"I doubt it."

"So if I decide you're cooking for me?"

He laughed. "You'll be the one who regrets it."

And so they started. Part of him considered losing on purpose, just to see what she'd do with her "power." On the other hand, she might actually decide to make him cook. And the ability to claim a kiss from her, anytime, anyplace...

Then two of her balls swooped up and into the fifty-point basket.

"Oh, game on. You didn't tell me you were a ringer." Hayden's next throw, an overzealous one, resulted in the ball bouncing around and ending up in the zero slot.

She beat him by twenty points. The machine spit out yellow tickets that could be redeemed for prizes. She held her strip up, compared it to his. "Hmm...my tickets are longer. I win."

"By one ticket. How about best two out of three?"

The music of her laughter stirred something deep in his chest. A primal ache that had nothing to do with sex.

Round two went to him.

During round three, Ronni distracted him. On purpose, he suspected. With a lot of butt wiggling. And the low-riding jeans she wore cupped her cheeks in a way that made his hands long to explore those curves. Every time she leaned over to roll a ball up the sloped alley, the powder-pink, short-sleeved tuxedo shirt pulled up, exposing a patch of creamy-white skin.

He wanted to press his lips there.

And everyplace else, from her forehead to her toes.

"That settles it," she said, dangling another string of tickets. "I win."

"You do. And I accept my defeat gracefully. What do you claim as your prize?"

"I'm going to have to think about it."

"What should we do with all these tickets?"

"I'm not exactly in the market for some cheesy stuffed animal." Ronni ripped one off, held it up, then tucked it into the front pocket of her jeans. "That's to remind us that you owe me." She added his to the collection in her hand and walked to the far alleys, where two girls played Skee-Ball under the watchful eyes of their parents. "Here you go, girls. Have fun."

"Thanks!"

Hayden offered Ronni his elbow. She hesitated only a moment, then threaded her arm through his as they headed out of the arcade building.

Dark clouds filled an ominously gray sky, casting a pallor over the amusement park. Worried parents glanced heavenward while their children, oblivious to the weather, scampered ahead of them.

"Uh-oh. Looks like rain. Sorry, Ronni, but we'd better get the bike home before the sky opens up."

"You made of sugar? Afraid you might melt?"

"No, I'm afraid of dumping us both onto wet pavement. I can ride in the rain, but I'd rather not. Especially with you on the back." He'd never forgive himself if he did something to hurt her.

Which was why, despite his flirting, he'd been restraining his impulses to touch, taste…love her.

As they wandered the blacktop paths back toward the park's entrance, she jerked to a halt in front of a refreshment stand. "Think we have time for a funnel cake?"

The scent of ozone hung heavy in the air, competing with the fried dough and hot oil smells coming from the small shack. "Much as I'm a fan of feeding you, I think we'd better pass for now. We can come back."

"Nah. We'll find something else."

In the parking lot, he revved up the bike, waited for her to climb on behind him.

An all-too-short ride later, he parked in front of his neighbor's garage just as scattered raindrops began to fall. "Timing's everything."

Already standing alongside him, Ronni held her hand out. "Give me the keys to your car. I'll move it out so you can put the bike in."

He shook his head. "It's a stick shift."

"I can drive a stick."

"Yeah, right. I remember when Ian tried to teach you to drive the pickup. I like my gears the way they are."

Another fat raindrop spattered the bike's gas tank.

"You're wasting time. I can do it."

The determined set to her jaw made him reluctantly pull the keys from his front pocket and hand them over. "That unlocks the garage's man-door, and this is the car key. Just back it out and pull over there." He indicated the space in front of the neighboring condo.

"Okay." Keys dangling from her finger, she dashed to the door, unlocked it and went inside. A moment later the overhead eased up. The Camaro's motor rumbled to life.

Hayden's shoulders tensed. He waited for the sound of grinding gears. But she smoothly zipped past him in Reverse. Nothing happened when she put it into first and pulled into the space he'd indicated, either.

He eased the bike into the garage. After shelving his gloves and their helmets, he went back outside through the overhead. Rounding the car to the driver's side as the rain took the form of an annoying mist, he yanked on the handle.

The door was locked.

Ronni grinned at him through the window. "Get in, pal, I'm driving."

"No, you're not." He rapped his knuckles on the glass. "Quit screwing around, Do-Ron-Ron. Unlock the door and switch over."

"Nope. I wanna drive it. Come on, Hayden, let me play with your toy."

"You want a toy? I've got better toys for you. Put the car back in the garage and I'll show you."

She sat quietly for a second or two—considering what he'd said? And unnerving the hell out of him. It had been a typical response for him, and though he wanted her in his bed, he hadn't expected her to take it seriously. "Fine. You can drive," he told her.

He ran around the hood of the car. Just as he reached the passenger door, the locks clicked open, and he slid into the seat. "The first time I hear even the hint of gears grinding, you're done. You understand?"

She saluted him. "Aye, sir. No gears."

True to her word, she didn't grind them at all. She headed for the other side of town, toward Fairview. The rain picked up to a gentle patter, just enough to need the wipers on the first setting.

"So who finally taught you how to drive a standard?" So much he still didn't know about her.

"Scott."

"How'd he manage what Ian couldn't?"

"Patience. Scott insisted everyone should be able to drive a stick. He didn't freak out the first time I ground the gears."

"Oh. Well, good. Glad to hear he had some redeeming qualities."

She shot Hayden a look. "Don't be mean. I wouldn't have married him if he was a total dick."

"No, it just turned out he couldn't keep his dick where it belonged."

When she flinched, his stomach twisted. "I'm sorry."

She shrugged. "That's as true as what I said."

"Maybe. But it hurt you. And for that…I am sorry."

She scoffed. "He hurt me a hell of a lot more." Her face hardened.

The urge to pummel Scott had Hayden fisting his hands. Why would a man who had a woman like this at home feel the need to go elsewhere? If you were going to commit to one woman, then it meant forever. Not just until someone else caught your eye. Or some other part of your anatomy.

Semper Fi. Too bad Scott hadn't been a Marine. One who'd truly embraced the Corps' motto, Always Faithful.

She turned the car right at the light at West Lake and Manchester.

"Walnut Creek?" he asked, happy for a diversion. "Most people go there to either fish or watch the sunset. We don't have poles, and even if it were time for sunset, it's raining."

"Yeah. I like to watch the rain over the lake, too. What's with you and the rain? Seriously, you'd think you were made of cotton candy."

"Rainy season in Panama with my unit provided enough rain to last a lifetime. Keeping your feet dry is one of the most important things they teach you in boot camp. In Panama during rainy season, that's damn near impossible. But that makes this look like a sunny Erie summer day. This isn't rain. It's a touch of humidity by their standards."

"Without rain, we wouldn't appreciate the beautiful sunny days."

"Quite the optimist, aren't you?" Which explained why she'd given Mangano a second chance. That second chance had come back to bite her in the tail.

"Something I've learned over the years. Dunno if it's

optimism, though, or pragmatism. There's always rain. Just get an umbrella and keep going."

At Walnut Creek access, where the creek flowed into Lake Erie, she veered off into the old parking lot on the right, away from the marina. The place was practically deserted. A few cars were parked near the main building, a few more down near the dock area, but over here, where she'd decided to pull in, there was nobody. She parked facing the lake and shut off the engine.

"See, made it here with no grinding."

"Good thing."

She popped off her seat belt, shifting to get more comfortable. He did the same. The rain pattered softly against the windshield. Out on the lake, small waves kicked up near shore.

"Show me your tat," he suddenly ordered, uncomfortable with the stretch of silence.

"What?" She turned partially toward him.

"Your tat. The one on your left leg. Show it to me and tell me the story behind it."

"You know about it?"

"Yeah. The day of the Memorial picnic, when I took you home, I took off your socks and shoes. Nice work."

She lifted her foot, crossing her left leg onto the right. Raising the hem of her jeans, she exposed a purple object strapped to the inside of her ankle.

"What the heck is that?"

"It's a purse. Perfect for bike riding." She showed him the pouch holding her cell phone.

"Compared to that huge thing you drag around most of the time, that's like nothing."

She laughed. "Tell me about it. I feel naked without my purse, but at least I can have some essentials this way. Cell phone, license, money, credit card, lipstick."

"Right. The *essentials*."

Velcro ripped as she unfastened it. She draped the purse across the gauges in front of the center console, then shoved down her raspberry sock, exposing the tattoo.

Hayden leaned in for a closer look at the Liberty Bell with the broken heart. Using one finger, he rubbed at the lines the sock had made in her skin. "Now tell me the story."

"One of Tam's friends did it for me, the day my lawyer finished the paperwork for the divorce. The day before we were going to file it. The day before I Skyped Scott in Iraq. Brokenhearted, but representing freedom, as well."

"Wow." Hayden traced the crack in the heart. Then he looked up at her, letting his finger linger on her flesh. "You ever reconsider filing that paperwork? Going through with the divorce? I mean, now that Nick and Vera know about what happened."

She opened her mouth to answer, then shut it again without saying anything.

"Truth, Ronni."

She lifted one shoulder. "I've thought about it."

A glimmer of hope speared through him. "What stops you?"

"Guilt. Fear. Responsibility."

The guilt, he'd known about. "What are you afraid of, babe?" He caressed her ankle.

"Doing something wrong. Again. Like I did with Ian."

"Totally different circumstances. What else?"

"Being judged by everyone. Hell, now that the media's on my story, can you even imagine what might happen if I filed those papers?"

The media interest had waned, but not died completely. She didn't have a mob of photographers stalking her anymore, but she still got regular requests for interviews.

"You can't spend your whole life miserable because you're worried about what other people will think."

"Sure I can."

"Well, you shouldn't." He let his fingers drift up the silky skin of her calf. "You deserve so much more. I don't think a little happiness is too much to ask for. You've had enough rain. You should have sunshine."

The patterns he traced on her skin drove her crazy. If she didn't do something drastic, quickly, she'd be begging him to move those fingers to more intimate places on her body. Bring her some happiness, indeed.

"You're right. And today is supposed to be about happiness, and living—enjoying life to its fullest. That's what Ian and I did on his last birthday. We did crazy, fun things. And you're bringing me down with this conversation." She jumped out of the car, into the summer drizzle. The car rocked as she slammed the door. She ran around the back of the car, into the wide, empty space of the parking lot.

She crooked her finger at Hayden.

He shook his head.

Tucking her hands into her armpits, she flapped her "wings" at him, clucking.

He raised both shoulders.

"Okay, your loss." She held her arms straight out, tilted her head back, closed her eyes. Warm raindrops dotted her face, caressing her skin. Waves lapped against the shoreline. Gulls cried overhead.

She let the rain wash over her, wash away another year of existing. Of intermittent pain. Worse, of brutal numbness that so often took the place of the pain.

At least when she hurt she knew she still could feel something.

Life was a gift. That was what Ian's final birthday had been all about. Milking the most out of every single second they'd shared that day. Every day.

Until he'd run out of days.

Tears leaked from the corners of her tightly closed eyes. He'd be so disappointed in her this year.

For selling herself short. For not embracing life.

For accepting less than she should.

She sensed a presence in front of her, and opened her eyes to find Hayden looking down at her. She hadn't heard him open the car door or approach.

"There's no crying on Ian's birthday," he said gently.

She swiped at her cheeks with the backs of her hands. "Just rain."

"My ass."

A chuckle collided with the lump in her throat and came out a sob. "And a very nice ass it is, too," she finally managed to say.

"Really? You think? These pants don't make it look fat?" He turned, gave a shimmy.

"No. You might want to avoid spandex, though."

He laughed, turning back toward her. "That's no lie."

Actually, it was a total lie. Spandex only made his rock-hard butt even more drool-worthy. But he had a healthy enough ego without knowing that.

He extended his left hand. "Well…since we're here. In the rain. With nobody around… Shall we dance? I hear dancing in the rain is the latest thing."

"Dance? With you?"

"Don't see anyone else around for you to partner with."

Damn. He'd danced competitively as a kid with Judy. Jordan had posted video footage of the pair dancing at Greg and Shannon's wedding last year. Stomping all over his feet would only make Ronni feel worse. "I'll just grind the gears. Remember you tried to teach me to waltz years ago? Right after Ian and I started dating?"

"Yes." Hayden's eyes darkened. Not with anger, more like with…desire? The rain flattened his spiked front hair. "I remember it pissed Ian off."

"You made him jealous."

"He had good reason to be. He knew how I felt about you then."

"W-what? How?"

Hayden clasped her right hand in his left, placed her left hand on his shoulder. The damp cotton of his turquoise T-shirt clung to his body, accentuating the definition of his muscles. "Stand up straight. I lead, you follow. We'll take it really slow."

Before she could protest again, he'd starting counting. Too focused on her feet to think straight, she did her damnedest to follow him. And keep her klutzy feet to herself. She skidded on some gravel.

He steadied her without missing a beat. His hand on her waist drew her closer, so near that heat radiated between them. "Eyes up. Look at me, not your feet. *One,* two, three, *one,* two, three… That's it."

After a few more basic steps, he started guiding her down the parking lot as gracefully as a couple in a ballroom. Before long, they were twirling in circles.

"Oh, my God, I'm doing it."

He smiled. "You are." A spark smoldered in his eyes as he drew her even closer. "At first the waltz was considered highly scandalous, because of the partners' proximity to one another."

"The original dirty dancing, huh?"

"Exactly. Though they didn't dare dance as close as this."

Joy bubbled up in her. Though Hayden detested the rain, here he was, waltzing her around a deserted parking lot, getting more soaked by the minute. Desire, sudden, hot and heavy, coursed through every cell of her body.

"How do you like dancing with the devil?" He grinned at her. "Remember at Nick's probation hearing?"

"I remember." He'd told her she didn't have to dance with the devil to help her son, just with him. "I like it."

When they whirled back toward the car, she tightened her grip on his shoulder. He smoothly eased them to a stop. "What?"

She reached into her front pocket, pulled out the yellow ticket. She held it up in front of him. "Prize time."

"Okay. What did you decide you want?"

Life. Passion. To feel worthy and desirable for the first time in almost three years. She could hear Ian's voice in her head, telling her that Hayden would take care of her.

She wasn't certain sex was what Ian had in mind, but got the distinct impression he would approve of her with his brother far more than he'd approve of her with Scott.

She drew in a deep breath.

"You." Voice trembling slightly, she continued, "Let's live a little. You lead, I'll follow. Just…take it slow."

CHAPTER TWELVE

"YOU'RE SURE?" Hayden's heart thudded against his ribs as if he'd just run across the city, not merely waltzed around an empty parking lot. "There's no going back."

She nodded, holding out the ticket.

Absentmindedly, he tucked it into his front pocket.

Then he took her face tenderly in both hands. She closed her eyes. He leaned down, lightly resting his forehead on hers. "I've waited forever for this." Every other woman he'd ever kissed had been a dress rehearsal, a practice run for this moment.

It took supreme effort to relax, to open himself to Ronni. He began by brushing his mouth over hers, side to side, then circling. He kissed her top lip, her bottom lip—once, twice—then sucked gently.

She sighed, and he pressed his lips fully to hers, inhaling through his mouth to capture that sweet breath. Her first surrender, first gift, to him.

Her eyes fluttered open, revealing her surprise. He eased off on the pressure, feeling the edges of her mouth turn up. "Slow enough?" he drawled.

Her head eased up and down, providing another set of sensations against his lips.

"Good." This time he started with the tip of his tongue, tracing the outline of her mouth, learning, memorizing its shape. One hand slid to the nape of her neck, the other stroked down her neck, shoulder, arm, then snaked around her waist to pull her flush against him.

She wiggled. Just enough to short-circuit his brain, as all the blood rushed south. "Mmm." He hummed in pleasure as he switched tactics, plunging his tongue into the warmth of her mouth. Running the tip along her teeth. Tickling the roof her mouth.

His pulse kicked up. His hand wandered to the seat of her jeans, exploring the curves he'd ached to touch. He needed to feel her without denim between them. Without *anything* between them.

He forced himself to pull back. Return to a softer, lighter kiss.

The sky chose that moment to open up and mimic a Panamanian rainstorm. A deluge. His already soggy clothes instantly adhered to his skin. Water dripped off the ends of her hair.

She glanced up at him, her eyes unfocused in a way that sent satisfaction coursing through him. He'd gotten to her as much as she'd gotten to him.

Ronni lifted a hand, shielding her eyes from the rain. "Do you think this is the universe's way of telling us to knock it off? Putting out the fire, so to speak?"

He laughed as he scooped her into his arms and ran to the car. "Hell, no. I think this is the universe's way of telling us we need to get indoors and out of these wet clothes as soon as possible."

Beside the Camaro, he set her on her feet, quickly opening the door and tucking her into the passenger seat. If it hadn't been wet, and this hadn't been his new baby, he'd have slid across the hood. Because he could. And because it was faster.

Instead, he settled for racing around the front end. A moment later, he slid in, dripping all over the driver's seat. In a hurry to get her home, he shoved the keys into the ignition, revved the engine.

As if his engine needed any more revving.

It would take at least ten minutes to get to her house. Hayden didn't want to let the mood go, let her start second-guessing herself.

Car idling, he turned sideways. Crooked a finger at her.

"I'm sorry you got so wet." She inched toward the center console.

"It was worth it. *You're* worth it." He beckoned her closer still, then mentally cursed the console and gearshift between them. For an alleged chick magnet, the car wasn't designed for making out.

Hayden toed off his sneakers, dropping them on the mud mats. Then he spun and knelt on his seat, pulling her into his arms despite the obstacles between them. Again he started off slowly. Lightly. Kissing her forehead, her cheeks, her nose, before making his way to her lips.

Then he pushed harder, deeper. Moved to her neck,

which she obligingly arched for him, granting full access. While grazing his teeth over her collarbone, he realized she trembled in his embrace.

He pulled back. "You cold, sweetheart?" Despite the summer temperature outside, and the steaminess inside, he turned on the heat, pointing the vents in her direction.

"N-not really," she stammered, her eyes tightly shut.

"Then what?" He ran his hands over her shoulders, rubbing her arms. "Ronni, look at me."

She cautiously opened her eyes, but instantly glanced down, not meeting his gaze.

"What's wrong?"

"I, um…" She fidgeted, and her voice dropped so low he could barely hear her. "I guess I'm scared."

"Of what? Dear God, not of *me?* I would never hurt you." He stroked her cheek.

"I know that. It's just…" Her jaw quivered. "I, uh, I've only ever been with two men in my whole life. Ian and Scott. And you, you've been with… I don't want to disappoint you."

"Oh, babe." He shook his head. Mangano had mangled her self-confidence so badly. If Hayden could restore it, maybe she'd find the strength she needed to retake control of her life. "You're a beautiful, sexy lady. Nothing about you could ever disappoint me. And anything that's come before today…doesn't matter. Life begins today, Ronni. My life, anyway. Give me your hand." He held out his.

She hesitantly put hers in it. He pressed her palm to the center of his soaked T-shirt. Normally this part of tantric foreplay involved both parties already being naked, but she needed it now. It also was meant to achieve more of a spiritual connection, but for the moment, he just wanted her to know how much physical impact she had on him. "Feel my heart pounding?"

She nodded.

"You made that happen." He moved her hand lower, cupped it around the raging erection he sported. He gritted his teeth for a moment, resisting the urge to rock into her palm. "And this? Does this feel like a man disappointed in you?"

A shy smile played on her lips as she shook her head. "I guess not."

"You *guess* not? Woman, if I get any harder, *you're* going to have to carry *me* into your house."

"Then I should probably let go now. 'Cause that's not likely to happen."

He freed her hand. Before she moved it away, she gave him a playful squeeze that left him groaning.

"That was mean. Remember paybacks?" Relieved to see her trembling had stopped, he eased back into his own seat, pulling on his shoes. "I'm going to make you moan twice as loud."

"I believe you." She fastened her seat belt and settled back with a sigh. "Damn. If kissing you is like that…"

Gravel popped beneath the tires as he headed out of the parking lot. "Yes?" Call him shallow, but he loved having his ego stroked by a beautiful woman just as much as he liked having certain parts of his anatomy stroked by the same.

"I can see why they line up for thirty days with you. Why they *settle* for thirty days with you. How does that work, anyway? Thirty days from the time you sleep with them, right? So, I've got until August 21?" She stiffened. "You're not going to dump Nick when you dump me, are you? 'Cause if you are, this is so off."

At the Walnut Creek exit's stop sign, he jammed on the brakes harder than necessary. "What?" He put the car in Neutral. "Thirty days? Dump Nick? Dump *you?* No foxtrot-ing way. On either count. What part of 'My life starts today' was unclear?"

"Umm…all of it? Hayden, I thought we were just going to—"

He slammed his fist into the steering wheel as what she thought became all too clear. "You thought I was going to break my number one rule—no married women—for a thirty-day fling? Sleep with you like you were just one of the others, then walk away? Well, you thought wrong, honey." His erection shriveled. Record time deflation. She may as well have dumped a bucket of ice water in his lap.

Love 'em and leave 'em didn't feel quite so good on this side of the equation. He'd always assumed that because the women he got involved with agreed to his terms, never had any complaints when it was over and were well-loved and well-satisfied during the relationship, he'd never hurt any of them.

Now he felt the need to break the "do not initiate

contact after the relationship is over" rule, get out his little black book, call a florist and send dozens of apology notes.

A car pulled up behind them. Hayden opened the window just far enough to stick his arm out and wave it around. There wasn't tons of traffic for them to worry about. More rain made it into the car before he got the window closed again.

"I'm sorry," Ronni said. She reached for his arm.

"Please don't touch me right now."

She recoiled, and he wanted to kick himself. Way to make her see how much more he needed from her. He eased the car through the intersection, his muscles still tight. As they headed up the hill, the wipers kept up a mad tempo against the deluge. When they stopped at the red light at the top, the rapid ratcheting of the blades across the window was the only sound.

Until Ronni's phone rang. She pulled it from the purple ankle purse still draped along the center console. A quick glance at it and she cursed. "What's up?"

Hayden divided his focus between his driving and her reactions—the sharp intake of breath, the tension that radiated from her within seconds.

"You had them take him to Saint Joseph's, right? Not the VA? After the last time there, I want him at Saint Joe's…. When?"

Shit. Something had to be wrong with Scott.

"I was down at Walnut Creek access. There's no cell coverage there." She glanced down at herself, smoothing her soaked jeans as if doing so would magically render them dry. "I'll head over to the hospital as soon as I can. Thanks." She snapped the phone closed, tucked it back into the purse, which she gripped in her hand.

"What's going on with Scott?"

"He's having trouble breathing. They think he's got pneumonia."

The word *pneumonia* seemed to slug Hayden in the gut, driving all the air from his lungs. He struggled to breathe himself, to maintain control of the car.

Fortunately, the storm began to lighten.

Double pneumonia had killed Ian. His fragile immune system, suppressed by the chemotherapy he'd been receiving, hadn't been up to the fight.

That he'd been despondent over the situation with Ronni hadn't helped.

Neither had the fact that Hayden, who'd sensed something else was wrong with his brother, had agreed to keep Ian's secret about feeling so much worse.

Was it possible Ronni was about to lose the second man in her life the same way?

When they pulled into her driveway, she'd already popped her seat belt. "I'm sorry, Hayden. This really isn't what I'd had in mind when I asked you to spend Ian's birthday with me." She leaned over, brushed her lips across his cheek. "And I'm really sorry I didn't get it before."

He snorted. "I'm sorry you didn't 'get it' before, too."

She offered him a weak smile at the innuendo. "We'll

talk later, okay?" With that, she bounded from the car, racing into the house.

After just a moment's contemplation, he got out of the car and walked to the trunk to retrieve his gym bag.

SHRUGGING A DRY SHIRT over her head, Ronni spoke loudly through the fabric so the speaker on her cell, which she'd set on her dresser, would pick up her voice. "I don't know, Tam. No bookings today, of course. My regulars know I take this day off every year. But I've got appointments tomorrow. I'll cancel or postpone them, but Mrs. Johnson really needs a cut and color tomorrow. Can you take her for me?"

"If I have to stay till ten tomorrow night, I'll fit her in for you," her friend declared. "Don't sweat it. You want me to sneak over and post a sign on your shop door? Family Emergency, blah, blah, blah? Urgent Bad Hair Days Call A Cut Above, and my number?"

"That'd be great." She grabbed yesterday's jeans from the laundry basket, jumped into them. "Hopefully this will resolve quickly, and we'll be right back to the same dull routine." A massive wave of guilt threatened to drown her. She'd been having a blast, making out with Hayden, while Scott had been transferred from the nursing home by ambulance.

"Keep me in the loop about Scott. And if you need anything else, you know how to find me. I'll swing by the hospital as soon as I can."

"Thanks, Tam." Ronni closed her cell and tossed it into her big purse. She dashed into the bathroom, flipped on her blow-dryer and hastily made some semblance of order from the mess. A few quick passes with a curling iron, and she looked at least fit to be seen in public again.

She'd called Lydia, just so Nick wouldn't be blindsided if everything went to hell in a handbasket in a hurry. Lydia had offered to keep Nick as long as she needed.

Ronni put off calling Vera until she could get to the hospital, speak to a doctor herself and assess the situation. Scott had battled pneumonia months ago and won. But the doctors had told her then that it would likely be something similar, some kind of infection, that would eventually take him.

As she pulled on dry socks, she paused to finger the tattoo. The way Hayden had touched her, kissed her... She shivered. He'd certainly aced the job of making her feel alive again.

But now Scott was in trouble. And it was her job to take care of him. She smoothed the white fabric over the Liberty Bell.

Freedom wasn't free. That was a common saying in the military community, whose members knew all too well that the cost was measured in lives. In limbs. In shattered psyches.

The only "exit strategy" Ronni had ever envisioned involved Scott's death. But now that the possibility loomed again... She didn't want her freedom to come at the price of Scott's life, even if that life wasn't much to speak of.

Even if his death had been the only way she'd ever seen their numb, not-really-alive existences ending.

She grabbed her bag, barreled down the hallway. Skidded to a stunned halt in the kitchen, where Hayden, now clad in dry clothes of his own, was polishing off a sandwich. "W-what are you doing here? I thought you left."

He stuffed the last bit of food into his mouth while he shook his head. He washed it down with several gulps of water. "Here." He handed her a sandwich in a plastic bag—which explained why several of the cabinets were open. "Let's move. I'm going to the hospital with you."

"Why?"

"Because I care about you. I'm not letting you do this alone."

A sense of comfort filled her. Though he'd been court-ordered into her life, he'd truly had her back since then. Which made her feel worse about the "misunderstanding" they'd had. "Even after before?"

He waved a hand. "I'm over that already. My own fault. You expected from me exactly what I always do." His shoulders rose. "Can't blame you for that, can I?"

"But what will people think if you're at the hospital with me?"

"First of all, I don't give a damn what people think. Secondly, they'll think that your *friend,* who's been at your place damn near every day so far this summer, is helping you with a family crisis. What's the big deal?"

"You're right. Let's go." She set the sandwich on the counter, picked up her purse and headed for the door.

"We'll take my car, and I'm driving," he announced.

"No, your car seats are wet. We'll be damp all over again. We'll take my car."

"Okay, but I'm still driving. This way I can drop you off at the hospital entrance and then park the car. Hand over the keys."

As soon as he'd backed the car from the driveway, he tossed the bagged sandwich at her. "Eat. I have the feeling it's going to be a long afternoon."

"My stomach can't take that right now."

He sighed. "I'm a health teacher. I know what I'm talking about. Your body can't run without fuel."

"Gosh, I never knew that. Thanks, Mom." She stuffed the sandwich into the pair of cup holders in the middle of the car.

They rode to Saint Joseph's without further conversation, Ronni wrapping the strap from her purse around her hand, then unwrapping it. True to his word, Hayden dropped her off at the hospital's main entrance, then went to park the car at the municipal garage next door.

The volunteer staffing the main reception desk checked the computer, which indicated Scott was still in the E.R. Ronni took the elevator downstairs.

The nurse at the triage desk in the E.R. checked her computer, then directed Ronni through the doors around the corner, to the private room where Scott lay, eyes closed, on a gurney with the side rails up.

Ronni leaned over the metal railing, stroked his hair. "I'm here, Scott." Heat radiated from him—a sign of the fever that raged as his body struggled with the illness. She grazed her fingers over his chin, over the roughness of his beard stubble. "No one bothered to shave you this morning. I'm sorry about that."

Each expansion of his chest appeared to take an effort. His breathing was raspy. Slow.

Ronni's own chest tightened. She swallowed a huge lump in her throat, blinking back tears. Despite everything that had happened, it still hurt to see him like this. She tried to convert that pain to anger. She had to advocate for him here, and being a puddle of mush wasn't going to help.

"Don't you do this to me, Scott," she murmured. "Not today. Not tomorrow, either, but definitely not today."

She glanced at the numbers on the monitor. She'd learned how to read them early on when Scott had come back to the States. Had had a refresher course the last time he'd had pneumonia. His oxygen levels were low. But he didn't have an oxygen mask.

No IV, either. As far as she could tell, he was being monitored, but not receiving any sort of treatment.

A young woman in a purple scrub top with bold pink flowers on it came into the room. "Oh. Hi. I didn't realize anyone was here with him. I'm Annette."

"I'm Ronni Mangano." She gestured toward the

bed. "This is my husband. Can I get an update on his condition?"

"Sure. Let me get the doctor for you, okay?"

"Thanks. Do you know if you've also got a call in to his regular doctor? Dr. Saunders?"

"I'll check."

Ronni forced out the next question, one she didn't really want to ask, but had to. "Is there still a copy of his end-of-life directives in his records?"

The nurse's eyes softened with sympathy. "Yes. We just need to know if, as his guardian, you still agree with it."

"I wrote it. I certainly agree with it. But I don't understand, if his O2 sats are so low, and you've read the document, why isn't my husband on oxygen?"

"I'm going to get the doctor for you."

HAYDEN HEARD Ronni's voice even before he entered the double doors to the E.R. area. He couldn't make out the words yet, but he got the tone.

She was pissed at someone. Big-time pissed.

He hustled down the hall, stopping several yards behind her. Fists propped on her hips, she squared off with a baby-faced doctor.

"If my husband was a rosebush or a houseplant, he'd get water, nourishment and, if needed, medication. And that's what I'm telling you. That's what his directive calls for. You start treating him right now, or I'll have you in front of the board of this hospital so damn fast you'll be treating yourself for a serious case of whiplash!"

"Mrs. Mangano, I'm just asking you to reconsider his quality of life. If—"

"Don't quality of life me. I know somebody gave you a fancy degree and a white coat, but you don't know everything. You're not God, even if you have a God complex. How would you like me to lock you in a closet with no food and no water and let you die like that?"

"I assure you, your husband doesn't feel anything."

"Okay, I'll knock you unconscious before I toss you into the closet. That makes it all better, right? 'Cause you won't feel anything?"

"Uh… Well, technically, I suppose it would. I wouldn't suffer at all."

"Is my husband unconscious?"

"Not precisely. I'm sure you know that PVS is a distinct category of mental state."

"So you're one hundred percent certain that he feels absolutely nothing."

"Yes."

"No possibility for error? None? Zero?"

"Well, uh…"

"Exactly. This is a top-rate hospital, Dr. Xavier. I chose it for that reason. Now you start treating him with antibiotics, with whatever other medications you think will help, whatever. Be a doctor. That's all I'm asking. If he stops breathing, you let him go. If his heart stops beating, let him go. But otherwise…get the hell in there and help him until Dr. Saunders arrives to take over his care."

"As you wish, Mrs. Mangano. Let me write out the orders."

"You do that," she muttered as the doctor strode away, head slightly bowed.

"Wow. Remind me never to get on your bad side," Hayden said. "I had no idea you could get so riled up."

She whirled around. "Hayden. I didn't know you were here already."

"That's 'cause you were too busy reaming out that doctor. Probably not the best way to win friends and influence people, but still damned impressive."

She shrugged. "He wanted me to not treat Scott's pneumonia. No antibiotics. No oxygen. Nothing." Her eyes glistened. "I can't...I can't do that. I'm already responsible for his condition. I can't...kill him. I have to do what I can for him."

There was her guilt again.

Hayden held his arms open. She moved into them, nestling her head against his chest. "Of course you do. I'd feel exactly the same way." Although if he were in Mangano's boots, he'd probably prefer death to the limbo the man was in. What good was life when you couldn't do anything at all? Couldn't feel anything at all? It wasn't life.

But Hayden sure as hell didn't want Ronni carrying even more guilt than she already did. He knew all too well how that felt. How it gnawed at you.

"I don't think he'd want to live like this." She snuffled into his shirt. "I don't want to live like this. But I can't..." She finally gave in, sobbing softly in Hayden's embrace.

"Shh." He stroked her hair, holding her tight. She didn't stay there long. A moment or two later, she shoved him away, swiping at her face with the back of her hand.

"Okay. Enough. I don't have time for that right now. I have to call Vera and let her know what's happening. And I have to shuffle around all my clients for tomorrow." She jerked her head in the direction of the E.R. exam room. "Can you please sit with Scott? Wow. That's a really weird thing to ask, isn't it? But...I don't trust that doctor. And I don't want Scott alone. If anyone comes in to do anything, you ask questions, okay? Find out exactly what they're doing, what medication they're giving, all of that?"

"If that's what you need me to do, you know I will."

She grabbed his hand. Gave it a quick squeeze. "Thank you." Then she headed for the doors, digging in her purse for her cell phone.

Once she'd passed through to the waiting room, Hayden entered the exam room.

Mangano looked even more like shit than he had in the nursing home. Something Hayden hadn't thought possible at the time.

Skin flushed with fever made Scott's five o'clock shadow more pronounced. Right. Ronni had given herself the day off from the nursing home and shaving duties in honor of Ian's birthday. "Can't even let the poor woman have a single day to herself, huh? We need to have a serious talk, mano a mano."

The way Mangano struggled to breathe kicked Hayden in the gut, bringing back painful memories of Ian's last hours.

Hayden leaned over the bed, adjusted the pillow, trying to open his airway more. "Your wife is a damn good woman. Way better than you deserve, that's for sure."

A nurse bustled into the room, an IV bag in hand. She skidded to a halt when she saw him. "Hayden…"

"Netti. You're his nurse?" He and Annette had been on very intimate terms a few years back.

"I am."

"Good." He took comfort—for Ronni's sake—in having Netti on the job. She was compassionate, and damn good at what she did. There was only one other nurse he'd prefer in a crisis, and that was his sister Elke.

Within minutes, Netti finished hooking up Scott's IV, then added another bag, responding to Hayden's questions, explaining exactly what medications the patient was receiving. She placed an oxygen mask over his face, turned the valve, then studied the monitor. One of the numbers immediately began to rise slightly.

"You think he'll make it?"

She shrugged. "This is generally what kills a PVS patient. Some kind of infection. But we'll see. His chart shows he had a bout of pneumonia four months ago and pulled through. Anything's possible." She patted

Hayden's arm. "If you need anything, hit the call button. Or stick your head out the door and yell. We won't come running, because he's DNR, but we'll come."

"Thanks, Netti."

When she left, Hayden leaned over the head of the bed again. "As I was saying, you don't deserve Ronni. And she doesn't deserve this hell you're putting her through. If you were any kind of a man, if you ever loved her, you'll let go of whatever it is that you're hanging on to.

"All I'm saying, dude, one military guy to another. You don't want to live like this, do you? So if you see a white light, you go for it. Of course, given the way you've treated your wife, the light might just be fire, but…a man's gotta do what a man's gotta do. Man up, soldier. Set her free.

"Set yourself free."

CHAPTER THIRTEEN

"My mom's in there with him?" Nick peered around Unk toward the hospital room's doorway.

"Yes."

"And they don't think he's going to make it this time?" He shifted his grip on the backpack over his shoulder.

"It doesn't look good, no."

The remnants of his dinner shifted uncomfortably in Nick's stomach. "Can you get my mom out of there? I want to see him, but I don't want her around when I do."

"Getting her to leave that room... I think you might have more luck if you just tell her you want some privacy with him."

Nick sighed. "Okay."

Unk moved to let Nick pass, then followed him into the room. Nick spared a glance at his stepfather. An oxygen mask covered his nose and mouth. Beard stubble dotted his jaw.

"Nick." His mom set a cardboard coffee cup on the bedside table, rising from a recliner in the corner. "I didn't think you'd come." She opened her arms.

With attention still on the shrunken man in the bed,

Nick hugged his mother. "I'm here. I—I need to see him. But…" He eased back from her embrace. "I need to do it alone. Can you…?" He jerked his head toward the door.

"Let me take you down to the cafeteria, Ronni, get you something to eat," Unk offered.

"No, thanks," she replied.

"All right, at least let me take you to the vending machines and buy you a candy bar."

"Please, Mom."

She stared at Nick for a long time, her brown eyes filled with hurt like he hadn't seen in a while.

He hoped she couldn't read the same thing in his.

"It's important to you?"

"Yeah."

She nodded. "Okay. There's a waiting room just down the hall. I'll be there when you're done."

"Thanks."

She tightened her grip on his arms again, yanking him back against her. "I'm glad you came," she said, her voice raspy.

"No problem." Actually, it was a big problem. But he had unfinished business with his stepfather. Things he needed to get off his chest before the guy…died.

And a long conversation with his grandfather had convinced him to come and say what he needed to say before it was too late.

Who were they all kidding? It had been too late to talk to Scott since the accident. But if Nick could talk to

his father, who'd been dead for thirteen years, he could
talk to his stepfather, who wasn't.

Quite.

Yet.

"Come on, Ronni." Unk gently disentangled them
and guided her toward the door.

"Just down the hall if you need me, Nick," Mom
called over her shoulder on the way out.

"Got it, Mom."

And then he was alone with the man in the bed.

Nick dropped his backpack on the floor and moved
closer. A machine beeped softly in time with Scott's
heart. A rattle gurgled each time he drew in a breath.
The skin on his face was pulled tighter than the last time
Nick had seen him, in the nursing home. But his eyes
were closed, not open and staring vacantly, as usual.

"You look and sound like shit," Nick said. "Maybe
they're right this time, huh?"

Don't curse, he imagined Scott telling him.

"I will if I want to." Nick grabbed the metal rail
on the side of the bed, struggling to find the words he
needed. But what came out wasn't what he'd planned.
"You're not my father."

How many times had he tossed that at Scott? Hell,
he'd even tossed it at Unk a time or two. When either
man tried to tell him what to do, or something he didn't
want to hear. "But—" Nick cleared his throat "—you
were my dad. For a while. You coached my damn Little
League team. Took me fishing. Let me sit on your lap
and steer the big tractor out at Dan's place."

Tears he hadn't expected trickled down his face. Nick swiped at them with the back of his hand. "It was good, dammit. We were a family. I loved you," he choked. "*Mom* loved you. Why'd you have to fuck that up?"

Nick leaned over, buried his face in the scrawny, hospital-gown-clad shoulder. A shoulder that had once held him so he could see a parade. "Why?" He wrestled with his tears, a losing battle.

A few minutes later, a large hand settled on Nick's own shoulder. He whipped upright, wiping his face, whirling to find Unk. "What part of privacy don't you get?"

"It was me or your mom. She sent me to check on you."

"I—I—I came to tell him what an asshole he is. And here I am, crying like a little girl. Over…over…"

"Over a man who filled the father-size hole in your life."

Nick nodded. "The man who cheated on my mother and broke her heart."

"Nothing's as black-and-white as we'd like it to be, Nick. There's a fine line between love and hate sometimes."

"That sucks."

"Yeah. It does."

Nick turned back toward the bed. "You're an asshole," he whispered, voice shaking. "Dad." Since he didn't know what else to say, he left it at that. Calling him Dad again, after all these years, said what he couldn't find the words for.

"THANKS, DOC." Hayden shook the physician's hand as the doctor strode from Scott's room on the fourth floor to continue his early morning rounds.

Hayden returned to Ronni, who still lingered at Scott's bedside. The past three days had played havoc on her. And the message the doctor had given didn't seem to have registered. "Ronni?"

She turned bleary, bloodshot eyes toward him. "Huh?"

"Crap, you're so out of it. Did you hear what the doctor just said?"

"I need more coffee."

"No. No more coffee. No more chocolate." He'd done his best to get something nutritional into her during their extended stay at the hospital. Amelia had hand-delivered dishes Finn had cooked specifically for Ronni. Hayden had ended up scarfing them down. The only thing he'd been able to entice her to eat had been Snickers bars. And coffee. "I'm done enabling you. You want coffee or candy bars, get them yourself. I'm done fetching them."

"That's mean."

"Cruel to be kind, babe. Ronni." He forced a hard edge to his voice that made her start. "You didn't hear a word the doctor said, did you?" She'd answered Dr. Saunders, said all the right things, but sleep deprivation combined with the intense emotions of the situation had set in. The lights were on, but nobody was home. She clearly didn't understand what had happened.

He took her hand, guided it to Scott's face. "How's he feel, sweetheart?"

"C-cooler."

"Right. And listen. Is he rasping and gasping anymore?"

She shook her head. "No. No. I can't hear him breathing."

"Exactly. Because he's doing better. Dr. Saunders thinks Scott has turned the corner. He thinks he's going to make it."

"Make it?" Her eyes widened. Her lower lip trembled, making him want to soothe it with his fingers. With his own lips. "He's…not dying anymore?"

"Probably not, no."

"Oh."

That was so not the response he'd expected. She pulled her hand free and raised it to her mouth. Then she turned and dashed toward the bathroom in the corner of the room with a speed he hadn't thought her capable of on her best day, let alone today.

Retching sounds echoed from the small room.

"Well, buddy, I'd like to officially welcome you back to the land of the semiliving." Hayden patted Mangano's shoulder, torn over the outcome. Despite his conversation with Scott days ago, he didn't wish death on anyone. But Ronni's torment—and Scott's, as well—would only continue. "Now, I'll go take care of your wife while she hurls her last round of coffee and Snickers."

The toilet flushed as he entered. Ronni knelt before

the porcelain god, a position familiar to anyone who'd
ever drank too much. Or had a migraine.

Or the emotional shock of a lifetime.

He rummaged through the toiletries his sister Elke
had dropped off. She'd visited several times a night, as
breaks from her own nursing duties on the sixth floor
permitted. She'd been a huge help, sitting with Ronni
and Scott, allowing Hayden to grab a quick shower or
catnap. The rest of the family, along with Ronni's friend
Tamara, had also provided support. Tam had brought her
fresh clothes every morning. The others had delivered
food, Ronni's precious coffee, and had helped take care
of Nick.

Hayden applied paste to a toothbrush, handed it to
Ronni.

"Thanks."

While she brushed, he uncapped the mouthwash
from the counter, offered that to her. She rinsed and
spit into the can. He extended his hand, helped her off
the floor. "Let's go. I'm taking you home and putting
you to bed."

"But—"

"No buts. I'll swing you over my shoulder and carry
you out of here if I have to. He's out of the woods. It's
time to take care of you."

Hayden waited, leaning against the wall, arms folded
across his chest, gritting his teeth while she stroked
Scott's face and planted a tender kiss on his cheek. Some
part of her still cared about the jerk. Not just as a responsibility. Actually cared.

And while her capacity to care, to forgive, was part of what made Hayden love her, it also made him want to punch something.

He did a mental double take. *Love?* A colorful litany of curses threatened to erupt, but he swallowed them.

Greg and Finn had been right, damn them.

He loved Ronni Davidowski. Ronni *Mangano.* And it looked as if her husband was going to live.

All those years of not wanting anything more than thirty days with a woman had caught up with him.

As he was fond of saying, paybacks were a bitch.

The woman he wanted, he still couldn't have. Not the way he wished to, anyway. He wanted his ring on her finger. His babies in her belly, with Nick as their big brother to look up to.

Wanted her forever.

And yet, when she stumbled toward him, with tears he wasn't sure were from joy streaming down her face, he knew one other thing with total certainty: he couldn't have her, but he couldn't walk away from her again, either.

"DON'T LEAVE ME," she murmured some forty minutes later, as he settled her on her queen-size bed. He'd repeated the ritual of removing her shoes and socks, but she'd crawled between the sheets without shedding anything else. "Stay with me. Please?"

She rolled onto her side with her back facing him, extending one hand out behind her. "Hold me. You've got to be tired, too. I don't want to be alone now. Sleep with me."

Though Hayden was utterly exhausted, his body went rock hard at the thought of climbing into bed with her. "If I get in there with you, we're going to do more than sleep." If he couldn't even have thirty days with her, then he'd take what he could get. If that meant one day, hell, one hour…he'd take it.

She waved her hand. "Sleep first. *More* later."

Though he wasn't sure she knew what she was saying, he toed off his shoes and socks and shed his T-shirt and jeans. Wearing only his briefs, he slid into the bed, curling around her. The curve of her breasts grazed his forearm as he wrapped her in his embrace.

"Mmm. Nice." She wiggled, grinding her denim-covered cheeks against his erection, sending pulses of pleasure through him. "Sweet dreams."

Erotic dreams, more likely. Still, holding her seemed right. He surrendered to sleep, praying that when they awakened, she wouldn't freak out, finding him in her bed.

Hours later, when he stretched and knuckled his eyes, the setting sun was slanting beams beneath the shade on the west-facing window, filling the bedroom with fiery light.

And he was alone.

He propped himself on his elbows. "Ronni?"

A cabinet slammed in the bathroom. She appeared in

the connecting doorway wearing a purple satin kimono. She tugged at the edges, as if to make sure it covered her.

And all he wanted to do was take it off.

"Sorry. Did I wake you?"

"Not exactly." He was fully awake now, though. Awake and on his way to ready. "Didn't expect to find you gone. Whatcha up to?"

She hesitantly picked her way across the bedroom to stand beside the bed, one hand fisted at her side. "Just showered and stuff."

"If you'd waited, I'd have been more than happy to wash your back."

A charming blush colored her cheeks.

"What's this?" He reached out, tapped her closed hand.

Her fingers slowly unfurled, revealing two condoms in her palm. The plastic crinkled as her hand trembled. "At the hospital, you said it was time to take care of me. I—I agree."

Hayden rose to his knees, shifted to the edge of the bed. He encircled her waist with his arms, pulled her flush against him. "Oh, I'm going to take care of you, babe. I'm going to take *good* care of you." He skimmed his lips over hers, a tease, a taste, a promise of things to come. Then he slanted his head and plundered her mouth fully, dancing his tongue with hers until the muscles in her body softened and she leaned into him.

He disengaged, running his fingertip over her now plump lips.

The slightly dazed but eager expression on her face captured exactly how he felt. "Hold that thought. Give me five minutes. Maybe six. No fair that you're all fresh and clean and I'm not." He leaped from the bed, spun her by the arms and sat her on the edge of the mattress. "Don't go away. Five minutes."

Ronni picked at the hem of the kimono as he vanished into the bathroom, giving her a terrific view of his gorgeous butt in his skin-hugging undershorts. Soon enough she'd be seeing it, touching it, au naturel.

The thought both thrilled and terrified her. She'd only ever been with Ian and Scott. And since Scott had obviously needed more than what she could provide in bed…

Still, Hayden had demonstrated his desire for her.

The shower turned on moments later. She set the condoms—who'd have ever thought she'd be raiding the just-in-case box she'd bought for Nick?—on the night table. Entertained herself by imagining Hayden naked in the shower. Lathering every inch of his body.

It kept the guilt at bay for a moment, anyway.

"I deserve this," she told herself softly, staring at the carpet. "At least once, anyway." Hayden had been totally amazing during the time in the hospital. Not only had he taken care of her, but Vera, as well. And more than once Ronni had returned from making a phone call to find him wiping drool from Scott's chin, though he'd always made the tissue vanish and been feet away from the bed by the time she'd actually gotten into the room.

Shouldn't have surprised her, given how hands-on he'd been with Ian's care. Still, this wasn't his brother.

It was her husband.

The husband she was about to cheat on.

Life is for living, Ian's voice whispered across her memory. *Promise me you'll never stop living.*

"Now there's a woman who's not thinking sexy things." Hayden's deep bass rumbled from the bathroom doorway. "I told you to hold that thought."

"Sorry." She swallowed the lump in her throat and raised her gaze to look at him. She never made it as far as his face.

A water droplet broke loose from his collarbone. She followed its path, down his eight-pack abs, until it blended with the smattering of dark hair that started near his belly button and traveled south to where her baby-blue towel rode low on his hips.

She pressed her lips together.

He chuckled, the rich, throaty sound vibrating through her core. She jerked her head upward again, this time meeting his eyes.

Merriment made them twinkle. "That's more like it."

He crossed the room in two quick strides, setting something beside the condoms, then pulling her to her feet. He grabbed the covers with one hand, stripping them down to the foot of the bed. "Please tell me these aren't your favorite sheets. Because I'm afraid we're going to make quite a mess of them before we're through."

"Not my favorites. Though they might be to-morrow."

He broke into a smug grin. "I like that."

He inched in front of her, reaching for the belt of her kimono and untying it. He parted the robe just enough to sneak his hands inside, wrapping them around her waist. He nuzzled her ear. "Your skin's so soft." His fingertips traced up and down her spine. Finding the strap to her bra. He ran one finger under the elastic. His fingers skimmed down again. Fondled the lacy fabric of her low-riding hipsters.

She'd chosen the sexiest lingerie she owned, a gift from Tam right after she'd found out about Scott's cheating the first time. The tags were on the bathroom counter.

"You have something on under here," he whispered in her ear. "Let's have a look."

She was fine until he had the kimono pushed low on her shoulders. Then she clamped her arms to her sides, stopping the slide of the satin any farther. She'd had a baby. Had he ever been with a woman who'd had a baby?

"Okay." He brushed his mouth over her collarbone. "No rush. We've got all night."

"Nick—"

"Nick is okay right where he is for one more night."

"Tomorrow—"

Hayden pressed his fingertip to her lips. "No talk about tomorrow. No talk about five minutes from now.

This is all about the moment, Ronni. Right now." He kissed her. "This moment." He nibbled her shoulder. Trailed his mouth along the curve of her neck. "This one. Get it?"

She nodded.

"Good." He sat down on the bed. "I'm not going to take anything you don't want to give, Ronni. So...whenever you're ready to slip off that robe, I'm ready." His eyes blazed with smoldering heat as he leaned back on his elbows, abs tightening in a way that made her long to touch them.

Made her wish that damn towel would loosen and fall.

"You've got gorgeous legs. I can't wait to feel them wrapped around me."

Emboldened by his compliment, deciding it was time to fish or cut bait, she shrugged off the kimono. It pooled around her feet. Leaving her standing before him in only the hot-pink, lace-covered pushup bra and matching panties.

She shivered.

His eyes widened. He drew in a deep breath. "Beautiful. Did you put those on just for me?"

She nodded, watching him through her lashes.

"Thank you." He rose from the bed again. "You give. I give." The towel joined the puddle of purple satin on the floor.

After a quick glance confirmed what she'd suspected—the man was built *everywhere*—she did her best not to stare.

He moved behind her, stroking her shoulders. His fingers lingered on her bra clasp. "This is beautiful. And I'm glad you wore it. But let's get rid of it. Okay?"

"Okay."

"Thank you." He placed his lips on her left shoulder blade while making short work of the clasp. A gentle push sent the straps sliding down her arms. He moved his mouth to her ear. "Take it off." His tongue traced the edge, then nipped at her lobe.

She shuddered as electric currents traveled from her ear to the apex of her thighs.

And he hadn't even touched her yet. Oh, yeah. She'd chosen the right man to be bad with.

She tossed the bra on the growing pile.

He skimmed his hands down her back again, then grasped her hips, rubbing the lacy material there. His thumbs lightly stroked her cheeks. "Panties now or later?"

If she was going to be bad, then dammit, she might as well be bad. Stop worrying. Live it up. If this turned out to be her only chance with him, she wasn't going to be passive. "Now," she said, and whisked them to her feet, then flicked them away with her toe.

She spun around, placed her palms in the center of his chest and pushed him onto the bed.

A moment later, she'd straddled his abs, pinning his hands over his head.

He grinned up at her.

"What?" she asked.

"You never stop surprising me. And that's a good thing. Go ahead. Have your wicked way with me."

She leaned down, pressing her breasts against his hard chest, keeping his hands captive. Just as she went to kiss him, he said, "I was going to give you a massage to get things started. But this is much better."

She sat back up. "A massage?"

He nodded. "What did you think the oil was for?"

She looked over at the table, then jumped off him, shoving him toward the edge of the bed. "Never let it be said that I interfered with your seduction plan." She threw herself facedown in the middle of the mattress, arms above her head.

His rich, deep laughter warmed her.

A bottle cap snapped open. He rubbed his hands together, then knelt alongside her, beginning with her shoulders. Oil lubricated the movements of his fingers.

Magic. The man wove magic with every stroke. Every once in a while his erection would graze her, igniting another firestorm of desire.

"So beautiful." He reverently laid one hand on her ass, caressed the skin. "Can I massage here?"

"Oh, hell, yes."

He chuckled. "You've embraced the spirit of the exercise very nicely."

He rose from the bed, asking her softly to turn over. She complied, to find him facing the nightstand again, pouring more oil into his palm.

Giving her a front row seat to his naked butt. She

sat up for an even closer look. There was something...
"Is that a tat? You have a tattoo on your ass? What's it
a picture of?"

He froze. His glutes twitched. She shifted to her knees
to examine it. A shield with four crossed swords.

Ian's name was inked on the shield, along with the
year of his birth. And his death.

"Ohmigosh. You did that for Ian? On your ass?"

Hayden's shoulders lifted, the play of his muscles
entrancing this close. "It was the only place we could
think of to put them where Mom wouldn't ever likely
see them. Not even accidentally."

"We?"

"Greg and Finn have matching tats. We got them
together. The first anniversary of Ian's death. I was on
leave from the Marines. It's what Marines do. They get
inked."

"I'm guessing most of them get an Eagle, Globe and
Anchor."

"Ink's personal. There's always a story. Just like
yours."

Touched by his tribute, she pushed him from the bed,
then stood and sidled up behind him, wrapping her arms
around him. Hugging him. "I think Ian would have been
pleased. Or at least amused."

Hayden let her hold him briefly. Then he spun in her
arms, pulling her to him. Clutching the back of her neck
in one hand. Crushing his mouth to hers.

Need coursed through his kiss. Hunger. And pos-
session.

She opened to him, let him plunder her mouth. Gave as good as he did.

Finally he tore himself away, raking his hand through his hair. "I'm sorry. That's not how this is supposed to be."

"Show me."

"What?"

The sun had sunk lower in the sky, leaving the room in comforting shadows. "Show me how it's supposed to be. Quit stalling and make love to me before you give me a complex, thinking you don't want me."

"Don't want you?" After retrieving a condom, which he placed within arm's reach, he sat on the edge of the bed again.

He patted his thighs. "Sit right here. Face me."

She did, sliding forward until the base of his erection created friction in exactly the right spot.

He grinned at her, rocking ever so slightly. Creating lovely zings of pleasure. He took her hand, placed her palm on his chest, as he'd done the day of the rainstorm, and held it there. Placed his other palm on her chest. "Look at me, Ronni."

She met his eyes, felt his heart thudding.

"Open yourself to me, sweetheart. Not just your body. Your spirit, too."

Hayden poured everything he had into loving her. Everything he'd ever learned. Wanting it to be the most amazing experience of her life.

Needing it to be.

He showered her with kisses. Touched every square

inch of her body. She gave him absolute trust. And everything else.

The first time she shuddered against him, moaning in pleasure, he damn near lost control. And he wasn't even inside her.

A situation he quickly remedied, pulling her down on the bed on top of him, then rolling so he was staring down at her.

He used his knee to urge her wider, knowing she was ready. More than ready. Edging into her was bliss. So damn tight. So damn…right. The intensity of their connection stunned him. "Don't close your eyes," he told her. "Look at me."

She locked gazes with him as he completed the process of making them one.

"Feel me." He swirled his hips, grinding into her.

"Hayden." The way she gasped his name snapped his already fragile control.

They spiraled up and up…and when she pulsed around him, he couldn't stop the inevitable. Something that hadn't happened to him since his early experiments with tantra.

So he went with it. Moaned her name. Claimed her mouth at the moment of his release. Then he pressed his face into the curve of her neck and murmured, "Mine."

"Hmm?"

"Fine." He pushed himself up on his arms as his thudding heart began to slow. "As in, holy crap, that was *fine*. Amazing. Incredible."

She hesitantly smiled. "Really?"

"Are you trying to tell me it wasn't good for you?"

The smile broadened as she shook her head. "For me? It was great. Fantastic. I just didn't know how it was for you."

"Okay, I'll tell you a secret."

She giggled, the sound causing just as much pleasure as the sex had. "Of course you will. You're JabberJaw."

He pretended to grimace. "You just undid years' worth of practice for me, and made me…finish…long before I should have." He slowly withdrew from her. "Don't move. Let me go take care of things, then I'll be back to take care of you. And in a bit, maybe I can try again to dazzle you with my renowned staying power."

She yawned, pressing a hand over her mouth. "'Kay. Think we both could use a rest before another round."

He kissed her forehead. "You did bring two condoms. Would be a pity to waste one of them."

"Mmm. It would."

In the bathroom, though, he got a shock. The condom had a small tear at the tip.

In all the years he'd practiced safe sex, he'd never run into condom failure.

His pulse kicked up again. He shivered as the sweat from their lovemaking chilled on his body.

Or maybe because of the condom.

The enormity of the situation left him frozen. He got checked for STDs on a regular basis, and always turned up clean, in no small part because of his fussiness in choosing partners. And Ronni had mentioned the emotional pain and frustration of having to get herself tested after she'd discovered Scott's cheating, so he didn't have huge concerns in that area.

But that she could get pregnant…

The sudden wave of joy staggered him. He leaned against the bathroom vanity.

If she got pregnant—with *his* child—she'd have no choice but to divorce Mangano. It would be pretty obvious it wasn't his baby bump.

And Hayden wanted her badly enough to hope it worked out that way. So despite that it would normally never occur to him to keep something of this magnitude from a partner, Hayden decided to. It would be his secret.

Fate had been at work with their relationship all along. He wasn't going to mess with destiny if it had plans for their future. He would, however, make sure Ronni knew how he felt about her and where he stood.

Returning to the bedroom, he slid into bed again. On his back, he pulled her to him. She laid her head on his shoulder, placed her hand between his pecs. He laced his fingers with hers, kissed the top of her head.

His heartbeat pounded, the sound heavy in his ears. Feeling the emotion was one thing. Confessing it… harder than he'd expected. Especially since he didn't anticipate a favorable response. Best to just jump. "I love you."

Her muscles tensed, and she went very still.

"Do you know how many women I've said that to?"

"All of them?" she whispered.

"None of them. Until now. Until *you*. I love you, Ronni."

"Oh, God, Hayden. Don't. Don't do that. Let me be the same as the rest of them."

"I can't. 'Cause you're not." His chest tightened. Funny how it hurt that she didn't return the words, even though he'd expected that. Because even if she felt it, Ronni wouldn't say it. Not while she was still married. Saying it would be even worse, more of a betrayal than what they'd just done.

"I can't give you forever, Hayden. Mine's currently tied up."

"I know." He stroked her hair, relishing the silkiness, wondering how long it would be before he got the chance to touch it—touch her—again. "But you could fix that. Back in the hospital, when we were leaving, you were crying. What were those tears about? Were those happy tears that Scott was going to be okay?"

She shook her head.

"I didn't think so. Why were you crying, babe?"

"Don't." Her voice caught on a sob, making him hate himself. "Don't make me say it. It's too ugly."

"No. Truth is sometimes hard to take, but it's not ugly. What made you cry?"

"B-because…I can't see another way out. His death, *my* death…"

"Hey!" He squeezed his arms around her. "Don't you

ever say *that*. Not even in passing. Nick needs you. *I* need you. In whatever form that takes. There's another way out. You've just got to be strong enough to take it. To say the hell with what people think of me, I deserve my own life, I deserve to be happy."

He rolled onto his side, facing her. "Divorce him, Ronni. Be with *me*. *Marry* me."

Her eyes widened.

"I swear, I'll never hurt you like he did. I'll be a Semper Fi guy. You know what Semper Fi means?"

She nodded. "Always faithful."

"That's right. I've found my forever woman. Let me make you happy. I do make you happy, don't I?"

Tears glistened beneath her lashes. "You do. Before you came back into my life, I was so numb, I didn't realize I'd forgotten how to feel anything. No pain, but no joy, either. You've returned that to me."

"I'm glad." He kissed her tenderly, with as much emotion as he could muster. Her lips trembled beneath his.

"Hayden…" She put her hand on his chest and pushed, creating some space between them. "I wish I could. I wish I were free. But…"

"You're not."

"No. And I can't…I can't…"

"Shh." He laid his finger over her mouth. "It's okay. I'll wait. Keep hoping you'll change your mind. Because I love you." For the first time, he truly understood. Why Finn had drunk himself under the table when Amelia had blocked him from Chip's birth, why he'd been willing to shut down his restaurant and pursue his family all the way to Maine. Why Greg had been so forlorn when Shannon had dumped him, insisting on driving past her apartment several times a day like a demented stalker.

Why his father had spent almost fifty years with his mother, through thick and thin, through the birth of twelve kids and the death of one.

Love truly was the glue that held it all together.

Even when it hurt like hell. Maybe *especially* when it hurt like hell.

Hayden had spent his whole adult life in short-term relationships just to avoid this kind of agony. Time to man up.

"We can't keep doing...this...either."

"I know. But for the rest of tonight, you're mine. I'm going to make this a night you'll never forget."

Then he'd do his damnedest not to go crazy with wanting her. And pray that something changed.

Something that would offer them a future.

CHAPTER FOURTEEN

"PLEASE?" The twentysomething with the long brunette hair offered him a pretty pout. One that just a few months ago might have stirred his interest.

Hayden shook his head. "Not tonight. I'm not in a singing mood."

Finn set his mug of beer on the bar. Slapped him on the back. "Sing something. The ladies are waiting on you." He looked at the woman. "Go tell them Hayden will sing for them."

She clapped her hands and scampered back to the table on the far side of the room. Giggles and cheers erupted.

The trio of brothers had taken to gathering for a beer on Monday nights at Down Home. This would be the last one, because next Tuesday Hayden had to report back to school.

He had gotten a reputation for his karaoke. Most times he did it just to annoy Greg and Finn, because the women always made a fuss over him. And though his heart wasn't in it, he'd been trying to keep things from his generally too observant brothers.

Keeping secrets was one hell of a lot of work.

Greg, on the other side of him, gave him a nudge.

"It's a country bar, pal. Perfect for your glum mood. Which has been going on for three weeks now. Ever since Ronni's husband got better."

"What are you implying?"

Greg shrugged. "Not implying anything. Except that you haven't been fit to live with since then."

"Luckily, you don't have to live with me anymore." Hayden took a long pull on his beer. He hopped off the bar stool, dragging the back of his hand over his mouth. "Fine. If it will get the ladies—especially you two—off my back, I'll sing."

Easily done, since no one else at the place had signed up. He picked his song, then ventured onto the stage, stopping in front of the microphone. Though he'd never try out for *American Idol*, he could carry a passable tune. Had used the skill in the past, like his dancing talents, to meet women.

But the only woman he wanted had pulled back from him.

Three weeks of hell had passed for him, knowing what kind of passion they shared, but couldn't have. His chest hurt every time he picked up Nick from her place.

The music started. He closed his eyes and pictured her face. That night. And poured his heart into McBride and the Ride's "Just One Night."

The lyrics conveyed exactly how he felt. If he died tomorrow, he'd be grateful for the night he and Ronni had shared. If that was all he ever got, he'd never regret it.

He hoped she felt the same.

When he finished, the small crowd broke into applause. The all-women table climbed to their feet, cheering. He swept a mock bow. The brunette who'd asked him to sing pinned him with a look that said she'd gladly take him home tonight, give him that one night he'd sung about.

He dropped his gaze to the floor, headed back to his brothers at the bar. They just stared at him when he sat down. "Now what? I sang, didn't I?"

"You slept with her," Finn accused.

"And didn't tell us," Greg added. "You don't keep secrets, Jaws."

"Gentlemen don't kiss and tell."

"That's never stopped you before," Finn pointed out. "And you mean screw and tell, right? Wow. That's sluttier than I expected from her."

"Watch your damn mouth!" Hayden grabbed him by the shirt and lifted him off the bar stool. Shook him like a terrier with a rat. Had his fist back and cocked, ready to rearrange Finn's pretty face when Greg captured his arm, throwing his full weight into holding him off.

"Stop, Hay!"

"Take it outside, boys!" the bartender yelled at them.

"No problem." Hayden dragged Finn toward the door. His brother stumbled, but hustled to keep up, not resisting at all. Greg let go to throw a twenty on the bar, then raced after them, all the while talking at Hayden's back, urging him to calm down, that Finn hadn't meant anything bad by his poor vocabulary choices.

In the parking lot, Hayden released his older brother with a shove that sent him stumbling. It was only fair to give him a chance to defend himself.

Once he found his footing, Finn just grinned at him.

"You lookin' to lose all your teeth that way?" Hayden lifted his fists.

"If you really think it will make you feel better, go ahead. Punch me."

"Are you crazy?" Greg stepped between them, arms out to keep them apart. "You *will* lose all your teeth. Don't encourage him."

"He's had a bug up his ass for weeks now. I'm just tryin' to shake it loose."

"By letting him use you as a punching bag? Great plan, but I don't think you'll like the results."

A squad car drifted by on the street.

"Hay, if you get busted for brawling in a bar parking lot, what kind of message does that send to Nick?"

"Same message we gave him the night the police cuffed him for protecting Jordan. A man protects his family. Defends his woman's honor."

"Crap, Hayden. You hear yourself?" Finn just shook his head. "*Your* woman?"

"Both of you, take a deep breath. Nobody's getting busted tonight. Finn, apologize. *Now*. Before Hayden pops you in the face and the police turn around and come back here."

Finn held up his open hands. "Sorry, Hayden. Didn't

mean any disrespect toward Ronni. Really. Just trying to find out what in the hell is going on with you."

"Good." Greg herded them toward his Tracker like a pair of ornery bulls. "Get your butts in the car. Hayden, passenger seat. Finn, in the back. Keep your hands to yourselves. Geez, I sound like Dad. We're going some-place way more private to finish this. Fresh?"

Finn shook his head. "Amelia's got something going on at the house tonight." Finn and his family lived on the second floor of the big old Victorian that housed Fresh on the first floor. "Basket party or something crazy like that. She will not be amused if we descend en masse. What about your place?"

"No. Shannon's so damn tired with being pregnant. We carry on and disturb her, and I'm in the doghouse for a week."

Hayden wished for the opportunity to get in the dog-house. "If we go to my place you're both sitting on the floor." He leaned his head against the window, letting the air-conditioning blasting on him cool his anger.

Finn had been baiting him. Stupid on his brother's part. But even the limited blowout had made Hayden feel better.

After stopping to purchase a six-pack, they pulled into their parents' driveway. Greg grabbed a flashlight from under the driver's seat, then they skirted the house, and headed into the woods. Hayden blew off more steam free-climbing to the tree house.

"Show-off," Greg said, reaching the top rung of the ladder, with Finn right behind him. Inside, they pulled out the battery-powered lanterns, providing the place with a bluish glow. Finn and Greg took seats at the game table. Hayden grabbed a beer, twisting off the cap, then wandered over to the bay window, glancing out at the dark shadows of the trees as they swayed in the breeze.

Memories of Ronni flooded him. He'd first held her right here.

"Hey, how long, exactly, after sex, before a woman knows if she's pregnant or not?"

Finn choked on his beer.

"Please tell me that's a rhetorical question," Greg said. "A question for a friend of a friend of a friend. Not to mention that *you* are in charge of teaching sex ed to teenagers. Now I'm really scared of public education."

Hayden moved away from the window. "I know the technicalities, thanks. I just wondered, since you guys have so much real-life experience in the area now, if you knew something I didn't." Like how the hell he could find out if she'd been at the fertile phase of her cycle that night.

"Start spilling," Finn said, using the bottom of his shirt to mop up the liquid he'd sprayed on the game table. "And don't leave anything out. Fine time for you to start keeping secrets."

"If she was at her most fertile, it would have been two weeks until her period," Hayden calculated out loud. "So she should know by now, right? I mean, if it's going to happen?"

"Depends on a lot of things. How long her cycles

are. How regular she is. Shannon's been watching this show on TV about women who have no clue they're pregnant and deliver full-term babies. She likes to yell at the screen about how the hell could they *not* know when there's a tiny creature squirming around inside them, kicking their bladder all the time."

"So then maybe Ronni *doesn't* know yet?"

"You tried to knock her up on purpose?" Finn asked.

Hayden turned a chair around, straddled it. "Condom broke. Never had that happen before."

"Holy crap. What did Ronni say? Surely she told you when or if she got her period? Or not, as the case may be."

Hayden fingered one of the dark squares on the chessboard built into the table.

Both his brothers groaned. "You didn't tell her, did you?" Greg said.

He shook his head. "Didn't want to give her the chance to take alternate measures. I'm sort of hoping…"

Finn and Greg exchanged a look.

"Told you he was hiding something big." Finn blew out a long breath. "But wow. I had no clue it was *this* big. Leave it to you, Hay. When you decide to keep a secret, it's a doozy."

"To love." Greg held up his bottle. "And the bat-shit crazy stuff it makes us do."

"Amen." Finn clanked his longneck into Greg's, then knocked into Hayden's. "May your swimmers have hit the mark, brother. And win you the girl. 'Cause we'd sure love to see you join us in the never-a-dull-moment adventures of marriage and parenthood. Well..." Finn's face colored. Amelia hadn't yet agreed to marry him. "Close enough to marriage, anyway."

Hayden would happily settle for the commitment Finn had. "I'll drink to that."

RONNI SAT in the shampoo chair, feet tapping the floor. Tam was in Do-Ron-Ron's bathroom.

With the stopwatch app on her cell phone.

And the test stick Ronni had peed on.

She had to be pregnant. Her breasts ached. Her nipples hurt like hell every time they rubbed against her bra. She'd been queasy every morning.

Not to mention exhausted to the point that she'd fallen asleep at the desk one morning before her first customer had arrived.

All the symptoms she'd experienced with Nick.

Her period had been due last Monday, just over two weeks after she and Hayden had made love. And while she wasn't always as regular as clockwork, when she put it together with the symptoms, it spelled *p-r-e-g-n-a-n-t*.

What was it with Hawkins sperm and her eggs? The attraction to the bad boys of the family went as far as a cellular level? No wonder she couldn't resist them.

And she could look forward to facing Lydia Hawkins with another surprise grandbaby.

At least this time she wasn't sixteen.

"No, instead you're married. Even better. Oh, and

just think, not just Lydia. The whole media will be after you." The press had resurfaced during Scott's trip to the hospital. Someone had talked. Whether from the nursing home, the ambulance squad, the hospital, somebody had alerted them to Scott being at death's door. Several shots of Hayden holding her elbow as he steered her out of the hospital the morning the doctor had pronounced Scott on the mend had appeared.

"Like my life is that interesting."

"You talking to yourself out there?" Tam called through the bathroom door.

"Yes. What's it to you?"

Tam sauntered out, pregnancy test in hand.

"Well? Well? Don't keep me in suspense." Ronni jumped out of the chair.

"It's negative."

"Huh?"

"Quick, gut instinct," Tam barked. "How do you feel right now?"

Ronni sank slowly back into the chair. She wasn't carrying Hayden's baby?

"Honey, how do you feel?"

"I—I don't believe it. I feel pregnant."

"Emotionally."

She draped her hand over her belly, looked up at her friend. "Sad. Disappointed."

"You wanted to be pregnant?"

Ronni nodded. Though only minutes ago she'd been scared to death about facing Hayden's mother, now all she felt was a big hollow ache. She swallowed hard.

"Cheer up, sweetie. You'll get another chance."

"When? When Scott finally gives up the ghost? How long is that going to be? I could be a doddering old woman by then. No eggs left. Even if Hayden really does wait, which I doubt. Why would he want to wait for me?" She shook her head. "No. This was my one and only chance."

"He'd wait because he loves you."

"He shouldn't wait. He deserves someone who can be there with him *now*. Someone…free to love him. To give him babies without worrying how the media is going to roast her over an open fire when the news comes out."

Tam threw the test stick in the garbage can behind the desk, then pulled the bag out and tied it up. "What would you have done if you had been pregnant?"

Ronni slowly climbed to her feet, ignoring the wave of dizziness that made the world spin. "Figured out how to divorce Scott."

"Why? You wouldn't let your first pregnancy force you into marriage with Ian. Why would you let being pregnant now lead to divorce?"

"Because…"

"Because why?"

Ronni sat back down. For several moments, she pondered Tam's question. "Because it's what I want. To be free from Scott."

"Exactly. Honey, you don't need the excuse of being pregnant to justify what you want. Scott already gave you all the excuse you need. Vera and Nick know about it. There are no more secrets holding you back."

The conversation she'd had with Amelia came back to Ronni. About obligation to herself. She wasn't defective. She wasn't unworthy.

Was she really responsible for Scott's accident? For his condition?

No. He'd brought the Dear John call on himself. And he'd been the one behind the wheel that day.

She'd proved to herself and everyone else that she didn't run away when life got tough, as she had when Ian had been sick.

In fact, divorcing Scott was going to be a whole lot tougher than just sticking around.

But it was the right thing for her to do.

Because she deserved more.

"I have to go see Vera. And call my lawyer. This is going to be complicated."

"All the good stuff usually is," Tam said.

HAYDEN STOOD in the classroom's doorway, returning cell phones he'd confiscated during his last period health class, when his own buzzed in his back pocket. "It's only the first day of school, so I'm being generous," he reminded the kids as they passed by. "No phones in class. Keep them put away or lose them."

"Sorry, Coach." One of his senior track stars—the boy had a good shot at a full scholarship—ducked his head, plucking his cell from Hayden's hand. "Won't happen again."

"Better not."

When the classroom was finally empty, Hayden

retrieved his cell, heading to the desk at the front of the room.

A text from Ronni? He flipped the phone open.

Hope your first day back went well. Can you stop by? It's important. We need to talk.

He sank down on the edge of the desk, sitting on a stack of course outlines. *Important? Need to talk?*

His chest tightened.

It had taken every ounce of strength he had to keep his distance from her for the past thirty days. To drop Nick off after they'd spent time together, and just drive away, without going in.

But the risks were too great. Odds were, he'd want to hold her. Touch her.

Beg her like a man possessed to divorce her cheating, soul-crushing husband.

Or ask her flat out if she was pregnant.

Maybe that's what she wanted to talk about? He scrambled off the desk. Instead of texting, he punched "1" on his speed dial, then shoved the extra course outlines into a filing cabinet. She answered as he flipped off the lights and locked the classroom door.

"I'm leaving school now. On my way. What's up?"

"I'd rather discuss it face-to-face. Especially if you're already on your way."

"Be there as soon as I can. Upstairs or down?"

"Up. No appointments this afternoon. Not at the salon, anyway."

That sounded interesting. "Okay. See you soon."

He broke his record—and numerous speed limits—getting there. Didn't bother knocking, either, just bolted in through the laundry room. "Ronni?"

He found her pacing the kitchen.

"Ronni?"

She froze. Stared at him with a deer-in-the-headlights look. "Hayden. Wow. That was fast. I didn't expect you quite yet."

"Sports car. Big engine. Poor example for impressionable young minds."

"Right." She glanced down at the table, where some papers lay next to the wooden salt and pepper containers.

He headed toward her. She edged away, bolted for the sliding glass doors. Stood with her fingers wrapped around the handle. "Why don't we talk outside?"

"It's hot out. Besides, I don't feel like getting bird crap in my hair today." He inched closer. Spoke softly. "What's got you tied in knots, babe?"

She turned to face him, her back against the glass panel. She blew out a long breath. "I wanted to be the one to tell you this. Didn't want you to find out through the grapevine or anything." She worried her lower lip between her teeth.

Hope flared. His heart started to pound. "Are you—are you pregnant, Ron? Because it's okay if you are," he hastened to assure her. "More than okay."

"W-what?" Her eyebrows drew together. "How

did you...?" She shook her head. "No. I'm not. You suspected...?"

His chest constricted. He'd once gotten into a barroom brawl with some fellow Marines against a bunch of Navy SEALs. Had had a SEAL stomp on his chest so hard he'd cracked two ribs.

That hadn't hurt at all compared to this.

"I...hoped." Guess there was no reason to spill his secret about the broken condom. Not if nothing had resulted from it. Damn.

The edges of her mouth turned up slightly, but her eyes didn't smile. "Me, too."

"You wanted my baby?"

She nodded. "I did. So much that I had myself experiencing all the symptoms of pregnancy."

"You're sure you're not?"

"Two home tests and a trip to my doctor. I felt so sure I was, even after the first negative test. And the second. But I'm not."

"Too bad." He'd had a family of his own that close, and it had slipped through his fingers. "So what's this all about? Something with Nick?"

She shook her head, brushed past him to start a new circuit around the table. She gestured at the papers. "Like I said, I didn't want you hearing this through the courthouse grapevine."

"C-courthouse?"

"Yes." She shoved the pile in his direction. "My lawyer will be filing these tomorrow. Once recorded at the courthouse, it's public information. I wanted to be the one to tell you."

Hayden picked the stack off the table but couldn't bring himself to look at them. He knew what he hoped they were, but didn't think he could stand the disappointment if they were something else.

"I'm divorcing Scott. His guardianship has been transferred to Vera, so she can represent his interests in the divorce action."

The papers fell from Hayden's fingers, scattering across the tabletop. He jerked his gaze to hers. "Say again?"

"I'm divorcing Scott. I've finally found the courage to go after what I want."

"And that's…"

"You. I want you, Hayden Hawkins."

Joy like he'd never experienced—except maybe the night they'd made love—coursed through him.

"This not-pregnant-but-wanted-to-be situation made me stop and think. Life's short, Hayden. I regret so much the time I missed out on with Ian. Two weeks I could have spent with him. Told him I loved him a few dozen more times. Kissed him. Touched him.

"I don't want to live with more regrets like that. I don't know how much longer Scott has left. But…I don't know how long I have, either. Or you. If Scott has two years left, but we only have one, I'd regret like hell that I didn't spend that time doing what I really want to do."

"What's that?"

"Loving you. Being with you."

"Having mad, passionate sex with me on a daily basis?"

Rich laughter bubbled out of her. The last bit of tension in his chest vanished.

"Yes, that, too."

He rushed around the end of the table. She extended her arm, palm up—the universal sign for stop. He reined himself in. "What? Why aren't we dancing? Kissing? Why aren't we celebrating?"

"It's not that simple, Hayden. There are things I need you to know."

"Nick's okay with this? I mean, I assume you've talked to him about it…."

"Yes, Nick's okay with it. He's…grown up a lot in the last few months. When I told him, he said he'd realized nothing is all black-and-white." She pressed her lips together. "That we could still love Scott, and be mad at him at the same time. That he understood why I wouldn't want to be married to him anymore. Out of the mouths of babes."

"Fourteen. One minute a man, the next… So what's the problem? What do I need to know?"

"If Vera dies before Scott does, I've agreed to resume his legal guardianship. I won't be his wife," she quickly added, "just his guardian."

"So you'd be in charge of his legal stuff? His medical stuff?"

"Exactly. Can you deal with that?"

"I think I can live with it. Hell, I think I can live with

you going to the nursing home to shave the guy every day. As long as every night you're in *my* arms."

"I think I can live with *that*." She lowered her hand, slipped into his embrace, snuggling into his chest.

He wrapped his arms around her.

"I love you," she said softly.

Music to his ears. Words he thought he'd have to wait a lot longer to hear. "You what?"

She gently slapped his shoulder. "Love you."

He'd never grow tired of hearing that. "I love you, too." He slipped his fingers beneath her chin, tilting her head up. "Paperwork hasn't been filed yet, but...I need to kiss you *now*."

This time the smile she gave him lit up her eyes. No more was she a ghost of the woman he'd had a crush on when they were young. No more a stricken woman whose cheating husband made her feel defective.

At her nod, he leaned down. Lost himself in her lips, her mouth, the warmth of her body melded against his.

Finally, they disengaged. As the fog of desire cleared from her eyes, somberness settled there. Then a fleeting bit of panic chased through them.

"What now?" he asked.

Her eyes grew even larger and her mouth opened for a moment before she spoke. "Who's going to tell your mother?"

He burst into laughter, rocking her in his arms. "I gave you my word, I've got your back, Ronni. We'll send her a postcard after we elope."

EPILOGUE

YEARS AGO, he'd promised his brother he would take care of Nick and Ronni. Today, he'd promise the same thing to them.

Make it official. Really make good on his word.

But he was going to be late to the courthouse.

Again.

The Camaro's tires squealed as Hayden took a corner a tad too quickly. His brother Greg braced his arm against the dashboard. "Take it easy. It would be great if you actually married Ronni before making her a widow, you know? She's already lost one Hawkins man before she officially became part of the family. Let's not make it two. Plus, I've got a new baby who really needs a father."

"We're going to be late." The jeweler had wanted Hayden and Greg to ooh and aah over his creations a lot longer than Hayden had patience for.

"She'll wait, I promise. After all the other hoops she's jumped through to marry you, including dealing with Mom to plan this low-key wedding instead of eloping with you, I don't think she's going to let a few minutes chase her away."

"It's not her I'm worried about. It's the judge."

"So we'll find another judge. The courthouse is full of them."

"No, it has to be Judge Madison. Ronni insists. He's the one who wrote out Nick's probation terms. She feels since he brought us together, it's only fitting that he marry us."

Hayden checked the dashboard clock one more time, as if that would get them there faster. One other potential problem loomed, as well. "Hope nobody's leaked it to the media. I'd like today to go without Ronni having to face them." Getting busted on his wedding day for beating a reporter didn't sound like a good idea.

Besides, he had plans for his wedding night. They didn't include being locked in a cell.

"Speaking of the media…" Greg flipped down the visor, checking his tie while they drove. "Just who was it, do you think, who leaked that video of Scott cheating on Ronni in Iraq?"

The media had been all over her when she'd filed the divorce papers, which were a matter of public record. But tones had changed after they'd discovered Scott's philandering ways. Ronni had gone from evil, cold-hearted woman to Erie's wronged sweetheart in the space of one short video clip.

"I'm not sure," he said. "But whoever it was, I'd like to shake his hand."

"Any suspects?"

"Yeah. There's a guy, Dan Abbott, from Scott's unit. I met him when Scott was in the hospital. The way he looked at Ronni sometimes… I think he did it. Despite what Ronni believes, I think he might be the one who sent her the video in the first place."

All the on-street parking spaces in front of the courthouse were full, but because they were holding a small reception afterward at the Erie Club, next door to the courthouse, it didn't matter. Hayden eased the car into the lot at the club and jumped out, tossing the keys to the valet. "Thanks, man."

Finn barreled down the steps of the club, turning his jacket collar up against the chilly March breeze. "'Bout time you guys got here. Thought maybe you got cold feet."

"Hell, no. Everything ready for later?"

"I checked with the chef myself. Tasted everything. It's all good." Finn had worked as a chef at the club before leaving to open his restaurant, Fresh. He'd insisted on handling the arrangements for the menu. Probably to the current chef's chagrin.

At the security checkpoint, they stripped off their coats, sent them through the X-ray machine. Passed through the metal detector and grabbed everything back on the other side. Hayden was partway down the hall when a voice called to him.

"What? You don't even say hi, let alone anything else?"

He turned to find Jeannie standing at the metal detector. "Jeannie. I didn't see you there."

"I'm crushed."

He grinned, spread his arms. "I told you one day you'd be sorry. Missed your chance. I'm a one-woman

man now. And in twenty minutes, I'll be a married man."

She placed her hand over her chest. "The women of Erie mourn their loss. Tell her she's a lucky girl."

"I'll do that!" He turned with a wave and bolted down the hallway, heading for the elevators.

"You're sure about this?" Greg asked him once the doors slid shut. "We've still got time to get you out of here." His brother smirked. Hayden had told him the same thing the day of his wedding.

Hayden slapped him in the shoulder. "Thanks. But I'm going through with it. I'm not taking any chances on losing her now."

And as soon as he got her home, they'd start working on another tie. A baby of their own.

He wouldn't mind if it took a few tries to make it work.

When the brothers entered the courtroom, the gathering of people—their immediate family, plus Tamara and Vera, who'd been extremely supportive of Ronni's choice—breathed a collective sigh of relief. Their mother wagged a finger at Hayden, pointing to her watch.

He shrugged.

Ronni, wearing an eggshell skirt with a long-sleeved jacket, both overlaid with lace, waited for him at the front of the courtroom. When she saw him, she smiled. Her eyes lit up.

Her skin glowed. Everything about her screamed happiness. Life.

A far cry from the first time he'd seen her in the

probation office downstairs. Or the day he'd taken her home from the hospital after Scott's bout with pneumonia, when she'd been a mere shadow.

He squared his shoulders.

"Stop preening," Greg muttered. "Now get your ass up there and marry the girl. Before *she* comes to her senses and changes *her* mind."

Hayden paused before the railing where Nick stood, looking uncomfortable in his suit and tie. They'd had to buy him a new outfit. The kid had grown two inches since the start of the school year.

Hayden stuck out his hand. "You're still good with this, right?"

"We're good." The boy gave him a firm handshake. "So long as you don't expect me to call you Dad. You've been Unk for so long, I don't think I could change if I wanted to."

"I don't want to replace your father, Nick. Ever. I'm good with being Unk."

The judge cleared his throat.

Hayden hustled to his place at the front of the courtroom, alongside Ronni. He laced his fingers with hers.

Judge Madison began the wedding ceremony, but Hayden hardly heard a word. He was too busy drinking in the sight of Ronni, knowing that from this day forward they were a team. Until the judge said, "Hayden and Ronni have chosen to write their own vows. Ronni? You begin, please."

She turned to face Hayden. Unlacing their fingers,

she placed one palm on his chest. The twinkle in her eyes told him what she wanted. He covered it with his own hand, and placed his other over her heart. She grasped his fingers. "Hayden. I love you. Every beat of my heart belongs to you. You've restored me to life. And I pledge the rest of that life to walk beside you. To be your partner. Your helpmate. Your lover. Forsaking all others. Forever."

"Lovely," the judge said. "Hayden?"

"I love you, Ronni. Semper Fi."

Her smile widened.

"Uh, is that it, son?" the judge asked.

"I think that says it all," Ronni responded.

"Do you have rings?"

"We do." Hayden dug in the pocket of his suit coat. Pulled out the two rings wrapped in soft white flannel. "Close your eyes," he ordered. "I don't want you to look until they're both on."

She shut her eyes. He maneuvered his ring to the first knuckle of his ring finger, did the same with hers. She pressed her fingertips to his, exploring it. "No cheating," he said.

"No," she said. "Definitely no cheating."

"I didn't mean... You don't have to worry—" he began.

"Shh. I know that. Now, finish marrying me so we can get on to the kissing, will you?"

The family laughed. Cameras snapped.

"With this ring, I thee wed." He pushed her ring to the base of her finger.

"With this ring, I thee wed," she repeated, doing the same.

"Open your eyes."

While the judge blathered on, pronouncing them man and wife, Ronni looked down at their entwined hands, at the rings he'd commissioned especially for them.

Narrow gold bands at the top and bottom anchored graceful gold script that circled around their fingers.

Semper fidelis.

"They're beautiful," she whispered.

"*You're* beautiful." Not sure if the judge had told them to kiss yet or not, Hayden leaned down to claim his wife's mouth.

Just as she'd claimed his heart.

* * * * *

COMING NEXT MONTH

Available June 14, 2011

#1710 FINDING HER DAD
Suddenly a Parent
Janice Kay Johnson

#1711 MARRIED BY JUNE
Make Me a Match
Ellen Hartman

#1712 HER BEST FRIEND'S WEDDING
More than Friends
Abby Gaines

#1713 HONOR BOUND
Count on a Cop
Julianna Morris

#1714 TWICE THE CHANCE
Twins
Darlene Gardner

#1715 A RISK WORTH TAKING
Zana Bell

You can find more information on upcoming Harlequin® titles, free excerpts and more at
www.HarlequinInsideRomance.com.

HSRCNM0511

REQUEST YOUR FREE BOOKS!
2 FREE NOVELS PLUS 2 FREE GIFTS!

Harlequin

Super Romance

Exciting, emotional, unexpected!

"THANKS FOR NOT TURNING ON THE LIGHTS," Tyler said. "I'm a mess."

"Not in my book." Even in low light, Alex had a good view of her yellow shirt plastered to her body. It was all he could do not to reach for her, mud and all. But the next move needed to be hers, not his.

She slicked her wet hair back and squeezed some water out of the ends as she glanced upward. "I like the sound of the rain on a tin roof."

"Me, too."

She met his gaze briefly and looked away. "Where's the sink?"

"At the far end, beyond the last stall."

Tyler's running shoes squished as she walked down the aisle between the rows of stalls. She glanced sideways at Alex. "So how much of a cowboy are you these days? Do you ride the range and stuff?"

"I ride." He liked being able to say that. "Why?"

"Just wondered. Last summer, you were still a city boy. You even told me you weren't the cowboy type, but you're…different now."

He wasn't sure if that was a good thing or a bad thing. Maybe she preferred city boys to cowboys. "How am I different?"

"Well, you dress differently, and your hair's a little longer. Your face seems a little more chiseled, but maybe that's because of your hair. Also, there's something else, something harder to define, an attitude..."

"Are you saying I have an attitude?"

"Not in a bad way. It's more like a quiet confidence."

He was flattered, but still he had to laugh. "I just admitted a while ago that I have all kinds of doubts about this event tomorrow. That doesn't seem like quiet confidence to me."

"This isn't about your job, it's about...your..." She took a deep breath. "It's about your sex appeal, okay? I have no business talking about it, because it will only make me want to do things I shouldn't do." She started toward the end of the barn. "Now, where's that sink? We need to get cleaned up and go back to the house. Dinner is probably ready, and I—"

He spun her around and pulled her into his arms, mud and all. "Let's do those things." Then he kissed her, knowing that she would kiss him back, knowing that this time he would take that kiss where he wanted it to go. And she would let him.

Follow Tyler and Alex's wild adventures in
SHOULD'VE BEEN A COWBOY
Available June 2011 only from Harlequin® Blaze™
wherever books are sold.

Finding Her Dad

Janice Kay Johnson

Jonathan Brenner was busy running for office as county sheriff. The last thing on his mind was parenthood…that is, until a resourceful, awkward teenage girl shows up claiming to be his daughter!

Available June
wherever books are sold.